D1011529

THE LAST
KIND WORD

ALSO BY DAVID HOUSEWRIGHT

Featuring Rushmore McKenzie

A Hard Ticket Home

Tin City

Pretty Girl Gone

Dead Boyfriends

Madman on a Drum

Jelly's Gold

The Taking of Libby, SD

Highway 61

Featuring Holland Taylor

Penance

Practice to Deceive

Dearly Departed

Other Novels

The Devil and the Diva
(with Renée Valois)

Finders Keepers

THE LAST
KIND WORD

David
Housewright

MINOTAUR BOOKS

❧ NEW YORK

THE LAST KIND WORD. Copyright © 2013 by David Housewright. All rights reserved. Printed in the United States of America. For information address St. Martin's Press, 175 Fifth Avenue, New York, N.Y. 10010.

www.minotaurbooks.com

Library of Congress Cataloging-in-Publication Data

Housewright, David, 1955–
    The last kind word / David Housewright.—First edition.
        pages cm
    ISBN 978-1-250-00960-9 (hardcover)
    ISBN 978-1-250-03739-8 (e-book)
    1. Private investigators—Fiction.   2. Undercover operations—Fiction.
3. Illegal arms transfers—Fiction.   4. Minnesota—Fiction.   I. Title.
    PS3558.O8668L37 2013
    813'.54—dc23

                                                    2013006984

Minotaur books may be purchased for educational, business, or promotional use. For information on bulk purchases, please contact Macmillan Corporate and Premium Sales Department at 1-800-221-7945 extension 5442 or write specialmarkets@macmillan.com.

First Edition: June 2013

10   9   8   7   6   5   4   3   2   1

For Renée
for reasons too numerous to mention

ACKNOWLEDGMENTS

I wish to acknowledge my debt to India Cooper, Cara Engler, Tammi Fredrickson, Keith Kahla, Alison Picard, and Renée Valois.

THE LAST
KIND WORD

ONE

The handcuffs weren't particularly tight, yet they pinned my arms behind my back, making it impossible to get comfortable. Eventually I was able to maneuver until one shoulder was leaning against the rear door of the deputy's patrol car, the other rested against the back of the seat, and my hands hung in the cramped space between them. I wiggled my butt, but it didn't help. The seat was made of hard vinyl so that it could be easily cleaned—it wasn't meant to be cushy. My fellow prisoner, his hands also cuffed behind his back, balanced on the edge of the seat and stared straight ahead with glassy and unseeing eyes. He looked walking-dead drunk. However, since he had spent the past few days in the Ramsey County jail being interrogated by FBI and ATF agents, I was betting on mild shock.

I turned my head to look out the window and watched a chunk of real estate whiz past, mostly forest. We weren't in the North Woods of Minnesota quite yet, although we were headed that way.

"Deputy," I said. He glanced at me through his rearview mirror. "What time is it?"

His smile made me think he used one of those teeth whiteners advertised on TV.

"What do you care, Dyson?" he asked. "Got somewhere you need to be?"

"Humor me," I said.

"Eleven thirty-five."

I continued staring out the window.

She's late, my inner voice told me.

I have a thing about punctuality, which means I spend a lot of time being annoyed. Waiting makes me grumpy if not downright angry, depending on whom I'm waiting for and how long. Nina says if I were less prompt myself I'd be a more agreeable companion. I suppose there's something to that. On the other hand, if you say you're going to be in a specific place at a specific time, then you should damn well be there. If I were wearing a watch, I'd be tapping the face with my finger by now. Only I had no personal possessions on me at all—just the orange short-sleeve jail scrubs and a pair of ill-fitting canvas tennis shoes furnished by the Ramsey County Detention Center.

I glanced at my fellow prisoner while pretending not to. He leaned forward until his head was pressed against the steel mesh curtain that separated the backseat from the front. He was muttering to himself. "Going to prison . . . never let us out . . ."

"You say something?" the deputy asked.

"No," Skarda said—that was his name, David Skarda. We had never met; still, I knew everything about him. For one thing, I knew he wasn't actually headed for prison, at least not yet. He was merely being transferred from one pretrial lockup to another—he was going to be tried in Grand Rapids, about

180 miles north of the Twin Cities, since he committed his armed robbery in Itasca County. He had originally been conveyed to the Ramsey County jail in St. Paul after he was apprehended as a convenience to the ATF and the FBI, which wanted to question him about the gun he was carrying at the time of his arrest. If he had been smart, he would have told them everything he knew. But he wasn't and he didn't.

Deputy Ken Olson—I wasn't supposed to know his name, either, yet I did—drove effortlessly, like a man who had spent many hours behind the wheel. We followed U.S. Highway 169 as it hugged Lake Mille Lacs going north. There were far better, faster routes that led from the Cities to Grand Rapids, yet none of them was as scenic. And none of them narrowed to a single lane in just the right spot.

"What time is it?" I asked again.

"Why?" Olson said.

"Lunch. I hear they serve a nice buffet in the Itasca County jail."

The deputy thought that was funny. "Relax," he said.

"Relax, relax," Skarda muttered.

"What's this?" The deputy spoke while watching the action unfold through his rearview. A red Honda Accord came up fast until it was hard on his bumper, swung wide despite the double yellow line, and passed him on the left. He laughed as it pulled ahead.

"A blonde," he said. "Some blond bimbo driving. Who else would be dumb enough to pass a police car illegally, and look at this—she's going fifteen miles over the speed limit. If it weren't for you two, I'd have me some fun."

"Don't mind us," I said.

A moment later I could feel the car surge forward. Itasca County was in the process of retiring its fleet of Ford Crown Victoria Police Interceptors in favor of the more economical

Dodge Charger the deputy was driving—if he had put the pedal to the metal, as the cowboys say, there would have been no contest. I saw Olson's eyes flicker down and to his right, and for a moment I thought he might be running the blonde's license plate on his onboard laptop. But then he sighed deeply, the Charger slowed, and he brought his full attention back to the road.

"Protocols," Olson said. He spoke as if it were the saddest word in the English language.

The Accord followed the highway into a sweeping curve and disappeared from view. A few seconds later, however, we caught up to it. The red car was fishtailing in the lane, and my first thought was that it blew a tire and the driver was trying to bring it back under control. The red taillights flared, and the car pulled to the side of the road and stopped, its nose on the shoulder, its rear on the highway, blocking us. The deputy brought the Charger to a halt several car lengths behind the Accord and watched intently.

"What the hell is she doing?" he asked.

Forget what you've seen on TV and in the movies about inattentive guards who regularly ignore barking dogs; sudden, unexplained noises; and the odd behavior of complete strangers. In reality, most are trained to react—hell, overreact—to anything out of the ordinary, and they are never, ever taken out by a single punch or karate chop. The deputy, however, wasn't one of them. When the blonde stepped out of the Accord he smiled brightly, showing all his teeth. I didn't blame him. She was wearing the longest hair, shortest skirt, and highest heels I had ever seen. She tottered toward us, carrying a highway map that hid her chest.

"You've got to be kidding me," Olson said. He put the Charger in park, opened his door, and slid out. "Lady, what are you thinking?"

The lady dropped the map. She was carrying an M26 Taser gun. She squeezed the trigger and two barbed electrodes exploded from the bright green nose, imbedding themselves into the deputy's chest and flooding his body with 50,000 volts, all before the map fluttered to the ground. The deputy's muscles locked up. He fell to the pavement like a square of shingles tossed from the roof of a two-story house.

The woman dropped the Taser, kicked off her heels, and went quickly to the deputy's side. She squatted next to him, her short skirt riding up high on her thighs, and searched his pockets for the key to the handcuffs. She took the key, removed the Glock from the deputy's holster, and padded purposely in bare feet to the Charger, where she found the latch that unlocked the back door. She moved as if every step had been carefully choreographed.

I slid out of the backseat and turned around. The woman unlocked the cuffs and gave me both the key and the Glock. I shoved the Glock between the waistband of my scrubs and the small of my back and followed her to the deputy. Olson was just starting to regain his senses as I cuffed his wrists behind his back. He said, "Huh, what?" while the woman and I dragged him to the patrol car.

"What are you doing?" Skarda wanted to know. His mood had switched from depressed to manic just like that. "What's going on? Is this an escape? Are you trying to escape?" His eyes were bright with the possibility even as he flattened against the far door. "Take me with you."

We ignored him, shoving the deputy inside; Skarda swung his legs up and away to give us room. The deputy shook off our hands and turned painfully until both his knees were planted on the floor of the car and his torso was folded over the backseat. His forehead was pressed against the hard vinyl as if he were using it to push himself upright.

"Stop this, stop it right now," Olson said.

I slammed the door shut.

"Luck," the woman said.

It was the only word she had spoken during the seconds—yes, seconds—it took to disarm the deputy. She gathered her shoes and ran to the Honda Accord. A moment later, she was motoring down the highway at a speed that invited arrest.

I slid behind the wheel of the Charger, shut the door, and put the vehicle in gear.

"You'll never get away with this, Dyson," the deputy said. His voice was hoarse and low.

"What did you say?" I asked. I accelerated down Highway 169 until I was going the speed limit and then set the cruise control.

"You'll never get away with this." This time he was shouting.

"I bet you say that to all the escaping prisoners," I said.

"Do you think the police are asleep up here? You think they don't know what you're doing?"

"No, actually, they don't know what I'm doing. That's why I took your car instead of hightailing it with the babe in the red Accord, so some citizen wouldn't see you parked in the middle of the highway and call it in. Time is my friend. It'll be hours before the county sheriff knows what happened, and by then I will be far away from here."

"This car is equipped with a GPS tracking device."

"It is?" Skarda asked.

"Cops want to make sure they can recover their vehicles if they're stolen," I said. "Did you know some guys started a cab company in Detroit a while back using nothing but stolen police cars? God's truth."

"Dyson, listen to me," Deputy Olson said. "We can still work this out. It's not too late."

I glanced at him through the rearview mirror and smiled. "Of course it is," I said.

"Goddammit!"

"Hey, hey, hey—use your indoor voice."

"What about me?" Skarda asked.

"What about you?"

"Take me with you."

"The plan is for one."

"Then, then you can, you can just let me go."

I shook my head slowly. "The cops'll pick you up in about ten minutes, and then you'll be screwed even worse than you are now. Isn't that right, Deputy?"

"That's right," he said.

"Believe it or not, I'm doing you a favor," I said.

"I'll pay you," Skarda said.

"Pay me what?"

"Fifty thousand dollars."

That made me turn in my seat. I stared at him briefly through the steel mesh before returning my eyes to the road.

"Where would a punk like you get fifty thousand dollars?"

"That's my business," he said.

"Fifty thousand dollars." I said it as if the number impressed me. "Who are you?" I asked, even though I already knew the answer.

"Dave Skarda."

"What did they bust you for?"

"Armed robbery."

"Armed robbery," I repeated slowly. "I won't ask if you have the money on you . . ."

"Well, no."

"Where is it?"

"My gang. Deliver me to my gang and they'll pay you."

"Your gang?"

"My crew."

"Uh-huh. Whaddaya think, Deputy? Think Dave here has a crew?"

"I think he's a wannabe gangster who's going to spend the rest of his life in Stillwater State Correctional Facility if he steps one foot out of this car."

"Hear that, Dave? Best keep your seat."

"Bullshit." He said the word as if he had invented it. "Bullshit, bullshit, bullshit. I'm not messing with you, Dyson. Fifty thousand dollars. On delivery. You have my word."

"Don't do this, Skarda," the deputy said. "It'll only be worse for you later."

"Shut up, just shut up," Skarda said. "Fifty thousand dollars, Dyson. I promise."

"If I take your word and you don't keep it—if you're lying you better say so now and no harm done cuz later's going to be too late."

"I'm not lying. Trust me."

Whenever anyone says "trust me" I automatically think the opposite, but I didn't tell Skarda that. "Okay," I said. "Okay. It's always good to have a Plan B."

"What does that mean?"

"It means—just be quiet for a while. Both you kids, be quiet. Daddy needs to think."

While I was thinking I maneuvered the patrol car north on 169 until it intersected Minnesota Highway 18 and I went east. Traffic was not heavy. It was June in Minnesota, and you usually get an inordinate number of city dwellers heading to lake cabins and other getaways "Up North." But it was also early afternoon on a Wednesday. I followed 18 until it merged with Highway 47 and I went south, effectively driving around the northern half of the enormous Lake Mille Lacs, where I had often fished for walleye. It was a pleasant drive, and I probably would have enjoyed it if I weren't on the run. Eventually 18 and 47 forked and I went east again. That's when the radio came alive. The signal was surprisingly strong and clear.

"Six-twenty-one," a voice said.

It was the patrol car's call sign. I heard the deputy use it when he cleared St. Paul.

"Hey, Dave," I said. "Keep the deputy quiet for a minute."

"What?"

"Six-twenty-one," the voice repeated.

I took the microphone from its holster and spoke into it.

"Six-twenty-one, go."

"Six-twenty-one, what's your twenty?"

Before I could click the SEND button and reply, Olson started screaming, "Ten-ninety-eight, ten-ninety-eight, officer needs assistance."

"Dammit, Skarda, what did I say?"

Skarda used his legs to brace himself against the door and then lunged to his side so that his elbows and shoulders fell on top of the deputy's head. The deputy screamed again, but this time Skarda's body muffled his voice.

"Six-twenty-one, say again," the voice said over the radio.

"Six-twenty-one," I replied. "Sorry 'bout that. I'm north on U.S. 169, just shy of State 210."

"Six-twenty-one, running a little late, aren't you?"

"Six-twenty-one, there was some traffic in Aitkin."

There was more muffled shouting from the backseat.

"Six-twenty-one, are you sure you didn't stop for a beer?"

"Six-twenty-one, I thought I'd wait until I got closer to home."

"Six-twenty-one, what's your ten-seventy-seven?"

"Six-twenty-one, ETA is one hour."

"Six-twenty-one, copy."

I took a deep breath and returned the microphone to its holster.

"It's okay," I said.

Skarda managed to roll off the deputy and sit up again.

The deputy sputtered his anger. "You're screwed, Skarda," he shouted. "I'm going to have your head on a plate."

"You have to take me with, now," Skarda said.

"We'll see," I told him.

"What does ten-ninety-eight mean, anyway?"

"Standard police code. It means prison break in progress."

"You two are totally fucked," the deputy said.

"I believe the basic code for that is ten-forty-five-F."

Less than an hour later we crossed Interstate 35, still heading east.

"My friends are up north," Skarda said.

"Mine aren't," I replied.

Deputy Olson didn't say anything. He simply sat in the back of the Charger and made angry breathing sounds.

We ended up on County Road 30 and followed it toward the Wisconsin border. Near the tiny town of Duxbury it turned from pavement to gravel; a giant plume of yellow and orange dust followed us down the road. This was no-man's-land, thinly populated, little traffic.

The radio crackled, its signal not nearly as vibrant as it had been.

"Six-twenty-one."

I ignored it.

"Six-twenty-one, do you copy?"

"Aren't you going to answer?" Skarda asked.

"Nope. Let 'em wonder."

The turnoff came up so fast that I was fifty feet past it before I could stop safely. I put the Charger in reverse, backed up, and then turned in. It was a logging road used so long ago that now it was little more than an overgrown trail with plenty of potholes that made the Charger bounce like a carnival ride. I followed it deep into the forest until we reached the edge of a small river—it might have been the Lower Tamarack; I didn't know for sure and never cared to ask.

"Six-twenty—"

When I turned off the engine, the radio went with it.

Trees—poplar, birch, and fir—surrounded us. The only noise came from the wind in the branches and the low gurgle of the slow-moving water. The sun was high in the sky, and there were few shadows on the forest floor. It was the kind of place where a guy might pitch a tent and try his luck with a fly rod, where most people dream of escaping to and Minnesotans generally take for granted.

"Gentlemen, this is where I leave you," I said.

"Here," the deputy said. "Here?"

"Your guys aren't going to be looking for me. They're going to be looking for you. First things first, right? It's going to take a long time to find you here, GPS or not. By the time they do and turn their attention to me, I'll be out of the country."

"Yeah? The average speed of a man hiking over unbroken ground is two miles per hour. How far do you think you'll get on foot?"

"All the way to where a car is waiting. Do you think I'm making this up as I go along, Deputy? C'mon."

"Dyson, you can't leave us here."

"Us?" Skarda said.

"You'll be all right until help arrives," I told them. "There hasn't been a bear attack around here in, I don't know, weeks."

"Us?" Skarda repeated. "You're taking me with you, right?"

"About that . . ."

"You promised."

"No, I didn't. Good luck to you, pal."

"Wait, wait, Dyson. What about the fifty thousand dollars? What about Plan B?"

"Yeah . . ."

"You can't leave me here. I helped you before. I helped you, remember? Remember? Forget the armed robbery. Even if I beat that rap, they'll send me to Stillwater for whatchacallit, aiding and abetting your escape. Right? Right?"

"How about that, Deputy?"

Olson's eyes were like roadside caution lights flashing SEVERE ACCIDENT AHEAD. "I look forward to testifying at your trial," he said.

"You owe me," Skarda said.

"Actually, you're going to owe me," I said.

I opened the back door and helped Skarda out. He was smiling when I unlocked his cuffs. The smile went away when I relocked them with his hands in front of him.

"What's this?" he asked.

"Fifty thousand dollars," I said. "The cuffs come off when I get the money."

"This'll make it hard to walk."

"Yes, it will." I shoved him more or less toward the northwest. "That way." While Skarda stumbled forward, I turned toward the deputy. "It's been a pleasure," I said. "Sorry I couldn't stay."

I locked him inside the patrol car and made a production out of dropping his car keys just outside the door where he could see them.

"Damn you, Dyson," he shouted. I turned and walked into the woods. "Goddamn you."

So far so good, my inner voice said.

I'm a city boy at heart. I can't imagine living anywhere that doesn't have a professional baseball team, jazz clubs, and a wide assortment of Asian, Mexican, Greek, and Italian restaurants. Still, there were times when the city boy loved to visit the Great Outdoors, fish in pristine lakes, hunt unclaimed forests, or just hike the countryside in search of wildlife you can't see close to home, especially birds. I love the sight and sound of birds. I have a clock at home that announces each hour with the warble of a different avis. Trust me when I say it's not the same as hearing them in the wild.

The air was clean and warm in the forest, and I found myself breaking a light sweat as we walked. It would have been a pleasant journey if not for the constant whining of my companion—"The cuffs are too tight, it's too hard to walk, where are we going, are we there yet?"

"What are you, eight years old?" I asked finally. "Shut up and walk."

"I want to know the plan."

"The plan is you stop talking or I'm going to leave you here. Can't you just enjoy the scenery?"

"I need to go to the bathroom."

"Oh, for God's sake."

Skarda was not a bad guy unless you want to hold being a Green Bay Packer fan against him. He was born in Krueger, Minnesota, went to the University of Wisconsin at Stevens Point, and returned home to work in construction until the bottom fell out of the housing market. As far as I knew, in twenty-seven years he had never committed a single transgression against God or country until they caught him outside the ticket booth of a country music festival with a ski mask over his face and a Kalashnikov submachine gun in his hands. After he relived himself against the trunk of a tree, we continued walking.

All the tricks the Old Man taught me about finding my way in the woods were as fresh in my mind as if I had learned them yesterday, including how to locate the points of a compass using nothing but the sun, a wristwatch, and a blade of grass. I didn't need any of them, however. I had been over this ground before, and I knew exactly where I was going.

Eventually we broke through the trees and found a narrow gravel road with a drainage ditch on either side. A Ford Explorer was parked on the shoulder about a quarter mile up from where we emerged from the forest. A man was sitting on the driver's side of the SUV, his body twisted so that his legs hung out the open door. We were about a hundred yards away before he spotted us approaching.

"I almost gave up on you," he said. "Who's he?"

Skarda had worn a worried expression on his face ever since I met him, so I didn't know if he was taken aback by my partner's question or not.

"Someone I picked up along the way," I said. "Dave, Chad, Chad, Dave."

"Jesus Christ, Dyson," Chad said. "We're using names?"

"Beats saying 'Hey, you' all the time."

I moved to the back of the SUV. Chad popped the rear cargo door. There was a nylon bag in the cargo bay, and I opened it to find several changes of clothes. I pulled out a pair of jeans and a shirt and gave them to Skarda.

"You'll have to wear your own shoes," I said.

Skarda held up his cuffed hands, a pleading expression in his eyes.

"Okay," I said. "But let's not do anything stupid, all right?"

To emphasize my point, I took the deputy's Glock and set it where I could easily reach it but Skarda couldn't before I unlocked one cuff. I left the other wound around his wrist.

While we were changing clothes, Chad talked and paced,

paced and talked. Mostly he was complaining about the change in plans, claiming that I was supposed to be alone. "Just you, you said. Just you. Everything's planned for just you." He was another guy who didn't appreciate the beauty of his surroundings.

After I changed out of the jail scrubs into a pair of blue jeans, a polo shirt, and Nikes—looking every inch like a tourist from the Cities—I picked up the Glock and turned toward him.

"Someone once said that genius is the ability to improvise," I said.

"What the hell is that supposed to mean?"

I brought the Glock up, went into a pyramid stance, and fired three times. Tiny volcanoes of blood exploded out of his chest as he fell straight backward against the gravel road, his arms and legs spread as if he were attempting to make snow angels.

Skarda screamed, screamed like a bad actor in a horror flick.

"What?" I said.

"You shot him."

"Of course I shot him. Are you telling me you wouldn't have?"

"He was your friend."

"If Chad was my friend, why did he sleep with my girl? Why did he turn me in to the cops and try to steal my money?"

"He—he helped break you out?"

"That's only because the money isn't where he thought it was. Chad broke me out so I would lead him to it, and once I did, he probably would have killed me. Are you paying attention, Dave?"

Skarda looked as if every word would be indelibly etched in his brain forever and he wasn't happy about it.

"Stay here," I said.

I slid the Glock between my jeans and the small of my back and crossed the gravel road to where Chad had fallen. I grabbed him under the shoulders, dragged him to the far ditch, and rolled him in. Afterward, I bent to go through his pockets. The depth of the ditch effectively hid Chad from Skarda's view.

"That hurt," Chad whispered. "Now I know why stuntmen make so much money."

"How's the deputy?" I asked. I was trying hard not to move my lips.

"Upset that you took him the way you did. I explained that we couldn't let him in on the scam for fear that he might give it away, but that we would tell his boss he agreed to cooperate with us so he won't be embarrassed."

I took Chad's wallet and stood up so Skarda could see me rifling through it. I pulled cash out and tossed the wallet away.

"Lousy hundred and eighty-seven bucks," I said. "What a schmuck."

Skarda was watching me closely, looking as if he wanted to run away very fast. I bent down again, and he moved to the door of the SUV, slid behind the wheel, and reached for the ignition. I stood up again, this time dangling Chad's car keys from a ring around my pinky.

"Hey, Dave?" I said. "Going somewhere?"

"I was just—I was getting ready. We should leave."

"Yes, we should."

I glanced down at Chad, and he winked at me. I climbed out of the ditch, crossed the gravel road, and moved to the Explorer.

"I'll drive," I said.

Skarda scrambled out of the SUV and went around to the passenger side. When he was safely inside, I told him to lock the loose cuff around the handle above the window.

"Why?" he asked.

"Good handcuffs make good neighbors."

"Huh?"

"One of Robert Frost's lesser-known works. Do it."

He did.

I fired up the Explorer, put it into gear, and headed down the road.

"Where are we going?" Skarda asked.

"To see a girl," I said.

TWO

The girl lived in White Bear Lake, not far from the former church that now housed the Lakeshore Players Community Theater. The city used to be a popular haven for the well-to-do who would travel twenty miles by train from St. Paul to vacation on the scenic lake that gave it its name. F. Scott Fitzgerald wrote about it; James J. Hill stayed there, and so did Pretty Boy Floyd and Ma Barker. Eventually the rich went elsewhere. Apparently they didn't care to rub shoulders with the many middle-class citizens who moved to White Bear Lake once the roads improved and car ownership became common. To reach it, we made our way down to Sandstone and crossed I-35 again, this time going from east to west. From there I drove south. Skarda wondered why we didn't take 35. I preferred to drive the succession of county roads that followed the original route of U.S. Highway 61, the legendary roadway that was made more or less obsolete between Duluth and St. Paul when I-35 was built. It was so much classier, although I didn't tell him that. Instead, I told him it was safer.

"The Minnesota Highway Patrol might be monitoring the traffic on 35," I said.

It wasn't the only question Skarda asked. The man seemed incapable of being quiet for more than a few minutes at a time. He wanted to know what I had been busted for, why I was being transferred to Grand Rapids, if I had done time, where I was from, and so on and so on. I refused to answer. Nor did I ask any question of him, which was part of the plan. Still, when he wondered if the girl we were going to visit was the blonde who drove the red Honda Accord, I told him, "Actually, she's a brunette, only there's no disguising those legs, know what I mean?"

Skarda said he did, yet I suspected he was only being polite because a moment later he asked if "the girl" was "my girl," the same one Chad had slept with. I told him it was.

"Are you going to kill her?"

"What the hell, Dave," I said. "Do I look like a homicidal maniac to you?"

He assured me that I didn't, and I thanked him. Just the same, by the time we reached the White Bear Lake city limits, I was humming "Delia's Gone," one of the last great songs recorded by Johnny Cash before he passed—the one where he claims if he hadn't shot poor Delia he'd have had her for his wife. If Skarda hadn't been cuffed to the handle above the door, I have no doubt that he would have jumped out of the car at the first stoplight.

We drove through what amounted to downtown White Bear Lake, reaching Stewart Avenue and driving south some more. I told Skarda what to look for—a white Colonial with an old-fashioned porch on the left side of the street. As we passed it, I said, "Sonuvabitch," and tightly gripped the steering wheel.

"What?" Skarda asked.

"Cops."

"Where? I didn't see anything?"

"That's because you were looking at the house when you should have been looking at the street."

Skarda turned in his seat and looked behind us.

"Don't," I said, and then, "Too late."

I stomped on the accelerator. The Ford Explorer surged forward. I pushed it up to fifty and took a hard left down a residential street. I did it the way they do in Hollywood movies and on TV—badly. I accelerated into the turn and braked to keep from losing control, which caused the back end of the Explorer to slide sideways and fishtail as I accelerated again. It was terribly inefficient but looked cool—that's why they do it in the movies—and gave Skarda the impression of desperate flight. I blasted through a right-hand turn and then another left, actually making the tires squeal.

Skarda got into it right away. "Unmarked cop car, a blue sedan, two blocks behind us," he said.

I hung another left followed by a right. I actually put the Explorer on two wheels, which was insane. SUVs have a higher center of gravity—do you know how easy it is to flip over one of those suckers? It shook me up so much that I actually made the next turn properly, slowing into the turn and accelerating out of it. Skarda kept looking behind us and didn't seem to notice.

"See anything?" I asked.

"No, yes, a white van."

I took a right followed by a second right, followed by a left, sometimes pushing the Explorer up to sixty. The streets were quiet, thank goodness, although I did have to lean on the horn to keep a Toyota from backing out of a driveway in front of us. I took another turn, this one more slowly. A block ahead of us I saw two cars idling in the middle of the intersection, one facing south, the other north, and my first thought was that they were a couple of neighbors chatting with each other, not worrying about clogging the avenue because only neighbors used it. Skarda didn't see it that way.

"It's a roadblock," he shouted.

I hit the brakes, slowing just enough so that I could safely turn down an alley.

"The cops are everywhere," Skarda said. "What are we going to do?"

"Hang on," I said.

I managed a few more quick turns until we jumped onto White Bear Avenue. I made a big production out of weaving in and out of traffic at high speed until we crossed Interstate 694. The Maplewood Mall was on our right. I pulled into its massive parking lot and hid among the cars there. I turned off the engine. All we could hear was the ticking as it cooled.

"I think we're all right," Skarda said. "I think we lost them."

'Course, there was no "them"—it was just Skarda's imagination running on overdrive. As for the white Colonial, it actually had belonged to a girl I once dated, an actor who went to Hollywood to try her luck about fifteen years ago.

"Oh my God, Dyson," Skarda said. Now that he thought he was safe, he was breathing hard and clutching his heart as if he were afraid it would leap from his chest. "That was close. When I saw the roadblock—I still don't believe you got us out of that."

"It was nothing," I said.

"You're a helluva driver, my friend."

"I expected something like this might happen," I said. "Still . . . this makes it difficult."

"What do you mean?"

"My money—I can't get to it. With Chad gone I figured my

girl—my ex-girl—wouldn't have the nerve to cross me again, only she did. She and Chad must have had a prearranged signal; probably he was supposed to call her, and when he didn't she called the cops. None of that matters. What matters is I can't get to my money now."

"Where is it?" Skarda asked.

I gave him a hard look that suggested that was the dumbest question I had ever heard.

"It's safe, that's all you need to know," I said. "It's safe. Only I can't collect it until things cool down. In the meantime, I have exactly a hundred and eighty-seven dollars in my pocket."

"So, what are we going to do?"

I patted him on the knee. "Dave, I like that you said 'we.' "

I gave it ten minutes, started the SUV, and began exploring the back rows of the mall's huge parking lot.

"What are you doing?" Skarda asked.

"Looking for a car to steal. This one's hot."

"Why here?"

"Store managers want to save the best spaces for their customers, so they usually have their employees park in the slots furthest from the mall. These are the people who'll be last to leave once the stores close up, so we'll be long gone by the time they report the theft. Ah, here we go. Useful and unobtrusive."

I slowed the Ford Explorer to a stop directly in front of a Jeep Cherokee with a swing-away tire carrier mounted on the back. After making sure there was no one nearby who could see us, I reversed a few feet, twisted the steering wheel, and eased forward until I nudged the Cherokee's bumper.

"Why did you do that?" Skarda asked.

"To check for a car alarm. Do you hear anything?"

"No."

"Well, then . . ."

I got out of the Explorer and again searched the parking lot. Assured that we were quite alone, I walked around the Cherokee, trying all the doors. They were locked. I cupped my hands against the windshield and peered inside. After a few moments I returned to the Explorer. Skarda spoke to me through the open window.

"Don't we need tools? A screwdriver at least?"

"The pen is mightier than the screwdriver," I said.

"What does that mean?"

"Check the glove compartment, see if there's something to write with."

Skarda opened the glove compartment with one hand—the other was still cuffed to the handle above the door—and found a pencil and a small notebook. I took them, returned to the Cherokee, and carefully wrote down the vehicle identification number that I read off of the metal strip attached to the corner of the dashboard. When I returned to the Explorer, Skarda said, "Now what?"

"Watch and learn," I said.

Not far from the Maplewood Mall was a community of new and used car dealerships. I found one that sold Jeep Cherokees and pulled into the lot. I left Skarda waiting in the Explorer while I walked inside. I went to the parts and service desk and told the mechanic that yet again I had locked my one and only key—along with my wallet containing my ID—inside my Jeep Cherokee. I asked if they could contact the manufacturer, give them the VIN, ask for the specs, and cut a duplicate key. They said that they could, that it would take half an hour. Fifty minutes and fifty dollars later, I walked out of the dealership with a new key. That's the part I told a visibly relived Skarda when I returned to the Ford Explorer. The part I didn't tell him was that the dealership had demanded proof of ownership before they cut the key, which I was able to supply with a call to the Minnesota Department of Driver and Vehicle Services because, well, I actually did own the Jeep Cherokee.

We drove back to the mall, parked the Explorer, unlocked the Cherokee, slipped inside, and started the engine. Yes, I again locked Skarda's handcuff around the door handle before we drove off. Despite that, Skarda was impressed.

"That was the slickest bit of car stealing I've ever heard of," he said. "I didn't know it was so easy."

"Like most things worth doing, it requires audacity. In any case, it beats the hell out of pulling ignition wires and breaking steering column locks. And look, we have a full tank of gas. So, where are we going?"

"Why ask me?"

"Hey, pal. You're Plan B, remember. I deliver you to your crew and your crew pays me fifty thousand dollars."

"Yeah . . ."

"You're not reneging on your part of the agreement, are you, Dave?"

"No, no, of course not. It's just . . . fifty thousand dollars."

"Don't worry about it," I said. "I'll settle for half; take it in cash. I'll scoot up to Canada and lay low until things cool down a bit, give it maybe a couple months just to be on the safe side, then come back for my money."

"Ummm."

"You had better not be messing with me, Dave. We had a deal."

"I'm not, I'm not messing with you, it's just . . ."

"You might not know this about me, pal, but I have a volatile personality."

"It's just that I need to make a phone call first, that's all."

"Once we get out of the Cities we'll find a pay phone," I said.

"Do they still have pay phones?"

They did. We found one in the lobby of Tobies Restaurant and Bakery in Hinckley, about halfway between the Twin Cities and Duluth. Because of its location, Hinckley had been a popular tourist trap since World War II. Travelers traditionally stopped there for a pee break, to purchase petroleum by-products, stretch their legs, or grab a quick bite. Since '48, Tobies had been the main beneficiary of this tradition, at least until the fast-food chains set up franchises across the street. It was crowded—it was always crowded. Admittedly, the food wasn't all that memorable, the service was what you would expect in a tourist town, and the congestion was exasperating at best. On the other hand, Tobies bakery served astonishing caramel rolls; they were so light, sticky, and sweet that I swear to God, they could kill a diabetic in thirty seconds flat.

I had to remove Skarda's handcuffs before we went inside. After I did, I showed him the Glock that I concealed beneath my shirt and reminded him that I was an exceedingly desperate man.

"You don't need to worry about me, Dyson," he said.

"Then I won't," I said, although I didn't mean it.

Tobies had a bakery, restaurant, coffeehouse, and lounge, plus banquet and meeting facilities in different buildings that seemed to be connected by Velcro. We entered through the bakery. I exchanged bills for change and found the telephone. Skarda pumped the quarters in, but I stopped him before he could dial.

"Who are you calling?" I asked.

"What do you mean?"

"Are you calling your family? Because that's the first place the cops'll look for you. They might already have a tap in place."

"We have prepaid cell phones. We only use them for business and then we toss them away." Skarda grinned. "I really do have a crew. We really do know what we're doing."

"How did you get caught, then?"

"How did you?"

He had me there.

"We're just a couple of John Dillingers, we are," I said.

Skarda placed his call. I positioned myself next to him so I could hear what was spoken through the receiver.

"Hello," a male voice said.

"Hello, Dad?" Skarda said. "It's Dave."

"Dave?"

"Yeah, Dave."

"Dave's not here."

The exchange made me laugh so loudly that people passing through the lobby turned to look, which is exactly what you want when you're the object of a police manhunt, people staring at you.

"Dammit, Dad, this is your son David speaking," Skarda said. "You know what, let me talk to Josie."

"Josie's not here."

"Who the hell is there?"

"Everyone's laying low. You're in trouble, boy."

"Tell me about it."

"The escape was on the TV. The *Star Tribune* got a story up on its Web site. They say this fella you're with, this Dyson, Nick Dyson, they say he's dangerous, a career criminal, that he's robbed banks and armored cars and shit." Skarda glanced at me out of the corner of his eye. "I don't think they care that much 'bout you, but they sure want this Dyson fella. If you ain't done it yet, you gotta get shy of him, boy. Get as far away from that psycho as you can."

Skarda took a deep breath and said, "Dad, the man is standing right next to me. He's listening to every word you say."

There was a long pause on the other end of the line before Skarda's old man spoke again. "Well, you shoulda said somethin' cuz now I feel bad."

"Dad, I'm bringing him to the cabin."

"The cabin?"

"You know, the cabin."

"Oh, oh yeah—the cabin."

"Tell Josie. Tell her that I owe the man some money. Will you do that?"

"Josie?"

"Yes."

"Josie's not here."

"Dad, I'm going to hang up. Tell Josie I'll call later."

Skarda hung up the phone.

"My dad," he said. "He's . . ." Skarda shook his head.

"Crazy?" I said.

"Old."

"I think I'd rather be crazy. Let's go."

My intention was to get back on the road as soon as possible—*keep moving,* my inner voice chanted—but the aromas wafting up from the bakery were too enticing.

"I haven't eaten all day," Skarda said. "How 'bout you?"

"Well, if you're going to insist, we could grab something and take it with us."

"Or we could eat here." Skarda gestured at the café on the

other side of the bakery. It had a cozy, hometown feel to it, as if it were trying to channel the corner drugstore where Judy Garland and Mickey Rooney once shared a soda. It might have managed it, too, if not for all the damn hanging plants.

"Quickly," I said.

We bellied up to the rounded glass display cases and started searching for bakery. I was thinking something simple, like a crispy elephant ear. I bent to take a good look at it. Plain or filled, I debated. That's when the deputy from the Pine County Sheriff's Department walked in. I saw his brown and tan uniform reflected in the glass before I saw him. He called out the name of the cashier, which I didn't get. She called his name in return. "Pat." I rose slowly and casually stepped aside, giving him room to search the glass case.

Skarda didn't notice the deputy at all until he nudged him while examining the cake donuts.

"Excuse me," the deputy said.

"S'okay," Skarda said. Then he saw the uniform, saw the badge, saw the gun in the black holster. He stood upright and still, a look of alarm across his face. I was terrified that he would do something stupid, like run, or worse, just stand there with that idiot expression until the deputy noticed and asked what his problem was, so I attempted to distract the cop.

"I always thought that thing about cops and donuts was a myth," I said.

The deputy kept looking through the glass, answering as if he had heard the remark a thousand times before.

"It started because for a long time the only places that were open past 10 P.M. besides bars were donut shops," he said. "So that's where officers working the third shift went on their breaks. Plus, they tend to be located in centralized areas, the donut shops, so they can be used for briefings." The deputy turned and smiled at me. It was a nice smile; made me want to contribute to the Police Benevolent Association. "Besides, who doesn't like a fresh donut?"

"No true God-fearing American, that's for sure," I said.

I watched Skarda over the deputy's shoulder. He took a step backward and swiveled his head back and forth as if he were searching for an exit. If I could have slapped him, I would have.

"What'll you have, Pat?" the cashier asked.

"Gimme a couple of fudge cake donuts and a café hazelnut."

"Coming up."

The cashier put the donuts in a small white bag with the name Tobies printed on the side and poured the coffee while the deputy reached in his pocket for his wallet. It was then that I noticed the name tag above his pocket read GARRETT.

"You know what," I said. "I got this." I put my hand in my own pocket and produced what was left of Chad's $187.

"Are you sure?" the deputy asked.

"It's my pleasure. Thank you for your service."

"Thank you," the deputy said.

A moment later, he left the bakery.

"That was nice of you," the cashier said.

"I'm a helluva guy." I turned to Skarda. "So, Dave. See anything you like?"

"I don't feel well."

And he didn't feel well again until I got him outside, into the Jeep Cherokee, and fifteen miles down the road.

"I'm sorry," he said. "I guess I froze back there."

"Uh-huh."

"It's just, after everything that's happened today, seeing the deputy appear out of nowhere like that . . . I'm not usually that easily frightened."

"Forget it. I wasn't exactly calm myself, especially after I learned his name."

"His name?"

"The deputy back there, his name was Pat Garrett. Do you believe that?"

"Who's Pat Garrett?"

"The lawman who gunned down Billy the Kid."

"Oh God, I'm going to be sick."

"You know Dave, I don't think you're cut out for this line of work."

We needed to eat, which was fine with Skarda as long as we didn't leave the car, so I stopped at the first fast-food joint we found with a drive-thru window. Skarda said he felt better after consuming a couple of Quarter Pounders with Cheese, although I couldn't say the same. *Note to self,* my inner voice told me. *Biggest drawback about being on the run, the food sucks.*

Afterward, we located a Target store, where I bought a $29.99 cell phone and a prepaid phone card with 160 minutes on it. Unfortunately, this required driving to a coffeehouse that allowed us to use an electrical outlet to charge the phone and activate it. There's a lot to be said about hiding in plain sight, although our last brush with honest, tax-paying citizens didn't exactly fill either of us with confidence. By then, however, Skarda was feeling better, so much so that he protested when I ordered a couple of straight-ahead black coffees. He wanted something called a caramel macchiato—when the hell did that become coffee? I turned him down, partly out of principle and partly because, after paying for the key, treating the deputy, and buying the cell phone, minutes card, fast food, and coffee—not to mention sales tax—I was down to exactly $59.35 in my pocket, a fact that I shared with Skarda.

"Don't worry," he said. "You'll get your money."

"Do I look worried?"

"I don't know. It's kinda hard to tell."

"This Josie, is she your wife?"

"My sister."

"Is she a member of your crew?"

"Yes, yes she is."

I slid the cell phone across the table. "I think it's time to call her. Tell her to get my money together."

Skarda took the phone, flipped it open, and completed the call.

"Put it on speaker," I said, and he did after first glancing around him to see if anyone else could hear.

"Hello," a woman's voice said.

"Josie? It's Dave."

"Dad said you called. Are you okay? Are you safe? Where are you?"

"Near Duluth. Have the cops been around?"

"No."

"No?" I said.

"At least none have knocked on the door and searched the place or anything," Josie said. "Is that Dyson?"

"Yes," Skarda said.

"Good evening, Mr. Dyson."

"Good evening, Ms. Skarda," I said. "Is that correct, your last name?"

"Yes. JoEllen Skarda. My friends call me Josie."

"May I call you Josie?"

"Please do."

"Josie, the police have you staked out. Could be they're watching to see if you go to your brother or he comes to you."

"This isn't the Cities, Mr. Dyson. There's not a lot of people, not a lot of traffic; not a lot of places you can hang around up here and not be noticed. If we were being watched, I think we would know it."

"Let's pretend, for safety's sake, that you are being watched and watched closely. Where could we meet?"

"The cabin. He'll take you to the cabin, but I have to ask—why do we need to meet?"

"Josie, your brother owes me fifty thousand dollars. He says you're good for it."

"What?"

"Wait," Skarda said. "I thought you said twenty-five thousand."

"What?"

"I'll accept twenty-five if you have the cash on hand," I said, "and I don't have to wait for it."

"What are you talking about?" Josie asked.

I leaned away from the table and gestured at the cell. Skarda took that as his cue to explain himself. When he finished, he said, "We'll pay him off at the cabin, okay, sis?"

"Are you sure?"

"Kinda between a rock and a hard place, you know?"

Josie sighed deeply. "Okay," she said. "I'll see you there. When?"

"Two hours. Maybe a little less."

"I'll be waiting."

"Love you, sis."

"Love you, too."

"Josie," I said.

"Yes, Mr. Dyson?"

"I don't have to threaten you, do I?"

She paused for a moment and said, "No, Mr. Dyson."

"Love you," I said.

Josie sighed as if she had heard lots of other men say those words without meaning them and hung up. Skarda deactivated the phone and leaned back from the table just as I had. He folded his arms across his chest.

"We're set," he said.
"So it would seem."
He smiled.
I smiled back.

THREE

Night falls harder in northern Minnesota than it does in most places. There are few cities, less ambient light—you can drive for tens of miles without seeing anything beyond your headlights except for the moon and the glitter of stars. We were on 53 heading north. I knew because the highway signs said so. Beyond that I had no idea where I was. Eventually we went northeast before catching a county highway with just the impression of traffic lines. The sign named Embarrass, Babbitt, Krueger, and Ely without listing how far away the towns were in miles. This was the heart of the Iron Range, as it was known in the Cities, or simply "the Range" to those who actually lived there—so named because of the rich iron deposits that had fueled the region's economy for a hundred years.

"Where are we going?" I asked. I had asked before, but Skarda was being as coy with me as I had been with him on the drive to White Bear Lake, telling me where to turn and little else. Finally I reached over and gave him an idiot slap to the back of his head.

"Where are we going?" I asked again.

"To the cabin."

"I got that part."

"It's a small place on a lake a few miles south of Krueger. We use it as a hideout."

"A hideout? What are you, the Cavendish Gang?"

"Who are they?"

"From the Lone Ranger, the gang that—never mind. Tell me about the cabin."

"It used to be owned by a stockbroker from Chicago. He died a year ago and his family has been trying to sell it ever since, only there are no takers. My sister is the real estate agent."

"I suppose the real estate market is pretty tough up here."

"Tough everywhere," Skarda said. "Anyway, it's isolated, which I guess is one of the reasons it's so hard to sell. We've been using it because sis thinks it's better that we're never seen together in public. You gotta remember, around here everyone's connected to everyone else. It's kind of like Kevin Bacon except you don't need six moves. Makes life complicated sometimes; hard to keep a secret."

"Your sister, Josie—I'm going to take a flyer here and say she's the brains behind this operation."

"I suppose she is."

I kept following Skarda's directions, turning onto a gravel road that became a potted dirt road and finally a long-grass and short-brush path that reminded me of the logging road where we had left the deputy—was it only nine hours ago? The path led to a clearing. In the center of the clearing the Cherokee's high beams swept over a small cabin. It was rust colored with white trim and supported on pillars of cinder blocks. There was a short flight of stairs that led to a sprawling wooden deck with benches, lawn chairs, a picnic table, and a charcoal grill. The cabin's sole door opened onto the deck. Skarda had said something about a lake, but I couldn't see it in the dark. I turned off first the engine and then the headlights. A square of light fell from a cabin window onto the deck, its edges engulfed by the night shadows. I spent a lot of time watching those shadows.

"Aren't we going in?" Skarda asked.

"Shhh," I said.

I reached up behind the seat and found the overhead light, sliding the switch so that it wouldn't go on when I opened the door.

"What are you doing?" Skarda asked.

"Shhh," I said again.

I opened the driver's door and slid out, the Glock in my hand, staying as close to the Cherokee as possible. I hugged the frame as I made my way around the SUV to the passenger door. I opened it slowly. It took a few anxious moments to manage it in the dark, but I eventually opened the handcuff that had chained Skarda to the door. I eased him out of the vehicle and then recuffed his hands behind his back.

"Is that really necessary?" he said. He added an "Oh, geez" when he felt the Glock.

"Listen up," I shouted. "I have the muzzle of a nine-millimeter handgun pressed against Dave's back. Anyone fires a gun, anyone makes a sudden move, anyone does anything at all that I don't like and I'll cut his spine in half. Do we understand each other?"

There was silence, so I shouted again. "Do you understand?"

"Yes," a voice said from the darkness on my right.

"Yeah, okay," said a voice on my left.

I nudged Skarda. "Dave, Dave, Dave," I said. "After all we've been through together, too."

"How did you know they were there?"

"What the hell, man? Did you really think this was my first rodeo?"

"We're just being careful."

"You had damn well better be careful." I spoke loudly so Skarda's crew could hear. "We're moving to the cabin now. How 'bout we all err on the side of caution, okay?"

"Okay," said a voice.

"Don't start nothing, won't be nothing," said the other.

"Really," I said. "You're talking smack?" I lowered my voice. "Any last words, Dave?"

"Dammit, Jimmy," he said. "Don't screw around."

"I won't," he said.

How the hell do you get yourself into these things? my inner voice asked. *You should be home watching the Twins on TV.*

Too late now, I told myself.

"Here we go," I said out loud.

I eased Skarda away from the Cherokee and pushed him forward in a straight line toward the square of light. We walked slowly more for fear that I would trip over something than fear itself. I saw nothing, heard only the sound of crickets and wind rustling the leaves of invisible trees. When we reached the deck stairs, I turned so that my back was to the cabin and Skarda was directly in front of me. Together we climbed the wooden planks sideways. When we reached the light at the top of the stairs, I turned Dave so that he was shielding my body while I slid along the wall to the door. I opened the door, backed across the threshold. Once inside, I spun Skarda around so that he was now facing the cabin and I was behind him again. A woman sitting at a small kitchen table caught my eye. She smiled at me, but that was meant only as a distraction. An old man dressed in a Che Guevara T-shirt was standing just inside the doorway. Long hair as gray as roadside slush fell to his shoulders. He was bracing the wooden stock of a 16-gauge double barrel against his shoulder. The business end was pointed at my head.

"Drop your gun," he said.

Instead, I quickly reached up with my empty hand and angled the barrel away so that it was pointing at the wall. At more or less that same time, I used the muzzle of Glock to violently rap the fingers the old man had curled around the shotgun where the stock met the trigger mechanism. He howled in pain, and I pulled the double barrel from his grasp.

"Damn hippie," I said.

The old man folded his fingers into a fist and shoved them under his armpit as if that would somehow ease the pain. Skarda turned toward him.

"Dad," he said. There was genuine concern in his voice.

I brought the Glock up and pointed it at Skarda's head. The old man moaned and said, "He broke my hand," and I pointed the gun at him. "Why did you hurt him?" the woman asked, so I pointed the gun at her. She was still sitting at the table, her chair turned so that she could leave it in a hurry. I couldn't see her hands, so I told her, "Let me see your hands." She brought them up and rested them on the tabletop. They were empty.

Skarda went to the old man. His hands were still cuffed behind his back, so there wasn't much he could do. "Let me see," he said.

The old man uncurled his fingers and flexed them cautiously. They might have been bruised—hell, I hoped they were bruised—but they were unbroken.

"Is he all right?" asked a quiet voice. Only it wasn't the woman sitting at the table. This voice belonged to a woman who had poked her head around the doorway that led to a room in the back of the cabin.

"Come into the light," I said.

She stepped through the doorway and into the room, moving cautiously as if threatened by life's sharp edges. She was young, no more than twenty-one I guessed, with golden hair that reached halfway down her back, a fetching figure, and smooth, milky-fresh skin colored with the tint of roses, skin I've seen only on northern girls. Yet it was her eyes that I found most remarkable. They were warm and wide open and so honest that meeting them made a fellow regret his long-forgotten sins. She would have been quite beautiful if not for the expression of despair on her face and the bruise under her chin.

"Are you Josie?" I asked.

"I'm Josie." I turned my head toward the woman sitting at the table while keeping the Glock pointed at Skarda and the old man. "What are you going to do?" she asked. Her eyes were tired, and her voice was filled with tension. She was about thirty-five, with hair that didn't know if it was red or brown. Her face was angular and clean-lined with a dusting of freckles across her nose and cheeks. She wasn't pretty, yet no one would have called her plain.

"Call your friends into the cabin," I said. "Tell them to leave their guns outside."

"Why should I?"

"Because you're an adult, not a child playing cops and robbers." I gestured at the old man. "Because I could have done a lot worse than rapping his knuckles."

Josie stood slowly and moved toward the door. When she did, I pulled Skarda backward so that he was standing between me and everyone else in the cabin. I rested the barrel of the shotgun on his shoulder just below his ear and pressed the muzzle of the Glock against his back.

"Jimmy," she called. "Roy. Can you hear me? I need you to come into the cabin. Leave your guns on the deck."

"Hell w'that."

Josie took a deep breath, closed her eyes, and gritted her teeth, giving me the impression of an elementary school teacher slowly counting to ten. "Must you argue all the time, Roy?" she said. "That's why no one likes you. Everything's a debate."

"People like me."

"Get your ass in this cabin right this minute."

A moment later I heard heavy footsteps on the deck. The door flew open and Roy stepped into the room. He was tall and clean-shaven, ten years older than Josie, with the furrowed brow of a man who would rather have his car stolen than admit he had forgotten where he parked it. He leaned down toward Josie, bringing his face within inches of hers.

"Don't talk to me that way," he hissed.

"Hey, pal," I said. He pivoted and looked at me as if he were surprised to find me standing there. I angled the barrel of the shotgun so it was pointed between his eyes. "Stand by the old man and be quiet."

His eyes narrowed, and he smiled with soft hostility. "Make me," he said.

"What, are you five years old? Get over there."

"Do what he says, Roy," Skarda told him. "I already saw him kill a man today. Shot him three times—"

"Hey, Dave, hey." I whacked Skarda's ear with the barrel of the shotgun. "You didn't see anything. Did you?"

Skarda rubbed his ear. "No, I didn't see anything," he said.

"Go stand over there, Roy," I said.

Roy moved next to the old man. The young woman joined him there. She set a hand on his arm, a gesture meant to assuage his anger and frustration. He brushed it aside and glared malevolently at her. She backed away.

"Jimmy," I said. "You still out there?"

"Yes."

"Come on in."

"You won't hurt me, will you?"

"Why would I do that?"

Apparently Jimmy couldn't think of a good reason, because he entered the cabin and moved to where the young woman was standing. He took her hand and squeezed it.

"Are you okay, Jills?"

She cradled his head and rested it against her shoulder. "It'll be all right, Jims," she said.

"It'll be all right, Jims," Roy said. The disdain in his voice was unmistakable. "What do you know about it?"

She looked from Roy to me. Her remarkable eyes darkened and she found a spot on the floor to stare at. Jimmy lifted his head from her shoulder and stood straight, but he did not release her hand.

"Nothing bad will happen as long as we all keep our heads," I said. I was still using Skarda as a shield, still balancing the shotgun on his shoulder. "Who are you people?"

"You know me," Josie said. "You know my brother. This is my father." Her gesture swept from the old man to Jimmy and the girl. "These are my cousins Jillian and James Neihart. This is Jill's husband, Roy Cepek."

Now we know where she got the bruise, my inner voice said.

"What is this?" I asked. "A family reunion? Never mind. All I want to do is get my money and get out of here."

"What money?" Roy asked.

"The fifty thousand dollars that Dave promised to pay if I broke him out of jail."

"We don't have it," Josie said.

"You said twenty-five," Skarda said.

"All right, I'll settle for twenty-five," I said.

"We don't have it," Josie said.

"Remember what I said about nothing bad happening? We might want to rethink that."

"Mr. Dyson—"

"How much do you have?"

"Nothing."

"Nothing?"

"I'm sorry."

I whacked Skarda's ear again. "Nothing, she said." He brought his fingers up to soothe his ear, and I whacked them, too. "Nothing," I repeated.

"I can explain," Skarda said.

"Volatile personality, Dave. Remember? I did warn you."

"Nick," Josie said. "Your name is Nick, right?"

"Dyson. Just make it Dyson. Let's not get overly friendly here."

"Dyson, we don't have fifty thousand dollars. We don't have twenty-five thousand dollars. We don't even have twenty-five hundred dollars. We're barely making expenses as it is."

"What do you have?"

Josie stepped forward. "We can give you a place to hide for a while. A place that's safe and no hard feelings, okay? I mean, we pointed guns at you and you pointed guns at us . . ."

"Here? Is this the safe place you're talking about?"

"Yes, and—"

"I've seen airport terminals with less traffic."

"And tomorrow, tomorrow we can give you some money and show you a place where you can cross over into Canada. That's where you're going, isn't it? Canada?"

"How much money?"

"A couple of thousand, anyway. That's the best we can do."

"Where are you going to get it?"

"We're going to rob a grocery store in Silver Bay."

"A grocery store?"

"Don't you know who we are?" Jimmy asked. "We're the Iron Range Bandits."

"What is that? A garage band?"

"We're in the news. We're famous."

I suddenly felt very tired. I let the barrel of the shotgun slip off of Skarda's shoulder and sat at the kitchen table. It was flimsy and wobbled when I leaned against it as if one of its legs were shorter than the others. I set the Glock on top of the table within easy reach and draped the shotgun over my knees.

"Famous," I said. "You're happy about that? God help me, I'm surrounded by amateurs."

"What's wrong with being famous?"

"What's your name again? Jimmy?" He nodded. "Jimmy, the last thing you want is to make the evening news. The very last thing you want is a nickname. See, the longer you stay out of jail, the less likely you are to go to jail. City cops, county cops, they have limited resources, only so many investigators. You pull a heist and they'll be on it like white on rice. They'll interview witnesses, examine the crime scene, study the film taken by hidden cameras, develop leads, talk to their CIs, check the strip joints and casinos and bars to see who's throwing money around, inquire at local banks to learn who's making large cash deposits, question the usual suspects—they'll do all those things. If after a period of time nothing pans out—well, they're going to have other crimes to solve, aren't they? So they'll redline your case, they'll rededicate their resources and retask their investigators to the cases they have a better chance of clearing, follow me?"

Jimmy nodded some more.

"However, if the media gives you a nickname, 'Iron Range Bandits Strike Again,' suddenly you're a priority. For one thing, you're making the cops look bad; you're hurting their professional pride. For another, a chief of police, a county sheriff, they have to run for reelection, right? Catching you helps their chances; letting you get away hurts them. Then there's the very real possibility that they might just say screw it and ask the Minnesota Bureau of Criminal Apprehension to step in, and they have investigators and resources to burn. No, sir, you do not want a nickname. You have a nickname, they're never going to stop looking for you."

"What do you know about it?" Roy asked.

"He's a big-time crook," Jimmy said. He meant it as a compliment.

"Yeah, big-time," I said. "I'm an escaped prisoner hiding out in the North Woods with the frickin' Waltons. Doesn't get much bigger than that."

Six pairs of eyes regarded me cautiously.

"Oh, hell," I said. "It's not like I have many options. Ms. Skarda, I will take you up on your kind offer."

I stood and tucked the Glock back under my belt. I broke open the 16-gauge, removed the two shells, shut it, and handed it to the old man. He took it from my hand as if he were planning to take it whether I liked it or not.

"Che Guevara," I said. "Really?"

"He wasn't afraid to stand up to the man."

"Get a haircut."

I handed Josie the key to the handcuffs, and she freed her brother. She wrapped her arms around him and hugged. She was shorter by about a foot, and her head slid beneath his chin. He hugged her back.

"I was so worried about you," she said.

"Have you heard from Liz?"

Josie squeezed him tighter. "No," she said. "What are you going to do?"

"About Liz?"

"About everything. You can't stay here, not in Krueger. Dyson's right. This is the first place the police will look. Even if they don't find you, so many people know you up here, can recognize you on the street—anyone can pick up a phone."

"Drop a dime," I said.

"What?"

I moved back to the kitchen table. Josie continued to hug her brother, but her eyes followed me.

"The correct phrase is drop a dime," I said. " 'Course, drop a dime, pick up a phone, it all amounts to the same thing—you can't trust anyone. Welcome to my world."

Josie gave her brother a quick squeeze before releasing him. "Have you eaten?" she asked. "Would you like a sandwich?"

"I'm starving," Skarda said.

Josie moved toward the refrigerator. I took a deep breath while she did and smelled fried everything—you could pull a handful of grease out of the air.

"Do you live here?" I asked.

"No one does. We use the cabin as a kind of staging area for our jobs. The only time we talk about our jobs is while we're here."

"When you're here, who does the cooking?"

"I do. Why do you ask?"

"Just curious."

"Tell me something, Dyson. Why did you help my brother?"

"It seemed like a good idea at the time."

"Tell me the truth."

"The truth is I was going to leave your brother handcuffed in the back of the squad car with an irate deputy. I took him with me because of the money, because of the fifty thousand he promised." I wagged a finger in Skarda's direction. "Don't think for a minute I'm not still annoyed about that."

Josie nodded her head, yet the expression on her face suggested that she wasn't satisfied with my answer.

"Ham and cheese okay?" she asked.

"Fine," I said.

While she got out the sandwich fixings, Skarda disappeared through the doorway where Jill had first emerged. I took a look. The front part of the cabin consisted of one large room divided into a kitchen, dining room, and living room. The back had two bedrooms with a bathroom between them. Skarda had stepped into a bedroom with two sets of bunk beds and a large metal locker. The other bedroom had a queen-sized bed and a small dresser. Besides that, the living room area had two sofas that could also be used for sleeping, and I saw a couple of foam mattresses that were meant to be tossed on the floor for additional sleeping space. The cabin was small, yet apparently built by someone who expected a lot of overnight visitors.

Skarda stepped out of the bedroom wearing a pair of worn cowboy boots. He was carrying the county-issued sneakers in his hand. He dropped them on the floor and kicked them beneath a sofa.

"I need a shower," he announced.

"That can wait," Josie said. "Eat first."

Skarda sat at the table. Josie slipped packaged ham, American cheese, lettuce, and tomato between two slices of white bread, set it on a paper plate, and slid it in front of him. She served me the same. Skarda ate as if he had just discovered food. Me, not so much.

"Coffee?" Josie asked.

"Thanks, sis," Skarda said.

Josie poured a mug for both of us. It was so strong you could eat it with a fork. I told her it was excellent just the same. As I ate and drank, the old man moved between the refrigerator and the kitchen table. He opened the refrigerator and produced a can of cheap beer, which must have been tough to do because he was staring at me the entire time. He opened the beer and took a drink, then sat at the table across from me. He kept staring.

"Something I can do for you, Dad?" I asked.

"You look like a narc to me," he said.

"You look like a district court judge."

The remark caught him by surprise. It took him a few beats before he realized that I didn't mean it. In the silence that followed, Josie drifted to Jimmy's side and whispered in his ear. He gave me a quick glance and disappeared into a bedroom. After he emerged, he walked right out the front door without a word. He was carrying something in his right hand, but I couldn't see what it was.

"You want a beer?" the old man asked.

"No, thank you."

"I don't trust a man who doesn't drink. Seems like he's hiding something."

"I don't trust a man who drinks too much. He doesn't hide anything."

He thought long and hard about that before replying. "Are you calling me a drunk?"

"Never crossed my mind." I don't think he believed me, possibly because I was speaking around a mouthful of ham and cheese at the time. "Tell me about this job of yours," I said. "This great grocery store heist."

"None of your business," Roy said. He was sitting on a sofa in the living room. I had to turn in my chair to see him. His young wife was sitting directly across from him. Her hands were folded in her lap and she was staring straight ahead. Her remarkable eyes now had the blank look of someone who had been gazing at an iPod too long.

"I don't know," Skarda said. "Maybe he can help; give us some tips."

"Us? You're not going."

Skarda turned in his chair and glared at Roy. "Who says?"

"The job was planned for five," Josie said. "Besides, what if someone recognizes you?"

"In Silver Bay? No one's gonna know me in Silver Bay."

"We can't take the risk."

"Well, then, who's going to be your inside man?"

"Jimmy."

"Jimmy?"

As if on cue, the young man entered the cabin. He was carrying a black box about the size of an old transistor radio with a collapsible antenna.

"Car's clean," he said.

Josie gestured toward me, and Jimmy stepped over and extended the antenna on his box.

"What is that?" I asked.

"It's a frequency finder that I bought on Amazon. We use it to detect GPS trackers and other bugs, hidden cameras, phone taps, that sort of thing. We once found a GPS transmitter in a bag of money we stole."

I stood without argument, spread my arms and legs wide, and let him move the antenna over me. At the same time, I glanced down at Skarda's feet, noticing his boots again.

"Nothing," Jimmy said at last.

"Good," Josie said. "We don't mean to offend you, Dyson, but—"

"Now do your cousin," I said.

"What?" said Jimmy.

"Do Dave. Check him out, too."

"C'mon," Skarda said.

"It'll only take a second," Jimmy said.

Skarda stood, and Jimmy ran the antenna over him while watching the box's black and gold face. When he finished, he said, "He's clean, too."

"Well, duh," Skarda said.

"Everybody happy?" I asked. "How 'bout you, Dad?"

The old man smiled at me. He was a happy drunk. I liked that.

"Like I said, we don't mean any disrespect," Josie told me.

"Please, don't apologize," I said. "This is the only smart thing I've seen you people do since I've been here."

"It's just that David escaping the way he did, escaping with you so soon after he was caught by the police, and both of you showing up here, it's such a coincidence."

"You have every reason to be cautious, although I doubt the cops would go to such extremes just to catch the Iron Range Bandits."

"You think you're something special, don't you?" Roy rose to his feet, although with his height it was more of an unfolding. He stood in the center of the living room, the legs straight without locking his knees, his feet about ten inches apart, his hands locked behind his back and centered on the belt. "If you're such a master criminal, how come you got caught?"

"I trusted a man who I thought was my friend. We all make mistakes." I was staring at Skarda when I spoke, and I saw his Adam's apple bob. I thought I also heard him gulp, but that was probably just my imagination.

"I'm not impressed," Roy said.

"I'm going to lose a lot of sleep over that."

"I'm impressed," Jimmy said.

"This coming from a kid who wanted to start a marijuana farm in the Superior National Forest," Roy said.

"Claire liked the idea."

"Claire?" said Skarda. "Claire hasn't got the brains God gave an aardvark."

Jimmy turned and looked me in the eye as if he expected me to defend Claire, whoever she was. Like I'm an authority on the intelligence of aardvarks.

"I had a spot all picked out," Jimmy said. "Deep in the forest where no one would have stumbled over it. I had processing equipment, packaging—in three to five months I would have been ready for distribution."

"What happened?" I asked.

"No one in this family is going into the drug business," Josie said.

"That happened," Jimmy said as he gestured toward his cousin.

"We're consumers, not dealers," said the old man.

Jimmy shook his head the way I expected Willis Carrier might have when his family pooh-poohed air-conditioning. He produced a laptop and plugged it into a phone jack. A few minutes later he had his browser up. He googled Nick Dyson and files appeared. The files were genuine. There really was a career criminal named Nicholas Dyson who specialized in robbing banks, jacking armored cars, and burgling the occasional jewelry store. We picked him because his physical description resembled mine—all we did was swap out his photo wherever we found it. The most recent file was from the Web site of the *Minneapolis Star Tribune* newspaper. It had booking photos of Skarda and me. In mine I had a scraggly beard and long hair that didn't appear fake at all.

"You get a haircut and shave after you were caught?" Jimmy asked.

"Wanted to make sure I looked like a sober, law-abiding citizen if my case came to trial," I said. "I was even going to wear a sweater like the one that guy wore in *Mister Rogers' Neighborhood*."

"You have an answer for everything, don't you?" Roy said from the living room.

He was being deliberately provocative, trying to goad me into a fight. Rushmore McKenzie would have ignored him, but then he had a job to do, and it didn't include beating up middle-aged punks with chips on their shoulders. Nick Dyson, on the other hand, had a reputation to uphold. He was a bad man, and if these people were going to do what he needed them to do, he might have to prove it.

"Roy," I said, "do you really want me to go over there and fuck you up in front of your pretty wife? I know you'll slap her around later to prove you're a man, but she'll see it and she'll remember. So will everyone else."

To show I meant business I stood up, took the Glock from where I had holstered it between my belt and the small of my back, and stepped away from the table. Jimmy went to his sister and pulled her out of the line of fire. The old man dodged out of the way as well. Skarda sat in his chair and watched. Roy eyed me cautiously yet did not move. It occurred to me that I might have played my hand too hard, forcing Roy to go all in even though neither he nor I wanted to. Fortunately, clearer heads prevailed. Josie stepped directly between us, slowly looking first at Roy, then at me, then Roy, and finally back to me again.

"I'm grateful for what you did for my brother," she said. "But gratitude has an expiration date. Like a sack of donuts, after a while it just goes stale. You know?"

"I'll be out of your hair by this time tomorrow," I said.

Josie glanced over her shoulder at Roy. He found something on the wall that seemed to demand his immediate attention and was pretending not to listen to us.

"Good," she said. "On that happy note, I think we should be thinking about sleep. Jill, you're with me in the master bedroom."

Jill drifted toward the doorway while watching her husband as if she expected him to stop her. When he didn't, she disappeared into the bedroom.

"Roy, why don't you, Dad, and Jimmy take the bunk beds. Dave, you stay out here with Mr. Dyson."

"In case I decide to run off with the silverware," I added.

Jimmy grinned. He was the only one who did.

Blankets and pillows were doled out. Jimmy, Roy, and the old man went quietly into their bedroom while the women went into theirs. Skarda bedded down on the sofa across from me. When he wasn't looking, I took the county-issued sneakers he had been wearing when we escaped and pushed them farther back under the sofa where no one could see them.

FOUR

I couldn't sleep; wasn't sure I wanted to. It was well past midnight and Skarda was snoring softly when I rolled off my sofa, went to the refrigerator, and found a beer. It was in a blue and white can, the kind of beer I would ridicule even before I quit the St. Paul Police Department to collect a seven-digit reward on an embezzler. But I was stuck in a North Woods cabin with Fagin and his pickpockets, and beggars can't be choosy. I took it out onto the deck, opened it, sat in a chair, propped my feet on the railing, and took a long pull. The air was crisp, yet I didn't mind. A half moon hung in the sky, its beams reflecting off the borderless black water just visible beyond the trees.

I drank slowly while my inner voice debated my options. It kept coming back to the same one—*Jump into the Jeep Cherokee and get the hell out of here.* Since becoming a man of leisure I sometimes worked as an unlicensed private investigator doing the occasional favor for friends. But the people I was working for, they weren't actually my friends, and this was frickin' dangerous.

On the other hand, so far everything had gone exactly as planned. Besides, there was something exhilarating about being undercover, knowing that at any moment you could give yourself away. I understood why some cops like it so much . . .

I blamed Harry, real name Brian Wilson, special agent working out of the Minneapolis office of the Federal Bureau of Investigation. I called him Harry because when I met him five years ago he reminded me of the character actor Harry Dean Stanton. He had been working at the time with an agent of the Bureau of Alcohol, Tobacco, Firearms, and Explosives named Chad Bullert. I blamed him, too.

Three days ago—was it only three days?—Bullert ambushed me in the clubhouse of the Columbia Golf Course in Minneapolis. I liked Columbia—it was a short course with narrow fairways that favored course management over distance. After playing eighteen holes, Harry and I had stopped in the clubhouse to talk it over. The waitress had just served our drinks when Bullert appeared, behaving as if meeting us like that had been as lucky as picking the Gopher 5. All of my internal alarm systems flared at once. It wasn't that I had any fear of Bullert, whom I hadn't seen since that frigid night in Lakeville. It was that he was wearing a suit, a tie, and black wingtips. Clearly he hadn't come to Columbia for a good walk spoiled, as Twain might have put it.

After taking a seat, Bullert said, "McKenzie, I was just thinking about you."

"Is that right?"

"How's the shoulder?"

I flexed it to show that my broken collarbone had healed nicely. "Good as new," I said.

"The concussion—no lingering symptoms, I hope."

"Nothing for a couple of months now, thanks for asking," I said. "Why *are* you asking?"

"I heard you got banged up a while back. Something about a museum heist." He was staring at Harry now, looking for assistance. The FBI agent's expression suggested that he was uncomfortable about giving it, although it occurred to me that Bullert would not have known I was going to be at the golf course if Harry hadn't told him. I took a sip of my beverage and waited for the shoe to drop. It didn't take long.

"Busy these days?" Bullert asked.

"I manage to keep occupied," I said.

"Doing favors for friends, I hear."

"McKenzie's a born kibitzer," Harry said.

Bullert pointed at my drink. "Buy you another?"

I rested the palm of my hand on top of the glass. "No, I'm good."

Bullert nodded.

Harry nodded.

I nodded, too, but then I hate to be left out.

"What?" I asked. "What do you want, Chad?"

"How come you never gave me a nickname like Harry?"

"I did. I called you Alec because you look like the actor Alec Baldwin, but I haven't seen you for five years so it didn't stick."

Bullert turned to Harry. "Do I look like Alec Baldwin?"

"No," Harry said.

"What do you guys want?" I asked.

Harry looked away as if he were too embarrassed to answer. Bullert wasn't so self-conscious. "I need a favor," he said.

"What kind of favor?"

"Will you help?"

"What kind of favor?"

"It's for your country."

Uh-oh, my inner voice said. *For Bullert to play that card so early in the conversation . . .*

"A wise man once said that patriotism is the last refuge of a scoundrel," I told him.

"What's that supposed to mean?"

"You wouldn't be shamelessly appealing to my love of country unless something went splat and now you need assistance cleaning up the mess. Am I right?"

Bullert gave Harry a sideways glance. Again he seemed to want help, and again Harry looked like he wished he were somewhere else.

"Have you ever heard of Operation Fast and Furious?" Bullert asked.

"Is that the title of the new Vin Diesel movie?"

"We're serious, McKenzie."

"Yes, I know about Fast and Furious. It was in all the papers."

"What do you know?"

"It was the name of a sting gone bad. A few years ago, the ATF—you guys—and some federal prosecutors supplied gun dealers with seventeen hundred weapons, the plan being that you would track the weapons and then arrest the dealers and their customers when they illegally resold them to the Mexican drug cartels. Only you screwed up—you lost track of the guns. Now they're popping up at crime scenes all along the border. There's evidence that they might even have been used to kill our own guys. Congress found out, hearings were held, disgruntled ATF agents and other whistle-blowers testified, high-ranking officials lost their jobs, the administration was embarrassed—just another sunny day in our nation's capital."

"We've recovered about half the guns one way or the other," Bullert said. "Still can't account for the other half, though."

"Butterfingers."

"A couple days ago, we got a lead."

"What lead?"

"I need to tell you something, but it must be held in strictest confidence."

I didn't respond. Again Bullert sought help from Harry. "McKenzie can keep a secret," the FBI agent said.

Bullert rubbed his face and then set his hands palms down on the table in front of him. He stared at the table, studying it carefully as if he wanted to commit it to memory.

"Some of the guns have shown up along the Canadian border," he said.

"Where?"

"Northern Minnesota."

"Ahh, c'mon . . ."

"We apprehended a man armed with an AK-47 that we sold in Arizona. He was attempting to rob the box office of a music festival near Grand Rapids; the Itasca County Sheriff's Department arrested him. There were five people involved. Four of them got away clean. Skarda—his car broke down, an old Saturn, blew a timing belt during the getaway. A patrol car rolled up; the deputy didn't even know about the robbery. He saw the AK on the seat and said, 'Hey.' "

"Top-flight police work all around," Harry said.

"The suspect's name was David Skarda," Bullert said. "We think he's a member of a crew called the Iron Range Bandits."

"The what?"

"That's what the *Duluth News Tribune* named them. They appeared about a year ago—robbed a couple of grocery stores, a bar known to cash payroll checks, never making much more than ten thousand dollars and usually less. So far they haven't hurt anyone that we know of. Sooner or later that's going to change, though."

"Yeah, it will," I said. Their fault, the victim's fault, nobody's fault—if they kept thieving, sooner or later someone would get shot. It was as inevitable as the rising of the sun.

"Skarda had no previous record, so we thought it would be easy to flip him, but he won't be flipped," Harry said. "Won't tell us anything. He's facing a four-year jolt and seems content to do it all."

"Which means he knows nothing about prison," I said. "Which means he's probably not a career criminal."

"Or it could be he doesn't want to rat out his family," Bullert said. "That's what the Itasca sheriff thinks. He wants to look into it. We're holding him back. We're holding everyone back—the BCA, too."

"Why?"

"The guns, McKenzie. We need to get those damn guns off the border."

"Just because Skarda is stand-up doesn't mean the rest of his people are. You lean on them, someone will talk."

"What if they don't? What if the gunrunners learn that we're looking into it and get spooked?"

"What if, what if—what do you want me to do about it?"

"We've arranged for Skarda to escape custody," Harry said.

"We want you to go with him," Bullert said. "Infiltrate the crew."

"Sure," I said. "Just like they do on TV."

"We're not asking you to stop the gunrunning," Harry said. "We're not asking you to arrest anyone. All we want is a name."

"And a location," Bullert said.

"But we'll settle for a name. Find out who supplied the AK to Skarda, and we'll take it from there."

"Why me?" I asked. "I don't have any undercover experience. You have agents who are trained for this sort of thing, who actually like this sort of thing. Why would you—wait a minute. Wait a minute! Why are we even having this conversation? I'm not a cop."

"You used to be," Bullert said. "A good one."

"Operative words being 'used to be.'" The expression on their faces told me everything. "You're working the case off the books, aren't you? It's a black bag job. You don't want anyone in Justice to know about it. You're afraid there'll be a leak, that someone will go running off to Congress and the hearings will start up again and everyone will be embarrassed and more supervisors will get fired."

"That won't happen if we recover the guns," Bullert said.

"If, brother. If."

"McKenzie, it's not just about our reputation," Bullert said. "Every time a crime occurs along the Mexican border, people, especially politicians, they start screaming about building electrified fences, building moats, for God's sake. Do you want them to start talking like that up here? With Canada? Do you want to see a fence along the Rainy River, the Great Lakes, the St. Lawrence Seaway?"

"It would be one frickin' long fence," I said.

"You know what I'm talking about."

"Yes, I do." I turned in my chair to face Harry. "What does this have to do with you? You're not ATF."

"I asked him for help," Bullert said. "I asked Harry if he knew someone we could depend on, someone we could trust. He mentioned your name."

I was still looking at Harry when I said, "I'm going to have to thank him for that one of these days."

"I want to get the guns, too," Harry said. "Before someone gets hurt. Do you know how many killings there have been along the Mexican border tied to ATF guns? This seems like as good a plan as any to get them back."

"You don't really believe that, do you?"

Harry shrugged.

"Will you do it, McKenzie?" Bullert asked. "Will you help us?"

It took about three seconds to decide. I leaned back in the chair again and spread my hands wide, palms up.

"Hell no," I said.

'Course, that was then. Now I was sitting on a deck in the North Woods overlooking a lake I could barely see in the dark. I felt movement behind me and turned my head in time to see the cabin door open slowly and a figure step out. White T-shirt, white shorts—even in the dark I could tell they were worn by a woman.

"Good evening," I said.

There was a startled intake of breath before the figure eased cautiously toward me.

"Mr. Dyson?" Josie asked. She kept her voice low, probably out of deference to her sleeping family, I figured, so I spoke quietly, too.

"Just call me Dyson," I said. "I thought we settled that."

"Why aren't you in bed?"

"I couldn't sleep—blame it on unfamiliar surroundings. How 'bout you?"

"I'm anxious about tomorrow."

"If it doesn't feel right, Josie, just walk away."

"Is that your professional advice?"

"As a matter of fact, it is."

"I wish it were that easy."

"You need to make it that easy."

"You don't understand. There are bills to be paid."

"I figured it had to be something like that."

"What do you mean?"

"There are only three reasons people steal—to feed their family, to take a vacation in Jamaica, or to pay for a drug habit. You guys don't look like meth heads to me, and this certainly isn't Montego Bay. That leaves Jean Valjean and his loaf of bread."

She moved to the railing, stepping between the moon and me, and I became aware of the shape of her body beneath the shorts and T-shirt. It was a nice shape, a body to arouse MILF fantasies in the young men at the minimart and gas station. Being older, of course, I was immune.

"Dyson, if you don't mind my asking, how did you become a criminal? I only ask because you seem so comfortable in the role."

"Me?" I flashed on Harry and Bullert. "You could say I fell in with the wrong crowd."

"Now I'm the wrong crowd." Josie's voice reminded me of a tenor saxophone. It was quiet and calm and totally without self-pity. "I'm the people my parents warned me about when I was growing up. I didn't mean to become a criminal, you know."

"No one ever does. It just kind of sneaks up on you."

"Everything went from bad to worse so quickly. First, the mines closed—I suppose we all saw that coming, but we were still unprepared for the consequences. Babbitt, the City of Babbitt, was hit hard. It has a high school built for two thousand students and an enrollment of a hundred and sixty. Last time I looked, a four-bedroom house was selling for forty thousand dollars and no takers. A couple of months ago the city's only grocery and drug stores burned down—maybe they'll be rebuilt, I don't know. In the meantime, people have to drive twenty miles to Krueger or Ely just to get a gallon of milk.

"Then the paper mill in Krueger closed, and no one saw

that coming. Two hundred and forty employees out of work, and that's not counting the loggers and truckers and all the others that depended on it. The mill was profitable, too; it was making money producing cardboard boxes for Kellogg, Budweiser, FedEx. Its parent company filed for bankruptcy for reasons that had nothing to do with us, though, and they just boarded it up. We were all hoping the company would sell the mill; we were told that was the plan. Learned that was a lie when the company decided to turn off the heat last January to save a few dollars—turn off the heat in the dead of a Minnesota winter. No matter how hard they tried to drain and winterize, there were so many feet of piping and odd angles—water pipes burst, equipment was destroyed, infrastructure damaged. The mill was built thirty years ago. Today, the place looks like ancient ruins. No one is going to buy it now—reopen it.

"All this on top of the housing crisis. Unemployment in Krueger is over twenty percent. It's about sixteen percent across the Range. One in six people is living below the poverty level. The government says it's a recession. Sure looks like a depression to me. My business—did David tell you I was a real estate agent, that I specialized in selling lake homes? My business went away, too.

"We're all supposed to keep a positive attitude, though. We're all supposed to carry on. That's what they tell us. Carry on. How? With what? There aren't any jobs, Dyson, minimum wage or otherwise, and there aren't going to be any. That's why the Range is losing population and the Cities are growing at double digits, because that's where all the jobs are. You either leave the only home you've ever known, where your parents lived and your grandparents and great-grandparents lived, or . . ."

"Or you steal," I said. "You don't need to justify yourself to me, Josie."

"Is that what I'm doing?"

"My experience, the reason most people are honest, seem to be honest, is because they've never had a reason—or at least the opportunity—to be anything else."

"You're saying we're all thieves at heart?"

"Not at all. Some people are painfully honest. That lovely little girl asleep in there—I bet she's been against what you're doing from the very start."

"Jillian doesn't understand the real world."

"From the bruise on her chin I'd say she's learning fast."

"Roy. I suppose it's been tougher on him than the rest of us."

"Oh yeah?"

"He was in the army."

"I gathered that."

"You did?"

"He's always standing at parade rest."

"You don't miss much, do you, Dyson? After he retired from the army, they gave him a management position at the paper mill. They hired him to systematically lay off the workforce so they wouldn't get their hands dirty. He hated doing it, just hated it, but he was used to following orders. He became terribly depressed. It didn't help that since he was the man handing out the pink slips, people held him personally responsible for what was happening. He was the face of the company; people didn't know whom else to blame. When he finished the job, the company fired him, too—fired him in an e-mail. This is a man who's known structure his entire life. Now he's adrift."

"Isn't that just too damn bad for Roy?"

"You're not a particularly compassionate character, are you, Dyson?"

"Compassion has its downside. For example, it makes you perfectly willing to forgive Roy for abusing his wife."

"I didn't mean it that way. I meant—it's hard sometimes knowing what to do."

"Think so? If Jill were my cousin, I'd know what to do. I'd beat the sonuvabitch to death for hitting her, and I wouldn't give a rat's ass what drove him to it. But as you suggest, I'm not particularly virtuous."

"You're a violent man."

"On the contrary. There are few people as laid-back as I am. I just happen to live in a world where violence is always an option, sometimes the only option. You live in that world now, too, whether you care to admit it or not. You're carrying guns into the grocery store tomorrow, aren't you? Tell me, Jo-Ellen, if it all goes bad, if someone gets between you and the door, will you shoot him? Will you take his life just so you can pay your bills? Will you become a killer?"

"Would you?"

"I don't have to make that decision. I'm not the one going into the grocery store, you are."

Josie stared into the darkness for a long time without speaking. The moon continued its slow arch across the sky. There were crickets and frogs and the rustling of leaves in the wind, and when she shifted her weight I heard the moan of wooden planks beneath her feet. Finally she turned and moved toward the door of the cabin.

"Good night," she said.

"Sweet dreams." I didn't mean anything by it, yet the words made her pause just the same.

"This is only temporary," Josie said. "Just until things get better."

I didn't know if she was speaking to me or to herself. A moment later she disappeared inside the cabin.

I slept surprisingly well. When I woke, the cabin was filled with activity. Someone said, "Where the fuck is Dyson?" Skarda and the old man stepped out onto the deck. "There you are," Skarda said. I was sitting in a lounge chair; the blanket I had retrieved after Josie went to bed was wrapped around me.

The old man shook his head like he was embarrassed for me. "You afraid we were gonna jump you in your sleep?" he asked.

I pulled the blanket away with one hand, giving him a good look at the Glock that I held in the other. "The thought never occurred to me," I said.

I made my way into the cabin. Roy and Jimmy were talking in hushed tones inside one of the bedrooms. Josie was in the kitchen. She was wearing boots, baggy coveralls, and a sweatshirt; her auburn hair was tucked beneath a baseball cap. She said "Good morning" in a quiet voice and offered coffee when I approached. I took a sip. It was strong enough to bring a dinosaur to its knees.

"Mmmm," I hummed.

"Most people don't like my coffee," Josie said.

"Wimps," I said. "Tell me, what are you made up for?"

"I don't want witnesses to know I'm a woman."

"Sweetie, I could tell you're a woman from a thousand yards, and it wouldn't matter how you're dressed."

She smiled slightly at the remark and nodded, also slightly, as if she appreciated the compliment but thought it was in questionable taste.

I sat at the kitchen table. It wobbled again, and I automatically looked down to see which of its flimsy legs was the culprit. Jill was already sitting there and staring wistfully out the window. There was a mug of coffee in front of her along with an untouched plate of eggs, bacon, and hash browns.

"Good morning," I said.

"Morning," she replied in a soft, middle-C voice.

I gestured at her food. "Not hungry?"

Jill smiled weakly and shook her head in response, and I had to fight the urge to cup her smooth, cool face in my hands, kiss her forehead, and promise her only laughter and love. I was a lifelong bachelor—not necessarily by choice—and the truth of it is, no matter how much we claim that we prize our independence above all else, bachelors tend to fall in love quite easily. I hadn't heard this beautiful, unhappy young woman speak more than a half dozen words, yet I was prepared to do just about anything to protect her. I suspect Nina would have understood. She had a sense of me that I didn't comprehend myself. She knew, for example, that I was going to help Harry and Bullert even while I was telling her that it was never going to happen. Maybe that's why she had yet to give me a definitive answer even though I had proposed to her three times over the past three years. She knew something I didn't.

"What do you think?" Jimmy asked. He wasn't speaking to me, yet I turned in my chair to examine him just the same. He was wearing a nylon jacket with an elastic waistband; the jacket zipped to a couple of inches below his throat. There was a discernible bulge above his left hip.

"Is that a gun in your pocket or are you just happy to see me?" I said.

"You can see it?"

"Unzip your jacket, let it hang loose. Let your arms hang at your sides." He did. The bulge disappeared. "Do you have anything a little more appropriate for the weather? A light windbreaker?" He shook his head. I stepped next to him and pulled the hem of the jacket away to reveal a 9 mm Browning stuck in his belt. "Are you left-handed?" I asked.

"No, right-handed."

"As a general rule, you don't want to cross-draw unless

you're sitting down. In any case, you'll want to practice, especially if you're all thumbs."

Jimmy reached across his body and pulled the Browning. Both the 4⅝ inch barrel and front sight caught on his jeans.

"That happens with big automatics like this," I said. "Listen, do you have a smaller gun? A .32 caliber snub-nose with a concealed hammer is my choice. It's less likely to catch on your clothes."

"I have a .38 S&W, but I don't know," Jimmy said. "It's smaller, and it only has five shots. The Browning has ten plus one more in the chamber."

"You point a gun at someone, it's going to look as big as a howitzer no matter what size it is. My opinion, a wheel gun is more reliable, less likely to jam, okay? It's not going to eject your empties all over the place, either, in case you left your print on a shell casing."

"But five shots . . ."

"Kid, if you can't seal the deal with five, an extra six isn't going to help. Trust me on this."

"What do you know about combat?" I glanced over Jimmy's shoulder to see Roy standing in the doorway that led to the bedrooms. He was carrying an AK-47 assault rifle in the port position.

"Whoa," I said. "Where did you get that?"

I reached for the rifle, but Roy turned his shoulder away like a child protecting a toy from his older brother.

"Don't touch it," he said.

"C'mon," I said.

Roy stepped away, showing me his back. "It's none of your business where I got it," he said. "What are you even asking for?"

Back off, back off, back off, my inner voice chanted.

"Hey, hey, hey," I said aloud. "Relax, man. I'm just curious. You don't often see this kind of ordnance."

"You come in here, pushing people around, and now you want to know where we get our guns—"

Skarda and the old man walked into the cabin. They must have heard the exchange on the deck. Skarda asked, "What's going on?"

Harry and Bullert wanted me to ask questions and get answers. At the moment, I couldn't think of anything more suspicious or foolhardy. It was like when you're doing time—ask for nothing, take nothing, offer nothing, see nothing, know nothing, never show interest in the activities of others, never take sides. Sooner or later the other inmates will realize that you want nothing from them. That's when they start talking to you. I needed to change the topic of conversation in a hurry.

"You're a real desperado, aren't you, Roy?" I said. "Ex-army puke, you think you know my business? Tell me something, Roy, what are you going to do if it rains?"

The question caught him by surprise—it kind of caught me by surprise, too. He hemmed and hawed and said, "It's not going to rain."

"Oh, you can predict the weather coming off of Lake Superior?"

"I'm just saying . . ."

"I'm just saying, I know my business and you don't. You're an amateur, Roy, and this gung ho we got the barn, we got the costumes, we got frickin' AKs, let's put on a frickin' show bullshit is going to get someone killed. Roy." I spun around, went back into the kitchen, scooped up my mug, and gave Josie my best Oliver Twist impersonation. "Please, may I have some more?"

As she poured, Skarda moved close to me. "What if it does rain?" he asked.

"People lower their heads when it rains," I said. "They don't look up, they don't look around, they don't loiter on the sidewalk, and they don't window shop. Store windows, car windshields, hidden camera lenses become distorted. Vehicles are made more difficult to identify. Sound is muffled. No one questions it if you're wearing a jacket"—I pointed at Josie—"or if you're wearing a hat. Rain, Dave, is your friend."

I glared at Roy when I said that last bit. He was standing in the living room, gripping the assault rifle tightly. He was angry because he thought I was trying to show him up—I could see it in his eyes. That's what I intended, although I knew it would work against me in the long run. An experienced, trained undercover operative would have handled it better, I knew, but at least Roy didn't think I was a police spy.

"We should be going," Josie said. "Everyone knows when and where we rendezvous, right?"

The general consensus was that they all did. The four thieves made for the door. Jill rose from the kitchen table to join them.

"You, too?" I asked.

"They need me to drive," she said.

I glared at Josie. She shrugged in return.

"Good luck, sis," Skarda said. He gave Josie a hug. She glanced at me over his shoulder.

"Break a leg," I said.

I was surprised that I meant it—absolutely break a leg if it keeps you from going into that grocery store.

Where did that come from? my inner voice asked.

Good question.

A few minutes later, they were gone. Skarda and I were leaning on the redwood railing that enclosed the deck, my coffee mug balanced on the top plank. The deck was about six feet above the ground yet seemed higher because it faced a hill that angled downward for about a hundred feet to the lake—Lake Carl, it was called. There was a wooden staircase that led to a wooden dock that jutted out into the lake with a pontoon boat moored to one side and a small fishing boat with a 25-horse Johnson tied up to the other.

"Do you want to go fishing?" Skarda asked.

"I don't think so." I took a sip from my coffee mug. "Tell me, why did Roy get all bent out of shape when I asked him about his assault rifle?"

"He doesn't want anyone to know where he got the guns."

"He didn't even tell you?"

"Nope."

"That's because he's chickenshit."

"No, no, he's not, Dyson. I know you two don't get along . . ."

"Listen, kid." Skarda was only a decade or so younger than I was, yet for some reason I thought of him as a kid. "I have never met a man who beat his wife who wasn't a coward at heart. All right? You want to know why he refuses to tell you about the guns—to save his sorry ass. If you guys get popped, he'll trade the intel to the cops for reduced charges or maybe no charges at all while the rest of you go down hard."

"You think so?"

"Why else keep it a secret?"

Skarda thought about that for a long moment before he said, "You know, when I was arrested, a man from the ATF said it would go easier for me if I told him about the AK-47 I was carrying. I didn't say anything, but . . ."

"You could have."

"If I had known anything. Dammit, Roy."

"I guess you can't blame a man for looking out for Number One."

"Yes, you can." Skarda tapped his chest. "I can."

We continued to stare at the lake. I learned later that the lake was just over eighty acres in size, which meant it easily made the cut—in Minnesota a body of water needed to be at least ten acres to be considered a lake. We had 11,842 of them.

"I hate this," Skarda said. "Waiting, I mean."

"Do you know where the supermarket is?"

"There's only one in Silver Bay."

"Do you have any binoculars?"

"Sure, why?"

"Let's go watch."

"Really?"

"I'd like to see the Iron Range Bandits in action. Who knows, I might even learn a thing or two."

FIVE

From Lake Carl we made our way along washboard gravel and paved county roads through the City of Krueger—Skarda hunched down in his seat so no one would recognize him—and then up to Ely. At Ely we turned east on Minnesota Highway 1 toward Lake Superior, driving sixty-two miles of narrow, twisting, curling, climbing, and plunging roadway that took my breath away. Forget the scenic wonders of the Superior National Forest it bisected—it was a road built to excite motorcyclists and sports car fanatics while terrifying motor home and bus drivers. Driving it in winter must have been exhilarating, to say the least. When we reached the sparkling great lake, we turned south and followed the highway five miles to Silver Bay.

Silver Bay was a company town built in 1954 for the employees who were hired to process the taconite that was mined and shipped by rail from Babbitt. It gained notoriety in the sixties when it was discovered that the Reserve Mining Company had been secretly dumping taconite tailings—a potentially carcinogenic waste—into Lake Superior to the tune of 67,000 tons each day. The company didn't stop, either, until the courts forced them to cease and desist in 1972, and as far as I knew, the tailings were still there. Most of the city itself was located on top of a hill that rose up from the lake. It had been built on an area where the trees and brush had been scraped clear with bulldozers; houses and commercial buildings had been carefully laid out with surveyor stakes.

The supermarket was part of a shopping center located on, yes, Shopping Center Road. The complex had three sides, with all of the storefronts facing a large asphalt parking lot. It was hailed as the largest shopping center north of Duluth when it was first built, although I seriously doubted it still held that designation.

To reach it, I drove down Davis Drive and then took a left, driving between the Silver Bay Public Library and a weathered brown-brick building built into the side of one of the city's few hills. There was a Silver Bay police car parked in front next to a white flagpole that flew both the U.S. and Minnesota flags. I crossed Shopping Center Road and parked the Jeep Cherokee at the edge of the lot, close enough to watch the supermarket and yet far enough away that I could quickly access any one of three potential escape routes. Cars moved in and out of the lot around us.

"When is the heist scheduled?" I asked.

"No idea," Skarda said.

"Well, we're early, otherwise the place would be swarming with cops. Tell me, Dave, did you know that Silver Bay had its own police department?"

The question seemed to surprise him. "No," Skarda said. "I thought—we thought a small town like this would get police service from the county sheriff. How did you know?"

"We just drove past it. Given Silver Bay's population, I figure a half-dozen officers counting part-timers. If they're halfway professional, and that's always a smart bet, I'd say they have a response time of about, oh, sixty seconds."

"Christ."

"I doubt there's any deity wants a part of this mess."

I brought the binoculars up to my eyes and looked through them. The grocery store was large and spacious, and I guessed that it served a great many more customers than those that lived in Silver Bay. It wouldn't have been a bad target if the cop shop weren't less than five hundred yards away. After a few minutes, I handed the glasses to Skarda. There was a café behind us that offered free Wi-Fi, and I asked him if he wanted a cup of coffee. Skarda said he did and would be happy to retrieve it.

"I'll get it," I said. "Remember, you're not actually doing anything illegal, so don't act like it. Whatever happens, just sit here. Calmly."

"Calmly," Skarda repeated, as if he weren't sure what the word meant.

I walked to the café. There were cars parked in the spaces in front of it, including a red Toyota Corolla with its windows rolled down. There was a man who looked too old to drive inside listening to the radio, something by Roy Clark, while he sipped from a travel mug. I went into the café and ordered two coffees to go from a woman who seemed happy to serve me. While she poured, I pulled the prepaid cell phone from my pocket after first making sure Skarda couldn't see me. Jimmy hadn't picked it up when he ran the frequency finder over me because it wasn't turned on—it wasn't transmitting or receiving—and apparently Skarda forgot I had it. I have a lousy memory for phone numbers, so after I inputted the 612 area code for Minneapolis, I substituted letters on the keypad that equaled Chad Bullert's phone number—LUNATIC. The phone rang just twice before he answered.

"It's me," I said.

"You okay?" Bullert asked. "We tracked the GPS transmitter in Skarda's shoe to a cabin near Krueger, but there's been no movement since."

"So far, so good. The boys and girls are using the cabin as a base of operations. If you want to take them, that's the place to go. If nothing else you can arrest them for trespassing."

"What about the guns?"

"They were acquired by an ex-army named Roy Cepek. He's carrying an AK-47 with him right now."

"Where did he get it?"

"Don't know. He's being pretty closed mouth, not only to me, but to his crew as well. He sure as hell didn't buy it at Walmart. I'm guessing he'd spill his guts if you picked him up."

"On what charge?"

"Aggravated robbery. In a few minutes he and the rest of the Iron Range Bandits are going to hit a grocery store in Silver Bay."

"Christ," Bullert said. "Tell me you're not in on it."

"You're another one who tosses that name around carelessly. No, I'm not in on it. I'm what you would call a material witness. Listen, the cop shop is a brisk five-minute walk from where I'm standing . . ."

"No, don't do anything. Let it play out."

"Let it play out?"

"The guns are the important thing, McKenzie. We can get the Iron Range Bandits anytime, but the guns—McKenzie, as a private citizen you are under no legal obligation to report any crime you witness."

"I don't know if that's entirely true since I am working with law enforcement. Besides, what if someone gets shot?"

"You just do your job and we'll take care of the rest."

Sure you will, my inner voice said. *That's why Nina insisted that I protect myself.*

After my meeting with Harry and Bullert at the Columbia Golf Course three days ago—actually, it was four, now—I went to Rickie's, the jazz joint in St. Paul that Nina Truhler named after her daughter, Erica. It was midafternoon, and the after-work happy-hour crowd had yet to arrive, although Nina's waitstaff was ready to receive them. A few of the waitresses called my name, and I felt a little like Norm in the *Cheers* reruns when I entered the comfortable downstairs lounge; the jazz was played in a performance area at the top of a spiral staircase that was never opened before 6:00 P.M. In the past five years I had never received a tab for anything that I had ordered in Rickie's, yet I always left a tip at least equal to the purchase price for whoever served me; thus I tended to be one of Nina's most popular boyfriends.

Jenness Crawford, Nina's assistant manager, was behind the bar. Before I had a chance to say a word, she poured a Summit Ale, my favorite beer brewed in St. Paul, my hometown, thank you very much, and set the glass in front of me.

"You're going to make some young man a wonderful wife," I said.

"Young man?" she asked.

I looked into her eyes, and she smiled demurely.

"I didn't know you were gay," I said. "No one tells me anything."

"Let's just say I'm keeping my options open. I'll tell Nina you're here."

I watched the woman as she made her way around the bar and into Nina's small office. I had known Jenness for years and just now learned that she played for both teams—which is why I worked as an *unlicensed* private investigator. Who the hell would give me a license?

A pair of cheaters was perched on Nina's narrow nose when she emerged from her office. In the past, she would have hidden them from prying eyes for vanity's sake. She had given up the deceit at about the same time her daughter had enrolled at Tulane University. It was a concession not to age, however, but to maturity—there is a difference, trust me on this. Beyond that, she looked as lovely to me as the day she had graduated from college. I had seen photos.

"How did you play?" she asked.

Before I answered, I leaned across the bar and kissed her on the lips.

"Lousy," I said. "I beat Harry by six strokes, though, and that's the main thing. Do you know what that SOB wanted me to do?"

"Give him mulligans? I know you hate that."

"He wanted me to go undercover."

I proceeded to give her a verbatim account of our conversation despite Harry's claim that I could keep a secret. He knew me. He knew Nina. If he thought I wasn't going to tell her everything, he was crazy. Afterward, she set her hand on top of mine and I felt a jolt of electricity that shot up my arm, through my chest, and straight down into my nether regions. She often had that effect on me.

"What?" I asked.

"Have you talked to Bobby Dunston?" she asked. "What did he say?"

"I haven't spoken to Bobby, but he's a commander in the Major Crimes and Investigations Division of the St. Paul Police Department, and I know exactly what he would tell me."

"You should talk to him. G. K. Bonalay, too."

"My lawyer?"

"And to that TV journalist you like so much."

"Kelly Bressandes?"

"Tell them everything you told me."

"Why would I do that?"

"Just in case."

"Nina, I don't think you heard me. I am not going to do this."

"Before you go—"

"Before I go? Do you actually want me to risk life and limb on some fool's errand?"

"No, but that's never stopped you before. McKenzie, it's been months since you've done anything silly. You're due."

"I can't believe you said that."

Nina propped her elbows on top of the bar and rested her face in her hands. She had the most startling silver-blue eyes I had ever seen, framed by jet black hair. When I first met her, the hair was short; then she grew it to shoulder-length; now it was short again, and I still didn't know which way I liked it best.

"Do you know how long I've been a bartender?" she asked.

"Since you were eleven?"

"Close. Do you know what I've learned in all those years?"

"To never pour beer into a frosted mug, because it creates condensation that dilutes it?"

"I've learned how to read people."

"You think you can read me?"

"Like a book, McKenzie. A graphic novel. Lots of pictures, little exposition."

"I am not going to do this job."

She smiled some more, smiled to the point of laughter, and gestured with her head toward the door. I spun on my stool in time to watch Harry, Chad Bullert, and a tall man dressed in one of the most expensive tailored suits I had ever seen walk into Rickie's.

"Tell them that," Nina said.

"I'll need a table," I said. "Not a booth. I want to be able to get up and walk away in a hurry."

"Oh, McKenzie. You're not going to walk away."

I had every intention of doing just that, though, if for no better reason than to demonstrate to Nina that I was captain of my ship, master of my domain, lord of my castle. Unfortunately, it didn't work out that way.

The tall, well-dressed man was introduced to me as Assistant U.S. Attorney James R. Finnegan. As I shook his hand I said, "I bet your friends call you Finny."

He seemed astonished by the assumption. "No," he said. "They don't." Then, "You have an interesting file."

"I have a file?" I asked.

"Of course you do. I read that you've been involved in gunrunning before. That's how you met Chad and Harry."

I looked at Harry. "Does everybody call you that now?"

"See what you've done?"

A moment later, Nina surprised me by appearing at the table to take our orders herself. Harry stood, bussed her cheek, and called her "lovely Nina," which I found irritating, then introduced her around. Finnegan shook her hand, said he was delighted to meet her, and asked, "Is it true that this place is haunted?"

"Uh-oh," Harry said as he took his seat.

I was tempted to look away, but it was like a traffic accident—you just have to watch.

Nina raised an eyebrow and smiled. Trust me when I say there was no mirth in it. "Do you believe in ghosts, Mr. Finnegan?" she asked.

"Not necessarily," Finnegan said. "The TV show . . ."

The TV program in question followed a team of self-described ghost hunters as they purportedly investigated paranormal activity around the country. Erica invited them to Rickie's without Nina's knowledge or permission. I suspect she was just trying to annoy her mother, who tended to take a flat-earth philosophy toward things like ghosts, ESP, UFOs, and government conspiracies.

"TV show?" Nina said. "What else forms your worldview, Mr. Finnegan? *Fringe*? *Lost*? *X-Files*? *True* freaking *Blood*? *The Vampire Diaries*?"

"I just—"

"Is this what the United States Justice Department has come to—getting its information from basic cable?"

Finnegan didn't answer, so Nina turned toward me as if I were somehow the cause of her frustration. I didn't so much as smile—I like excitement as much as the next guy, but I'm not suicidal. I pointed at Finnegan.

"Give him the bill," I said.

She did, too, or rather Jenness Crawford did. Nina remained out of sight. It occurred to me that it was no coincidence that the morning after the TV program's camera crew arrived at Rickie's, Erica flew off to New Orleans.

The moment Nina left, Finnegan said, "I don't know about ghosts, but clearly she—"

I raised my index finger in warning and cleared my throat. Finnegan glanced at Harry, who was shaking his head slowly from side to side, an expression of dire warning on his face.

"Yes, well, a very nice club," Finnegan said. "I hear the music is sensational."

"So is the food," Harry said.

Finnegan took a deep breath and exhaled slowly. He didn't smile. I doubted he had much of a sense of humor—he had the look of a man who decided long ago life was a very serious proposition. He began speaking in that earnest, sincere way career politicians have.

"McKenzie," he said. "It's just McKenzie, correct? Not Mr. McKenzie?"

"McKenzie will do."

"McKenzie, normally I would attempt to appeal to your altruistic nature. I would tell you about all the people who will suffer if we don't get those guns off the border, the men and women—and children—who will be hurt or killed. I would tell you how the damage done to the Justice Department's reputation would make it more difficult for us to do our work, how it would compromise our ability to secure our borders and protect our citizens. However, I'm informed that Special Agents Bullert and Wilson have already addressed that argument."

Everyone nodded in agreement.

"Next, I would make threats. I would refer to that rather lengthy document we've compiled on you and your many, should I say, indecorous actions?"

Oh, let's, my inner voice said. *Indecorous—my, my, my.*

"I have been assured, however, that you are not a man who is easily intimidated," Finnegan said. "I am also aware that you and your investment counselor—H. B. Sutton, I believe is her name—have grown the reward you accepted to nearly five million, so a bribe is certainly out of the question."

"Sounds like an impasse to me," I said.

"On the other hand, perhaps you might be enticed by the age-old system of barter. That is your preferred method of exchange, is it not—favor for favor?"

"What do you have to trade?"

Finnegan took a business card from his pocket and slid the card, faceup, across the table to me. The top listed his name, title, and assorted means of contact under the crest of the U.S.

Department of Justice. I turned it over and found the word "allegation" written there.

I repeated it out loud, and Finnegan grinned. "I love that word," he said. "What was it that the Reverend Jesse Jackson once said? 'I not only deny the allegation, I deny the alligator.'"

"What does this mean exactly?" I asked.

"Call my office day or night, use the code word, and the next voice you hear will be mine."

"I don't get it."

"It's a get-out-of-jail-free card," Harry said.

"Let's face it," Bullert said, "the way you live your life, sooner or later you're going to need it."

"Your buddy Governor Barrett is not running for reelection," Harry reminded me.

"So?" I said.

"So now we're your friends in high places," Finnegan said. "And a man like you can never have too many friends."

"I made myself clear to Finnegan," I told Bullert over the cell phone. "I'm in until the bullets start flying. I'm in as long as no one gets hurt. If these guys shoot someone . . ."

"Let's hope for an uneventful criminal enterprise, then," he said.

"Christ."

"In the meantime, we'll check out this Roy Cepek. Could be he got the guns through a military connection, an army buddy turned merc, maybe."

I ended the call, erased Bullert's number from the log just in case, deactivated the phone, and returned it to my pocket. Shortly after, my hands filled with cardboard coffee cups, I opened the café door with my shoulder and stepped into the parking lot. The Corolla was still there; the elderly man still inside, although Roy Clark had been swapped for Loretta Lynn—I guessed this was what amounted to Golden Oldies in Silver Bay. I returned to the Jeep Cherokee and handed Skarda his coffee through the open passenger window.

"You were gone so long," he said. "I was starting to get worried."

"I took a minute to use the john," I said. I circled the SUV and entered through the driver's door. "Anything interesting happening?"

"Just the armored car."

"What armored car?"

Skarda handed me the binoculars, and I studied the blue vehicle, the name Mesabi Security printed on its side. It was a decidedly old armored truck with streaks of rust along the wheel wells and rocker panels. The driver sat in the cab, the window rolled down, his elbow propped on the door frame. A second guard exited the supermarket carrying a nylon bag. He set it on the ground behind the truck where the driver couldn't possibly have seen him, opened the rear compartment, tossed the bag inside, and then climbed in after it.

"Very, very sloppy," I said.

"Hmm?"

"The armored car guards. I could take those clowns with a slingshot. Okay, look—you had better contact Josie and have her call off the job."

"I can't. I don't have a cell phone. What happened to the one we bought yesterday?"

"I tossed it. Look, we have to head them off somehow."

"Why?"

"Because there's no money to steal. The armored car guys just drove off with it."

"No . . ."

"What do you think they were here for? To buy Milky Ways and Slushies?"

"No . . ."

"Stop saying that."

"Look."

Skarda pointed. I followed his finger to a car that pulled to a stop directly in front of the grocery store. Jill was driving. Jimmy got out of the car. His jacket was hanging open as he nonchalantly walked into the store, pausing for a moment while a woman pushed a loaded shopping cart past him. Exactly seven minutes later a second vehicle approached from the opposite direction. The old man was driving. Roy stepped out holding his AK-47 in the port position again and scanned the parking lot like a hunter searching for game. Josie—the way she was dressed she looked to me like a woman who was trying hard not to look like a woman, not unlike the feminists who marched for the Equal Rights Amendment when I was a kid. She was carrying a shotgun when she emerged from the passenger side. Together, she and Roy entered the supermarket.

The sky suddenly seemed to grow dark and ominous to me, even though it remained bright blue with puffy white clouds to everyone else. I rested my head against the top of the steering wheel.

"Well, this is an unfortunate turn of events," I said.

"If everything is going according to plan, Jimmy has his gun on the store manager and is forcing him to open the safe."

"Which is empty, now."

"Roy is guarding the door while Josie moves from cash register to cash register, forcing the cashiers to empty their drawers into a grocery bag."

I rotated in my seat and gazed out the window toward the Silver Bay Police Department. I saw no movement, but that didn't mean anything. More likely the department's patrol cars had all received the 911 by now and were converging on this very spot with the greatest possible dispatch. I started the Cherokee just in case.

Seconds seemed like minutes, and minutes—it felt like I was sitting through *Avatar* again. I listened intently, for what I wasn't sure. Terrified screams, I suppose. Gunfire.

"Here they come."

Skarda was pointing again. Jimmy was first out the door, carrying a white tote bag by the handle with one hand and his clunky automatic with the other. He was followed closely by Josie. She was clutching a plain brown grocery bag to her chest as if it contained baby formula. Roy came out of the super-market a moment later, backside first, training his weapon on the entrance as if he were expecting a swift counterattack. Jimmy was in Jill's car and the car was motoring halfway out of the parking lot before Josie reached hers. She shouted some-thing as she climbed in, and Roy turned and jogged after her. He jumped into the car, and the old man stomped on the gas, spinning his tires like a teenager trying to impress his rivals.

That's when the Silver Bay PD arrived.

The patrol car came slowly up Shopping Center Road with-out siren or lights.

I saw it first in my sideview mirror and again when I twisted in my seat to look at it through the rear window. It was dark blue and scary as hell. At the same time, I saw the elderly man backing his red Toyota away from the café and steering it toward the entrance to the parking lot. At his cur-rent speed, I estimated that he would reach the entrance just before the cop car did.

"Hold on," I said.

I cranked the wheel of the Cherokee and hit the accelerator. The coffee cups spilled out of the cup holders and fell to the floor of the passenger side, the tops popped off, and coffee splattered Skarda's feet and ankles.

"What are you doing?" he shouted.

I ignored the question and sidled up next to the Toyota just as it entered Shopping Center Road in front of the cop, its sideview mirrors nearly touching the Cherokee's driver's-side door. I leaned hard on my horn. The elderly man looked at me, panic etched across his face—and did exactly what I wanted him to do. To avoid a collision, he spun his steering wheel violently to the left away from me, stomped on the accelerator, and promptly crashed into the Silver Bay Police Department patrol car. There was no squealing of tires, no blaring of horns, just a satisfying crunch as the Toyota's fiberglass composite front end folded around the cop's high-grade steel push bumper.

I drove straight ahead, crossing Shopping Center Road, shooting down the alley between the public library and the police department, hanging a hard right on Davis Drive and then another on Outer Drive. I followed it at high speed past Blazers Northshore Auto, Silver Bay Municipal Liquor, and the City Arena to U.S. Service Highway 11. We were not followed. It wasn't until we were a good five miles out of town that it occurred to me that the Silver Bay cop might not have received a call about the supermarket robbery at all; he didn't have his lightbar and siren working. He might simply have been patrolling in the wrong place at the wrong time. Skarda, however, didn't see it that way. He was full of praise about how my superior driving skills once again not only made good our escape, they also delivered his family from sure arrest.

"You'd make a great Iron Range Bandit," he said.

I started laughing out loud, but, of course, Skarda didn't get the joke.

It took several hours to return to Lake Carl, mostly because of the roundabout way I took to get there. The Iron Range Bandits were gathered on the deck when we arrived. None of them looked pleased. They were drinking beer from a cooler set beneath the picnic table; the empties suggested they had been drinking a lot. There were five stacks of U.S. currency on the table along with the white tote bag and paper grocery bag, both emblazoned with the name of the Silver Bay grocery store. A single rock had been placed on top of each stack to keep the bills from blowing away in the light breeze. Neither of the bags moved despite the wind, and I decided there must be something inside weighing them down.

"Where have you been?" Josie wanted to know the moment Skarda and I started up the steps that led to the deck.

"Silver Bay," Skarda said. "We were watching."

"I told you to stay here."

"You're lucky we didn't. The cops came just as you were leaving the parking lot. If it wasn't for Dyson, they would have caught you."

There was a murmur of voices. Josie turned to me. "Is that true?" she asked.

"More or less," I said.

"Did any of you know that Silver Bay had a police force?" Skarda asked. "Did you know that the police station was five hundred yards away from the shopping mall? You could see it from the parking lot."

"I only know that we took $2,347," Roy said. "A lousy $2,347. That's $469 each."

"And they say crime doesn't pay," I said.

"I need more than that," Jimmy said. "I have a townhouse to pay for. I'm getting married."

"No one gives a shit about your problems," Roy said. His face was flushed with anger and alcohol.

"Shut up, Roy," Josie said.

"You shut up. This is your fault. You're the one who picked the supermarket. $469. We can't live on that."

"None of us can," Jimmy added.

"What are we going to do?" the old man asked. He had been standing at the railing and now moved to a frayed lawn chair at the head of the picnic table. He lowered himself into it the way the elderly sit when they're afraid something might break. He sure got old in a hurry, I thought.

"Ask your daughter," Roy said.

"Josie," the old man said. "Josie, what are we going to do?"

"I don't know," Josie said. She turned her back to the people on the deck, leaned against the railing, and stared out at the lake.

"I knew I should have kept the marijuana farm," Jimmy said. "Out in the forest, on public land, no one around to bother you. I would have had a huge crop by now."

"You would have been in prison by now," Roy said. "You rode around in an old Cadillac so everyone would think you were a player."

"I told you, that was all about marketing."

"No one in this family is going to deal drugs," Josie said.

"This is better?" Jimmy asked.

"It would have been okay if you had gotten there half an hour earlier," Skarda said.

"What are you talking about?" Jimmy asked.

I went to the cooler, lifted the lid, retrieved a can of beer, and closed it while Skarda answered.

"An armored truck picked up all the money just before you arrived. We were going to warn you, but it was too late," he said.

"Is that true?" Roy wanted to know.

"You didn't do your homework," I said. I reached for the

two bags and looked inside. They both contained personal checks made out to the grocery store as well as some receipts.

How are these people not in jail? my inner voice asked. *They're not even smart enough to destroy incriminating evidence.*

"Maybe it's a sign," Jill said. "Maybe it's someone telling us we should quit. We should stop doing this."

Roy cursed and raised his hand to hit her. Jill made no attempt to escape. Instead, she cringed, raised one shoulder and ducked her head behind it as if she knew exactly where the blow would fall, and screwed her eyes tight in anticipation. Rushmore McKenzie wanted to step in to protect the girl. Nick Dyson did nothing. *Stay in character, stay in character,* my inner voice chanted. Fortunately, the blow didn't fall. Roy simply cursed again and turned away. I opened the beer and took a long sip.

"What we should have done," Skarda said, "was rob the armored truck. Dyson said the guards were sloppy. He said we could have taken it with a slingshot."

"That's not what I said, not exactly anyway," I told him.

Josie turned to face me. "How much money does an armored car carry?" she asked.

"Depends on the customers," I said. "Sometimes millions, sometimes only a few hundred thousand dollars."

"A few hundred thousand," Jimmy said. "That would be more than enough."

"Forget it," I said. "You guys can't even stick up a supermarket properly."

"You can teach us," Josie said.

"Me? I'm just passing through, remember? I'm going to Canada."

"With only four hundred and sixty-nine dollars?" Jimmy asked.

"Josie insisted we give you a share, I don't know why," Roy said. "Jimmy's right, though. How far do you think you'll get on four hundred and sixty-nine dollars?"

"I'll get more," I said.

"How?" Josie asked. "With what? A stolen car? A deputy's gun?"

"It's a start."

"You're on the run, remember? Every cop in the state is looking for you."

"Dyson, you said it would be easy," Skarda told me.

"No, I didn't," I said. "Listen to me. Forget what I said about the local cops before. You hit an armored truck—that's a federal beef. The FBI investigates whenever federally insured money is stolen, and they never stop looking for you. Never. They're worse than the frickin' Mafia. When they catch you— there's no parole system for federal prisoners, no time off for good behavior. They'll convict your ass for aggravated bank robbery with a deadly weapon—which is how they look at armored truck heists, like they were bank robberies. You could draw a sentence all the way up to twenty years, and you'll serve every single day."

"You said—"

"I didn't say, Dave. You weren't listening. That's the problem, you guys don't listen. Jimmy didn't listen about the automatic. Roy doesn't listen to anything. You think you're hardened criminals. You're not. We're talking about real cops and robbers now, and people can get killed."

"You can teach us," Josie repeated.

"C'mon."

"What about it, tough guy?" Roy said. "You're supposed to be this criminal mastermind. What about it? Are you chicken?"

"You're damn right I am."

"Dyson," Jimmy said. "You told us about the FBI and all that. What's the upside? There's always an upside, isn't there?"

"You mean besides the money? The FBI has never solved more than thirty or forty percent of the armored truck robberies committed in any given year, so the odds are slightly in your favor. Unlike with a bank, there's little chance that the money will be marked. Also, you get to hit the truck at a time and place of your own choosing. If you work it right, you can do it where there are no witnesses. Or at least fewer witnesses than in a bank—no tellers, cashiers, customers, no security cameras. The problem is, it's an armored truck, emphasis on armored. The only way to get into the rear compartment where they keep the money is with a carefully guarded key, which requires an inside man that we don't have, or with explosives. Have you ever seen *Butch Cassidy and the Sundance Kid* where they accidentally blow up the train? You want to avoid that, which means the best way to do it is when the guards are outside the truck. Except these guys are macho men. They're like Roy here; they all think they're tougher than Israeli commandos. You can't expect them to give up the money without a tussle."

"It can be done, though," Skarda said.

"If it's done right."

"You can teach us," Josie said. "You need real money. We need real money. We can do this together."

"Sounds like a marriage made in heaven," Skarda said.

"Shut up, Dave," I said.

"Dyson." I turned to face Roy as he spoke. "I don't like you, but if you agree to help us, I'll do everything you tell me to do. No arguments."

Will you stop beating your wife? my inner voice asked.

"We will all do what you tell us," Josie said.

I looked at them, one after another, my gaze sweeping from Josie to Skarda to Jimmy to the old man to Roy and finally to Jill. She was the only one who didn't look me in the eye.

"Roy," I said. "The AK-47. Where did you get it?"

"That's for me to know."

"Well, we're off to a great start."

"Roy," Josie snapped. "Tell him."

"I can't say."

Can't or won't? my inner voice asked.

"Unlike what you might have heard, we're not going to do this with slingshots," I said. "We're going to need firepower. Maybe AKs, maybe more—we might even need plastic explosives, Semtex 10, I don't know yet. The question is, can you get it or are you just blowing smoke?"

"I can get it."

"How much lead time do you need?"

"I don't know."

"What do you know?"

"It's going to be expensive."

"It always is. When the time comes, I'll need to meet with your people. I don't know what kind of relationship you have with them, and I certainly don't want to put you on the spot, but if this is going to happen, I'll need a face-to-face. Can you arrange that?"

"I think so."

"Okay."

"We're going to do this, then?" Josie asked.

Off in the distance I could hear Bobby Dunston laughing.

The evening after I met Harry, Bullert, and Finnegan at Rickie's, I went to Bobby's house in Merriam Park, the blue-collar neighborhood in St. Paul where we were both raised. Bobby bought the house from his parents when they retired to a lake home in Wisconsin; growing up I had spent almost as much time there as he had.

"This is insane," he told me while I paced the living room floor. Shelby Dunston was sitting on a blue mohair chair in the corner, her right leg tucked beneath her. Nina sat like that sometimes, I could never figure out why.

"You're not seriously considering doing this?" Bobby asked.

"Yeah . . ."

"McKenzie, you're not police anymore. You would be so exposed."

"That's why I have the letter explaining my actions on be-half of the Justice Department, why I had Finnegan sign it—five copies. One to you, one to G. K., one to Kelly Bressandes—"

"That tramp?" Shelby said.

"The others I've squirreled away for safekeeping. Nina insisted."

"I don't understand. Why do you need the letters?"

While Nina was a dark beauty, Shelby was all sunshine and windswept wheat fields. Nina's most dominant feature was those astonishing eyes. With Shelby it was her smile—the kind of smile that could encourage even the most conservative of us to do no end of foolish things. God knows I had. I met her at a party in college about three minutes before Bobby bumped into her, spilling a drink on her dress. It had pretty much been widely accepted that if Bobby hadn't married her, I would have. Bobby and I had never spoken of this, probably the only subject we hadn't discussed at great length since meeting in kindergarten. On the other hand, he asked me to be best man at his wedding and godfather to his eldest daughter, tolerated it when I spoiled both Victoria and Katie with ridiculous gifts, and thanked me when I made them the sole heirs to my estate, such as it was. From that I gathered he wasn't particularly anxious about my relationship with his wife, which, when you think about it, was kind of insulting.

"Have you ever seen *Mission Impossible,* the TV series, not the movie?" I asked. "You know that line they always say, 'Should you or any of your IM Force be caught or killed, the secretary will disavow any knowledge of your actions'? The letters are to make sure that doesn't happen to me."

"They won't necessarily protect you," Bobby told me. "I don't care if Finnegan is an assistant U.S. attorney. No one can give you permission to break the law."

"That's what G. K. said. Really, though, is it any different than busting a dealer and then letting him work it off, wear a wire while he makes a couple of buys from suspects higher up on the food chain?"

"The dealer might not be arrested for those specific crimes, the ones he commits while he's helping the cops, but that doesn't mean he's going to get a free pass for everything else he does. What I'm saying is, there are limits, McKenzie. If you cross too far over the line"—he waved the letter at me—"this isn't going to be worth the paper it's printed on."

"Point taken."

"Do you want my advice?"

"Always."

"Grow up."

"That's a pretty tough thing to do, Bobby. It's why so few people succeed at it."

I moved to the railing and gazed out on Lake Carl. The setting sun made the calm water sparkle. It occurred to me that wetting a line wasn't such a bad idea, but I ignored the thought and spun to face the six people on the deck. They were all staring at me—Jill included.

"We'll look into the possibility," I said. "I'm making no promises until we sort it out. No promises, all right? But we'll take a look to see if there's anything there, see what we have to work with. In the meantime, no more jobs. No more crimes. No guns. No fights. No heavy drinking. I want you all to become model citizens; go through your day as if nothing is happening. You'll be given your assignments as we go."

"What do we do first?" Jimmy asked.

"You mean besides getting a better grade of beer? We're going to find an armored truck to rob."

SIX

It was easy to justify my behavior to myself. I was getting the Iron Range Bandits off the street—no thefts, no guns, no danger to themselves or their potential victims. I would go through the motions of organizing a stickup until everyone was comfortable, I would convince Roy to lead me to his friendly neighborhood gunrunner, and then I would turn the lot of them over to the ATF, FBI, BCA, Silver Bay PD, county sheriff, and whoever else wanted a piece. In the meantime, I wouldn't be compelled to participate in any criminal activities myself, which would please Bobby Dunston no end. The more I thought about it, the more clever I felt. Not to mention quickwitted, resourceful, and ingenious. I went to bed thinking I was smarter than Ernest Hamwi, the man who first thought to serve ice cream in rolled-up waffles. When I woke the next morning, I was just as impressed with myself.

This is good, my inner voice told me. *You're doing God's work.*

"You da man," I said aloud as I did a little dance.

I thought I was alone in the cabin. Josie poked her head around the doorway that led to the bathroom and looked at me.

"Did you say something?" she asked.

"Hmm? Me? No."

"Thought I heard something."

She stepped into the living room. Gone were the boots, baggy coveralls, sweatshirt, and ball cap that she used to disguise herself the previous day. They were replaced by flip-flops; khaki shorts that revealed long, slender legs; and a light, pink sweater that Josie had buttoned from her waist to just below her chin. She had allowed her auburn hair to cascade around her shoulders.

"Dyson, what are we going to do first?" she asked.

"Get some breakfast," I said.

Josie had grilled chicken on the deck the evening before, and I hadn't eaten anything since, although I had consumed plenty of cheap beer. Afterward, everyone except Skarda and myself departed to their separate homes, taking their thin stacks of currency with them. Jill didn't get a share, and I had asked Josie about that.

"It's the way Roy wants it," she told me. I took that to mean Roy was desperate to keep Jill under his thumb. Give her money and she might use it to leave him.

Only Skarda and I had remained overnight. When he wasn't looking, I took the grocery bags filled with checks and receipts and stashed them beneath the cabin.

Early in the morning, we went fishing, using the late owner's boat and equipment; he had a nice Shakespeare rod and reel outfit and an impressive tackle box. Yet despite Skarda's promise of fish, we were both skunked. While we were on the lake, I unceremoniously dropped the Glock overboard, making sure Skarda saw me do it. When he asked why, I told him there was an unsubstantiated rumor that it had been employed in the commission of a felony and I didn't want the authorities to get the wrong idea should they find it on me. "Never keep the gun, Dave. Never." He nodded his head in agreement as if my advice had come straight from the mount. 'Course, I didn't mention that I dumped the Glock to make sure nobody discovered it had been loaded with blanks. (You had to give Bullert credit; he didn't leave much to chance.)

By the time we got off the lake, the Iron Range Bandits were already gathering on the deck. I went inside and changed clothes. I didn't have much to choose from, just the stuff we had tossed into the nylon bag in the back of the Explorer before staging the escape. I thought I was the only one in the cabin until Josie appeared.

"What are we going to do after breakfast?" she asked.

"It's like I told Jimmy last night. We need to find an armored truck and follow it around for a few days. Armored trucks generally have a tightly choreographed routine of stops and starts—supermarkets, bank branches, department stores, casinos, anyplace with an ATM. What we're looking for is a weakness, something we can exploit. I remember there were these two armored car guards working outside San Francisco a couple years ago. Turned out they always stopped at the same coffeehouse. They'd stop there at different times of the day, but it was always the same coffeehouse. One afternoon a crew met them at the front door with guns, took their keys, forced them back into the truck, drove to a prearranged location, looted the truck, and left them tied up in the back. Feds said the crew got away with the proverbial undisclosed amount of cash. I'm here to tell you that it was nearly eight hundred thousand dollars."

"How do you know?"

"How do I know what?"

"How do you know . . ." Josie was watching my eyes. They told her to stop asking questions, so she did.

I'm getting good at this, I thought.

"Where do we start?" Josie asked.

"I'm not familiar with the area, so I'm going to need someone to drive." I pointed at her.

"Me?" she said.

"Can't use Dave. He and I are still wanted, and while it's unlikely that anyone will recognize me, Dave is known up here. All things considered, I think it's best that Roy and I keep our distance as much as possible. The old man—with due respect, he's too old for what I have in mind, and Jimmy, he's a little too enthusiastic. That leaves you."

"Jillian . . ."

"I want her kept out of this. She should never have been involved in the first place."

"You seem to have taken quite a fancy to her."

"She's the little sister I never had."

"Is that it? She's quite beautiful, you know."

"I make it a point not to lust after any woman who hasn't voted in at least three presidential elections."

"I don't think Jill's voted in any yet. Besides, she's married."

"There's that, too."

"If you need a woman . . ."

"Excuse me?"

"I'm just saying . . ."

"Josie, are you offering yourself to me?"

She blushed, actually blushed—you don't often see that in a grown woman. Her eyes grew wide, her freckles sparkled, her mouth opened, and she took a step backward.

"No," she said. "I should say not. I mean—I meant a married

woman, Jill is a married woman, and Roy—Roy has a temper and, and there are others who would be willing, that you can, but not—dammit."

She spun on her heel and quickly walked out of the cabin, letting the door slam behind her.

"Oh, well," I said.

I joined her on the deck a few moments later. The Bandits watched me expectantly. I didn't want them to think too much, so I told them what I had in mind.

"Josie will be my driver," I said. "Jimmy, you're the tech guy." Jimmy grinned widely and jumped up from the picnic table as if he had been chosen first in a game of dodge ball. "I want you go to your computer and locate all of the cash-intensive businesses you can. I don't mean in a ten-mile radius, either. I mean throughout the Iron Range. Compile a list. Afterward, I want you to mark their locations on a map of the area. A big map."

"I'm on it," he said.

"Roy, you're my procurement officer. We're going to need vehicles, coveralls, gloves, masks, nylon restraints like the kind cops use, weapons, of course—I'm not sure exactly what we'll need, but I need you to think about where we're going to get this stuff, anyway."

"Are we going to buy or steal?" he asked.

"We'll steal the cars." Roy's pupils grew larger. "Don't worry, I'll show you how."

"You should have seen how he stole the Jeep Cherokee," Skarda said. "It was beautiful."

"Dave," I said. "You talk way too much."

"Sorry."

"Try to work on that."

"I will."

"Which reminds me—I don't need to tell you all to keep quiet about this, do I? You're conspiring to commit a major felony. You can be arrested just for that alone. Please, please don't tell your friends. Don't tell your relatives. Don't get drunk and brag about it in a bar. If you want to stay out of prison, this is a secret you take to your graves."

"Hear, hear," said the old man. He seemed to have recovered nicely from the Silver Bay raid. He was wearing a tie-dyed T-shirt and sitting in his frayed lawn chair at the head of the picnic table. An unlit joint hung from his lips. The look in his eye suggested it wasn't his first of the day. I asked the obvious question.

"Are you smoking dope?"

"It's medicinal marijuana," he said.

Does he have cancer? my inner voice asked. I glanced at Josie for confirmation. She was rolling her eyes. *I guess not.*

"It's important that we keep a clear head," I said.

"You got a job for me?" the old man asked.

"Not today."

He spread his arms wide. "Still say you look like a narc."

"Keep it to yourself."

"What do you want me to do?" Skarda asked.

I gestured at the old man again. "Take your father fishing. And keep out of sight. You're hot, remember?"

"So are you."

"No one will recognize me. You, on the other hand, are known hither and yon. Don't worry about it, Dave. You'll have plenty to do when the time comes."

"Should I be doing anything?" Jill asked. Her voice was so soft I barely heard it. I found her eyes. They betrayed her apprehension.

"No," I said. "I won't ask you to do anything on this job.

You'll be left completely out of it. All I want you to do is go home and pretend that you're not surrounded by a bunch of lowlife maniac thieves, okay?"

She didn't quite smile, but her face seemed to brighten a bit just the same. "Thank you," she said.

Roy glanced from Jill to me to her and back to me again. "What do you mean, she's out of it?" he asked.

I ignored the question, although I knew it would come up again, and soon.

"One more thing, people," I said. "I'm not a big believer in this honor among thieves BS. Everything you heard about being a stand-up guy and not snitching, not informing—forget that. It's okay to look out for yourself. I highly recommend it. All I ask is that you give everyone the same courtesy that the CIA asks of its operatives—a twenty-four-hour head start. If you're arrested, don't even give out your name, rank, or serial number. Keep absolutely quiet for twenty-four hours; give the rest of us a chance to run and hide. After that, I advise you to do whatever you need to to protect yourself, and good luck to you."

"Hear that, Roy?" Skarda asked.

"What's that suppose to mean?" Roy said.

"Your gun dealers—you've been keeping their names a secret so that you have something to trade to the cops if you get arrested, make a deal to help yourself while the rest of us go to prison. Well, now you've got our blessing."

"You don't know what you're talking about."

"Dave," I said. He looked at me, and I ran my thumb and index finger across my lips like I was closing a zipper.

"I was just saying," he said.

"Okay." I clapped my hands together and rubbed them back and forth. "Let's get to work."

Josie and I left the deck and circled the cabin to where

Josie's Taurus was parked. We were going to take her car because my Jeep Cherokee, after all, was stolen. Roy followed us. I kind of figured he would.

"Wait a minute, Dyson," he called.

"What do you need?" I asked.

His fingers curled into fists as he approached, and his eyes darted from my hands to my chin, nose, eyes, throat, groin, and knees—they were target glances, something I was taught to look for when I was at the police academy. *The sonuvabitch is going to throw a punch,* my inner voice warned. I waited.

"What is this bullshit?" he asked.

"Could you be more specific?"

His fists tightened and his teeth clenched. "I saw the look you gave my wife."

"What look?"

He stopped with his left foot forward and his right foot back, a pugilistic stance. He cocked his right arm. I hit him hard in the jaw with a left jab, but he took it like a bitch-slap from an old man with arthritis. I hit him again with my right, this time putting all of my weight into it. He fell backward, bounced against the cabin wall, and slid slowly to a sitting position. For a moment he looked like a pile of laundry before being tossed into the washer.

"Dyson," Josie shouted.

"What? I'm supposed to wait until he hit me?" I moved close to Roy and leaned in. "You were going to hit me, weren't you, Roy?"

He nodded even as he brought a hand up to cradle his jaw.

"I guess you're upset that I cut Jill out of the crew, am I right?" He nodded again. "Maybe you think I have the hots for her." His eyes locked on mine. "Not true. It really isn't. She's out because she doesn't have the stomach for any of this; she doesn't have the heart for it. Jill's gone along with you so far because you made her. Every step of the way, though, she's been thinking she should run—you can see it in her eyes, in her demeanor. Your slapping her around isn't helping any, either. All it does is make her want to run that much more. Where do you think she's going to run to, Roy, if you keep punching her out? She's going to run to the cops, and then we're all screwed."

"She won't go to the police."

"What's stopping her, Roy? Her undying devotion to you? I have no doubt that Jill loved you once, but I think you've pretty much beaten it out of her. I understand that times are tough; I understand that they're tougher on some than on others. Beating on the one person who has vowed to stick with you for better or for worse, tell me how that helps? Look, your personal life is your business. If you don't love your wife, that's fine with me—"

"I love my wife."

"I hadn't noticed, but that's not my concern. My concern is staying out of prison, so Jill is out of it. It wouldn't kill you to be nice to her until the job is over, either. You might try to remember why you married her in the first place—I bet you had some pretty good reasons."

I stepped back and offered Roy my hand. He took it, and I helped hoist him off the ground.

"No hard feelings, okay?" I said. "I need you, Roy. These kids, they don't know which end is up. If we're going to pull this off, it'll be you and me doing the heavy lifting. I know I've been giving you a hard time since I arrived. That was just to establish hierarchy for the kids. You're army; you understand what I'm talking about."

He nodded, and I patted his arm.

"Good man," I said. I started walking toward Josie's car. Roy called to me.

"Dyson. When this is over, I'm going to kick the shit out of you."

"Roy, Roy, Roy," I said. "When this is over, you're going to be too busy counting your money to even think about that."

A few moments later, Josie and I were in her car and heading toward the county road. She had an amused expression on her face. I knew she wanted me to ask her about it, so I did.

"You handled that really well," she said. "You not only got Jill out of the robbery, you got Roy to agree with you. He doesn't even seem all that angry that you punched him. How did you do that?"

"I read a business book once, *The One Minute Manager*. It taught me everything I know about running a crew."

"Did it teach you how to be a criminal?"

"No, that I learned reading Donald Trump's autobiography."

Krueger was a "city" in name only. The entire community could have fit easily inside Target Field with room left over for an executive golf course. There was very little of it that I could not see from the road: an orange-brick schoolhouse next to an overgrown football field and an outdoor hockey rink, the boards still up even though the ice had been gone for months now; a gas station/minimart at the crossroads; a bar, restaurant, hardware store, bait and tackle shop; a building that looked like a barn with KRUEGER VOLUNTEER FIRE DEPT. painted above the door. A half-dozen businesses made up Krueger's downtown, with an abundance of empty parking spaces in front of them. Houses packed close together, some new, most old, surrounded the downtown. They thinned out as we drove; there were longer and longer stretches between neighbors until there were no neighbors at all. Yet I could see plenty of people living their lives—a mother with a stroller, young kids running through sprinklers, older kids playing baseball; a young man working a barbecue grill while his buddies watched, plates in hand; an elderly couple walking down the road, their arms linked.

"A great place to live, I just wouldn't want to visit here."

I was speaking to myself. Josie heard me, though, and added, "Until the jobs went away."

"Not much worth stealing."

"No, not much. Do we have time enough for me to make a quick stop at my office?"

"Sure."

Josie's office was also her home, located on the intersection of paved and gravel county roads. It was small and square and built to resemble a log cabin. A sign clearly visible from both roads read LAKE DREAMS REALTY—SERVING ELY-KRUEGER-BABBITT. She stopped for mail and then went through the front door. I followed. The office was all blond wood, including the large desk that sat at an angle in the corner. Next to the desk was a rack filled with brochures, most citing tourist attractions, area businesses, and financing options. One noted that "Ely ranks 12th on the *Field & Stream Magazine* 2008 list of Best Fishing Towns in America." Another stated that "Real Estate is an important element of any long-term investment plan." Across from the desk four chairs surrounded a round table. A PC was in the center of the table; its screen saver read "Browse our listings of affordable lake homes."

Beyond the office the house was set up like an efficiency apartment. A doorway behind the desk led to a kitchenette and tiny living room; a staircase in the living room allowed access to a second-floor bathroom and a large bedroom.

While Josie went to her phone and checked her voice mail, I clicked the mouse and skimmed the real estate listings.

There were three pages of them. All of the listings had gorgeous photographs and enticing copy; a third were highlighted with the words "Recently Reduced Price" written in red. Josie hung up her phone and cursed loudly. I turned away from the PC to look at her.

"Client just backed out of a sale," she said. "A hundred and eighty-five thousand dollars."

"Sorry."

"I needed that eleven-thousand-dollar commission."

Josie sat behind her desk and sorted through the stack of mail. "Bill, bill, bill, flyer, request for money, request for money, bill, flyer, and one, two, three preapproved credit card applications. What am I going to do, Dyson?"

"I think you've already made that decision."

"Am I a bad person?"

"Most bad people don't ask that question. We are not prone to introspection."

"We?"

Stay in character, stay in character, my inner voice chanted.

"I have no pretensions about what I am," I said aloud.

"What are you?"

"A thief."

"I googled the Iron Range Bandits last night. They're blaming the Silver Bay robbery on us."

"Lucky you."

"They don't seem to have any suspects, though. I mean, nothing to connect us to the robbery."

"Sweetie, if they did, they wouldn't tell the newspapers."

"They mentioned you, though, and don't call me sweetie."

"Me?"

"You're the unidentified suspect that caused a traffic accident that allowed us to escape."

"It's like I once told you, I'm a helluva guy. Did I tell you that? I'm sure I did."

"Where are you from, Dyson? I mean, where is home?"

"I don't remember."

Dammit, did you say that out loud? my inner voice asked. Truth was, I couldn't remember where Dyson was from. *You should have done a better job studying his profile.*

"I don't have a home, Josie," I said aloud. "I had to give that up."

She studied me from across her desk for what seemed like a long time. "Will I have to give up my home?" she asked.

It was a good question. My deal with Harry and Bullert was for information identifying the gunrunners. I made no promises concerning the Iron Range Bandits, and like Bullert said, I was under no legal obligation to report their crimes. It was possible I could do what I came there to do and leave them out of it.

But they're thieves, my inner voice reminded me. *How many jobs have they pulled?*

That's not my problem, I told myself.

Whose problem is it?

"I don't know, Josie," I said aloud. "We'll see."

A few minutes later, we were back on the road. We drove northwest until we reached Ely. Compared to Krueger, Ely was a teeming metropolis with thirty-eight resorts, twenty-seven outfitters, six bait shops, thirteen restaurants, twelve bars, nine motels, and two B&Bs, plus art galleries, museums, gift shops, golf courses, parks, and the International Wolf Center. Nearly all of its businesses catered to tourists lured to the area by the fabled Boundary Waters Canoe Area. It had a listed population of 3,700 people, although that number more than doubled during the summer months when people from the Cities opened their lake homes. Which wasn't to suggest that it was all sunshine, lollipops, and rainbows. Many of the joys of Ely ended fourteen miles east in the charred remains of the Pagami Creek Forest Fire.

A lightning strike caused the biggest fire in state history, burning over a hundred thousand acres of jack pine, black spruce, white cedar, balsam fir, birch, aspen, ash, and maple trees in the BWCA and even threatened the tiny town of Isabella. Plumes of ash actually settled on the roof of Miller Park in Milwaukee over four hundred miles away. Despite that, the U.S. Forest Service—which allowed the blaze to burn unchecked for over three weeks before stepping in—was pretty much nonchalant about the situation, suggesting that a fire every now and again was necessary to clean up the forest. Josie, for one, was skeptical.

"Tell that to the people who rely on the tourist dollars that the BWCA brings to the area, the resorts and outfitters and whatnot," she said. "As if the Range didn't have enough problems."

Josie wasn't a particularly good driver. She tended to behave as if there were no other traffic on the road. Still, I had her drive back and forth and around Ely for nearly an hour. She became quite nervous when I had her motor past the county sheriff's department substation on East Chapman and Second Avenue East—twice. Eventually I found just what I was looking for.

"Hey, a Dairy Queen," I said.

I made her stop, and we both ordered Blizzards; she had Cappuccino Heath Bar, I had M&M's. We ate them while sitting in the car in the parking lot. While we ate, a county sheriff's department patrol car parked two spaces down from us. Josie flinched and gave me a panicked look. I rested a hand on her thigh. Her skin was soft and warm beneath my fingers. I left them there while we watched the two deputies enter the DQ. One was short and thin with sandy, receding hair. The other was tall with a beer belly that rolled over his belt buckle and hung there as if it were looking for a place to sit. We could see them ordering through the store's large windows.

I did not move my hand, so Josie did it for me, taking my fingers and setting them on my own thigh. "Look," she said. "They're paying for their treats with the free coupons they're supposed to dole out to the kids that they see wearing bicycle helmets."

McKenzie would have been outraged by the sight; Dyson, not so much.

"Scandalous," I said. Josie gave me a look that suggested she was disappointed in me. "We're not exactly Ken and Barbie ourselves," I reminded her.

"These two—James and Williams—they stopped my father a few months ago. My old man, everyone up here knows he does grass. It's not a secret. So they stop him for no particular reason and search his car."

"Is this before or after your cousin decided to go into the drug business?"

"Before, and Jimmy—Jimmy was never in the drug business. We put a stop—do you know he had pictures on his cell phone? He went around showing people photos of his plants and fertilizer and equipment."

"Gotta like a man who takes pride in his work."

"But that was—ridiculous."

"Go on with your story."

"My dad, they stopped my dad. He wasn't carrying, okay; didn't have anything on him. That didn't faze James and Williams. They supplied a baggie of grass for him, pretended they found it in his trunk and told him—they were laughing when they told him, the old man said—that it felt like it weighed more than two ounces. In Minnesota if you're caught carrying less than one and a half ounces of grass it's a three-hundred-dollar fine. More than that, it's a felony starting at five years in prison and a ten-thousand-dollar fine. As a favor, though, as a favor to my father, they said they'd call it one and a half ounces and he could pay them the fine, pay them the three hundred dollars. This wasn't a bribe, oh no—Dad said they were very clear about that. They claimed the law was being upheld and my father was being punished for his crime—which he didn't commit. The difference was they didn't have to do paperwork, didn't have to bother the overworked court system, and the old man wouldn't be going to prison, thus sparing the state the expense of another mouth to feed."

"I bet your old man paid," I said.

"Of course he paid. He was so frightened—going to prison. The odd thing is that Dad smokes a lot more grass, drinks a lot more beer, now than he ever did before it happened. Look, Dyson, it's not just him. Everyone pays. Don't tell me the county sheriff doesn't know about it, either. All the other county deputies, they ride one to a car. James and Williams, they ride together—they're always together. Makes it easier for them to intimidate people."

"James and Williams, is that their first names or last?" I asked.

"Last. I think their first names are Eugene and Allen. Bullies with a badge."

"Well, we all have to make a living," I said—or rather Dyson said. McKenzie had been a cop for eleven and a half years. He wanted to beat the hell out of the two sonuvabitches and then make sure they never carried a badge again.

We remained in the car eating ice cream. At least I ate ice cream; Josie seemed to have lost her taste for it. James and

Williams finished theirs before we finished ours and drove off down Sheridan Street, the name the locals gave to Minnesota Highway 1 as it passed through Ely. It was the main drag. Hell, it was the only drag.

"This isn't going to work," I said. "Everything is on the same damn road, all the major businesses. If we stop and start along with the armored truck, I don't care how many car lengths we stay behind, how many times we pass it and then wait down the road for it to pass us, we're bound to be spotted. Especially if we're going to repeat it over a three-, four-day period while looking for the best place to hit 'em. We could run a three-car rotation in Ely, a city like Ely, only what about the long stretch of single-lane highway between Ely and Tower or Virginia? It would look like a frickin' parade."

Josie stared at me. I wasn't sure she knew what I was talking about.

"Okay," I said. "We'll go to Plan B."

"There's a Plan B?" she asked.

"There's always a Plan B. I just don't know what it is yet. Call your cousin. Let me talk to him."

A moment later, Jimmy was on Josie's cell phone.

"Jimmy," I said. "I want you to look up the address for Mesabi Security."

He did. "Their main office is in Duluth, plus they have a terminal in Krueger," he said.

"A terminal?"

"That's what it says on its Web site."

"Hang on." I lowered the cell and looked at Josie. "Does Mesabi Security have an office in Krueger?"

"Not an office. Just a parking lot."

"Parking lot?"

"They keep some of their trucks there."

I stared at her for at least a half-dozen beats, marveling

that this woman had made a considered decision to engage in a life of crime. She ate a spoonful of her melting ice cream to be doing something instead of staring back.

"You didn't think that might be pertinent information, Jo-Ellen?" I asked.

She twirled a lock of auburn hair around her finger and dragged it across her mouth. "Please, mister. Don't scold me. I'm just a little girl from the Iron Range."

"Sure you are."

I studied the Mesabi Security Company's truck terminal from the parking lot of a roadhouse located on the other side of a county road about three miles east of Krueger. There wasn't much to it—a small shack and parking lot about the size of a gas station that had been carved out of the forest and surrounded by a high chain-link fence with razor wire strung along the top. There were eight vehicles—three cars, three SUVs, and two pickup trucks—parked inside the enclosure. A short driveway led from the county blacktop to the gate. The gate was open. A large padlock was attached to a thick chain hanging on the fence post. The padlock was open. There was no one in the yard. If there was someone in the office—and I assumed there was—I couldn't see him.

Josie kept twisting in her seat to look at the entrance to the roadhouse. It was called Buckman's, and it looked like it had been there since the last time the University of Minnesota went to the Rose Bowl—1962.

"Should we go inside?" she asked.

"Why? Are you thirsty?"

"Won't people be suspicious if we just sit here?"

"A man and a woman spending time together in a car outside of a bar—no one's ever seen that before."

"They know me here." That caught my attention. "They'll think I'm spending time with you."

"Perish the thought."

"You know what I mean."

I gestured casually at the shack across the county blacktop. "Do you know who works here?"

"No. Why would I?"

"It's a small town."

"Not that small."

"Sweetie, my high school graduating class was bigger than this."

"That doesn't mean we know everybody, and don't call me sweetie. Besides, the man who works there, he might not even be from Krueger. People don't necessarily live near their work up here. Distance doesn't mean the same to us that it does to people in the Cities."

"Distance, though, that's why this place exists. I'm guessing Mesabi Security has a lot of clients up here. Instead of commuting all the way from Duluth, especially when the weather's iffy, they roll some of their armored trucks out of this terminal. Judging by the number of cars in the lot, I'm guessing three."

"Is that a good thing?"

"Time will tell. Do you have a map?"

"Glove compartment."

I opened it, found a three-year-old Explore Minnesota Official State Highway Map, and handed it to Josie.

"Tell me your cell phone has a camera."

She did. I asked her to show me how it worked. Afterward I told her to drive the car to the shack, get out, and ask the attendant for directions.

"Directions where?"

"Josie, I don't care. I just want you to distract him for a few minutes."

"Why?"

"So I won't be seen while I take photos of the padlock."

"Why do you want to do that?"

"God, you're worse than your brother."

"What a terrible thing to say."

"Do me a favor. Before you walk into the shack, undo a couple of buttons on your sweater."

"I most certainly will not."

"Just a thought."

I slipped out of the Taurus and walked casually down the county road. Josie drove her car out of the roadhouse parking lot to the nearest intersection, flipped a U-turn, and came back, pulling up in front of the shack. As soon as she disappeared inside, I jogged across the blacktop and followed the short driveway to the gate. The padlock was made by Abus, a company I had never heard of. I took photos of each side, plus the top and the bottom. Less than a minute later, I was back on the blacktop and walking away from the terminal. Six minutes after that, the Taurus pulled up, and I jumped into the passenger seat.

"What took you so long?" I asked.

"The attendant wanted to chitchat."

I glanced at Josie's chest. She had undone the top three buttons of her sweater.

"I don't blame him," I said.

Josie knew exactly what I was talking about. She tried to rebutton her sweater with one hand while driving with the other. The car swerved over the centerline.

"Want me to do that?" I asked.

"I hate you, Dyson. Honest to God I do."

SEVEN

Grand Rapids was a real city with a population of about eleven thousand built on the Mississippi River where it was still narrow enough that you could pass a football from one side to the other. That put it in the heart of Minnesota's northern resort and recreation area, making it a prime retail center. The stores there sold everything I needed, including an Abus Solid Steel Chrome Plated 83/80 RK padlock. It had taken me about five minutes using Josie's office computer to identify it from the photographs and another three to locate the nearest store that sold it.

Josie was skeptical when I announced we were taking a road trip. "G. R. is in Itasca County," she reminded me.

"Yes."

"Itasca County Sheriff's Department—you escaped from them the day before yesterday."

"Yes."

"Aren't you worried that they're looking for you, that they might find you?"

"Nah."

Famous last words.

It took us nearly ninety minutes to get there with Josie driving. Along the way I kept fiddling with the buttons, searching the available radio stations for something worth listening to.

"What are you looking for?" Josie asked.

"Jazz."

Josie slapped my hand and punched the button for KGPZ, the FM station out of Coleraine. The announcer referred to it as a "real country" station and proceeded to play Taylor Swift.

"Where I come from, the person driving the car gets to pick the radio station," she said.

"Country-western, though?"

"It's the voice of the people."

"It's pop music. It stopped being the voice of the people when Johnny Cash died."

"Take that back." Josie's jaw was set, and her hands clenched the steering wheel with anger.

Is she really going to fight over this? my inner voice asked.

"I mean it," she added.

Yes, she is.

"I apologize," I said.

Josie knew I was less than sincere, yet she said, "That's better," just the same.

"You're nuts," I told her. "You know that, right?"

"Do you want to drive, Dyson?"

"Yes. Yes, I do."

"Well, you can't."

I only knew Grand Rapids well enough to drive through it, so it took a while before we found the locksmith that stocked the Abus padlock. I matched it against the photos I took on Josie's cell phone and paid the man in cash. He asked if I needed a receipt. When I answered no, he put the bills in his pocket instead of the cash register and thanked me for my business. I found myself nodding as I left the store. Even when I wasn't pretending to be a hardened criminal, I appreciated any effort that kept taxable income out of the hands of the government.

Afterward, we headed for an electronics megastore off of Highway 169 where a fetching young lass with eyes that matched the color of her shirt gave me a quick tutorial on the pros and cons of a variety of GPS transmitters. We settled on a passive GPS logger that recorded locations, speed, and time and, when plugged into a computer's USB port, displayed the data it collected on an interface powered by Google Maps.

"It has a motion sensor," the tech told me with a pretty smile. "When the vehicle isn't moving, the device will go into sleep mode to conserve battery power."

I bought three, plus magnetic boxes to put them in.

"You should be ashamed of yourself," Josie told me when we entered the checkout line.

"Now what did I do?"

"Flirting with that salesgirl. She's young enough to be your daughter."

"She wasn't a salesgirl. She was a trained tech assistant—it said so on her name tag."

"I was standing right there, too. Who knows what she thought."

"Probably that we had a boring sex life that could only be improved by her technical expertise."

"You're disgusting."

Not me, I told myself, Dyson. Dyson was disgusting, and he was kind of enjoying it. After I paid for the electronic devices, I made sure I was walking behind Josie as we left the store.

"My, my, my," I chanted.

"Stop it."

"It must be jelly cuz jam don't shake like that."

Josie turned sideways to glare at me as she passed through the automatic doors. "Now you're just being obnoxious," she said—and walked directly into the arms of Deputy Ken Olson of the Itasca County Sheriff's Department, hitting him hard enough that they both nearly fell over.

"Excuse me," she said.

"Are you all right?" he asked.

"I wasn't looking where I was going."

"Don't worry about it."

It was then that Josie noticed the uniform, noticed the badge. She took a step backward. Her voice became thick with anxiety. "My mistake," she said.

Deputy Olson smiled his pearly whites at her. He looked over her shoulder at me. His eyes grew wide, the smile disappeared, and he rested his hand on his Glock—apparently he had replaced the one I had stolen. Josie saw the movement and her expression displayed her panic. Like her brother's, her face didn't hide anything.

"No harm done," I said.

I moved closer to the deputy. I was counting on the fact that Bullert had briefed him after the escape and had even told Olson's boss that Olson had been in on it from the beginning so he wouldn't be disciplined for his incompetence.

"Beautiful day, isn't it, Deputy?" I added.

Olson read my eyes. He removed his hand from the butt of the Glock and visibly relaxed.

"It is, sir," he said. "Anyone who wonders why we suffer through Minnesota winters should come up here on a day like this. Are you sure you're okay, miss?"

Josie nodded a little too vehemently.

"Are you from around here?" the deputy asked.

"No," I said. "Just visiting friends. I should be back in the Cities in a couple of days."

"Enjoy your stay."

The deputy offered his hand, and I shook it.

"Thank you," I said.

A moment later, Josie and I were crossing the parking lot, my hand gripping her elbow. We walked to her Ford Taurus as casually as I could make her.

"What just happened?" she wanted to know.

Instead of answering, I directed her to the passenger side, took her keys, unlocked the door, and eased her inside.

"I'll drive," I said.

She didn't object.

A few minutes later we were heading out of town.

"He recognized you," Josie said. "I saw it. He even reached for his gun."

"He thought he recognized me. When I came up and started chatting with him like we were old friends he realized, no, I couldn't possibly be the same guy. If I were the same guy, I'd be running or shooting it out. I wouldn't be asking him how he was doing."

"You were so calm. You just—you just talked to him. How could you do that?"

Because you're not actually wanted, my inner voice said. *You had nothing to be afraid of. You can't tell her that, though.*

"We all have a fight-or-flight response mechanism built into our DNA," I said. "It's an instinct that's left over from when our ancestors slept in trees. Animals have it, too. The trick is knowing when to suppress it, knowing when being smart is preferable to doing battle or running like hell."

She stared at me for a few beats after that and then asked

the question I knew was coming. "Why are you doing this? You're so intelligent, you're so—you could be doing anything you want."

"I am doing what I want. Few people enjoy their work as much as I enjoy mine."

"You don't have to steal."

"Neither do you."

Josie shifted in her seat and gazed out the passenger window. She didn't speak until I started fiddling with the radio stations again. "Just pick one," she said.

She was angry, only I don't think she was angry with me.

The sun was still high in the sky by the time we returned to Krueger. I drove Josie's Taurus past the Mesabi Security terminal again. It was the same as it had been hours earlier: eight vehicles parked inside the enclosure, no armored trucks to be seen.

"What should we do?" Josie asked.

"I don't think the attendant would fall for the same trick twice no matter how many buttons you open."

"Thanks a lot."

I glanced at my watch. "Let's come back in an hour."

We did, this time stopping in Buckman's lot. Two of the armored trucks were now parked within the enclosure, and most of the other vehicles were gone, leaving just a single car and two pickups. It was after 8:00 P.M., but thanks to daylight savings time, dusk was still a long way off.

"Go inside the bar," I said. "I'll meet you there in a minute."

"What are you going to do?"

"We can't afford to wait. The third truck could arrive at any moment and we'll lose our chance."

Josie kept staring at me.

"Go inside the bar," I repeated slowly.

Josie gave it a beat and then scampered out of the Taurus. When she disappeared into Buckman's I left the car and walked swiftly across the county blacktop to the terminal's driveway and down the driveway to the gate. I was carrying my Abus padlock. It was unlocked. When I reached the gate, I slipped Mesabi Security's padlock off of the chain and replaced it with my own. Careful not to accidentally close the shackle on Mesabi's padlock, I returned to Josie's Ford Taurus and set it gently on the driver's-side floor. The entire process took less than ninety seconds, and as far as I could tell, no one saw me, yet I was sweating profusely. A moment later, I entered the roadhouse.

It was a polite bar despite the smell of stale beer rising from the warped wooden floor—the kind of place where a restless woman could come in alone, survey what was available, maybe even sample the merchandise, and leave without necessarily being tackled in the parking lot or followed home.

I found Josie sitting at a small table just inside the doorway with a man who seemed to be in his midtwenties. It was hard to tell because he was hunched over his beer and the bar's lights had been dialed down to give patrons a sense of privacy. I let my fingers brush Josie's shoulder as I walked past just to let her know I was there. She surprised me by reaching back and giving my hand a squeeze without once taking her eyes off the young man.

"How's your mother?" she asked him. She asked the question softly with a concern in her voice that told me she had a natural and genuine sympathy for anyone who was in trouble.

I made my way to the end of the bar and found a stool. The

Twins were on the coast playing the Angels, and the pregame show was on the flat-screen TV.

"What can I gitcha?" the bartender asked.

He didn't pour Summit Ale, so I ordered a Sam Adams that he served in the bottle.

"You come in with Josie?" he asked.

"I did."

"Love that girl. Always cheerful, always cheers the place up. She knows, no one else seems to know but she does, acting all miserable all the time, it ain't gonna make the world a better place, is it?"

I couldn't argue with that, I told him.

"How's business?" I asked, just to be polite. I didn't expect much of an answer. The bartender gave me one anyway.

"If it improved one hundred percent it would still be lousy," he said. "Since the big shock, since the mill closed, it's been deader than—I got my customers, my regulars, the truckers and loggers and guys from the mill, they still come in, but all they order is beer now." He gestured at the bottle in front of me. "They buy a beer and nurse it all night long; taking no pleasure in drinking it, neither. The only reason they come in at all is because they can't stand being cooped up in their homes no more, you know?"

It was terrible, according to the bartender. Tough times all through the region. An economy in free fall. Everywhere you looked, men and women out of work through no fault of their own. Corporations, some of them founded when his father was a boy, were folding like carnival tents. Banks failed. Retailers from national chains to the ma-and-pa shop on the corner were locking their doors and throwing away the key. Yet even though it was happening to everyone, he said it was hard not to take it personally. Especially in small towns like Krueger and Babbitt that had been built around one company or one industry, towns whose very existence had been decided on the whim of overpaid, overpampered executives who had never even seen the place.

That was only part of it, the bartender said. Because of the lack of jobs, people were abandoning the area's small towns and cities. Which reduced their tax base. Which lowered their general funds. Which caused them to slash the services they could afford to provide the citizens who remained. Which encouraged more people to leave. Which lowered tax collections even more. Which put entire communities at risk.

"A city like Krueger," said the bartender, "we're one disaster away from bankruptcy, and not a big disaster, neither. A roof collapses on the municipal building, a sewer pump burns out, a water main breaks—that's all it'd take."

Listening to him and watching the men and women who sat in twos and threes at the tables and in the booths, I felt the despair of the unemployed. I began to wish that the bar would suddenly disappear along with all the other buildings in Krueger, and the people, too. I wished that none of the Scandinavians, Slavs, and Italians who had initially settled the region had come there and that it would all revert back to the wilderness from which it sprang. I wished we all could start over again knowing what we know now, hating fewer people and admiring others not so much. I wished . . .

I glanced Josie's way just in time to see her open her bag, pull out her wallet, peel off several of the bills she had helped steal in Silver Bay, and press them into the young man's hand. He didn't want to take them, yet she insisted. The gesture reminded me of a poem I was taught way back in St. Mark's Elementary School, something by Robert Browning.

'Twas a thief said the last kind word to Christ:
Christ took the kindness and forgave the theft.

In that moment I felt the acid taste of guilt crawl up from my stomach into my throat; guilt because I didn't have the same needs that these people had, the same concerns; guilt because I was a millionaire who had done precious little to earn my money. The reason I couldn't be corrupted like Josie and the Bandits, the biggest reason anyway, was that I didn't need the dough. Assistant U.S. Attorney James R. Finnegan had been right about my finances. Yet if I had been wallowing in debt, if my child needed medical care, if my home was about to be foreclosed on, if my wife was threatening to leave me, I might have thought differently.

No, no, no, don't go there, my inner voice told me. *These guys are criminals, and the why isn't important. Think about their victims. Think about how terrified they must have been to have guns pointed at them—an AK-47, for Christ's sake. The Bandits hadn't physically harmed anyone, yet that would change if they kept on—think about that. Coming around to Josie's way of thinking would be a very dangerous thing indeed. Stockholm syndrome, I think they call it.*

Josie cupped the young man's cheek, then patted his arm before leaving the table and making her way down the bar to where I sat. I looked away so she wouldn't think I was watching her. I turned my attention to the baseball game. By then the starting pitcher was just finishing his warm-up tosses. Josie pulled up a stool. The bartender made her a vodka Collins without being asked, and she thanked him. He asked her how she was doing, and Josie said she was fine. Then he said, "Dave okay?"

"Excuse me?" I asked.

"Dave, her brother," the bartender said.

"I know who he is."

"Dave's okay," Josie said.

"Tell him, anything he needs . . ."

"I'll tell him." To me she said, "I'm hungry. Are you hungry?"

"I could eat."

"A couple of menus, please."

The bartender said, "Sure Josie," gave me a what's-your-story look, and moved down the stick.

"The bartender knows that your brother is hiding up here?" I asked.

"In a small town, people don't need a newspaper," Josie said. "You only need a newspaper when stuff happens that people can't see or hear about for themselves. In a small town, it doesn't take long before everyone knows everything."

"I do not find that comforting."

The bartender reappeared, gave us menus, and disappeared again. The menu recommended Buckman's "World Famous Cheeseburger." I had never heard of it, but then I didn't get out much.

After the bartender served us, Josie leaned in and whispered, "Are you sure this is going to work?"

"I'm guessing that the first person to arrive at the terminal in the morning, probably the attendant, has the key. He unlocks the padlock, unwinds the chain, opens the gate to the enclosure, and then hangs the padlock on the chain without locking it because, why would he? That just makes extra work for himself later. The last person to leave, and maybe it's the attendant again, he closes the gate, wraps the chain around it, and locks the padlock. We're hoping he doesn't notice we switched locks. Later tonight, we'll sneak over there, unlock the padlock with our key, get inside, place the GPS loggers on the trucks, then switch our lock with Mesabi's again. Tomorrow they won't even know we've been there."

"What if they have security cameras?"

"If they do, they're hidden pretty damn well, because I couldn't find them."

"What if we get caught?"

"Nonresidential burglary for a woman like you without a record, they'd slap your wrist and make you promise not to do it again."

"What about you?"

"What about me?"

"What will they do to you?"

"What can I say, sweetie? I've been living on borrowed time for years now."

"Don't call me—"

"Sweetie, I know."

"I wish I knew more about you."

"Like what?"

"Anything. Everything."

"Let's see. I like jazz. I like baseball. I like the ballet, believe it or not. I prefer whiskey if I'm going to drink to excess and beer if I'm not. When I read—and I read a lot—I'd rather have a real book in my hands instead of one of those electronic gizmos. I like to cook. I don't believe in saving money, and I'll never marry because I refuse to impose my lifestyle on anyone I care about. What about you?"

"Me? You'll think I'm making fun of you."

"Give it a try."

"I don't like jazz or baseball or whiskey or beer, and I've never been to the ballet. I'm a lousy cook. I don't read much that's not business related. I think everybody should save their money, and I desperately want to fall in love and get married."

"Sounds like the beginning of a beautiful friendship, Josie." To prove it I clinked her glass with my beer bottle.

We sat at the bar and watched the Twins. I nursed the Sam

Adams, much to the bartender's chagrin—hey, I had work to do—while Josie had multiple vodka Collinses. Possibly the drinks loosened her up, because she turned out to be a pleasant companion despite her refusal to accept the sacrifice bunt as a sound baseball strategy. "Why would you deliberately make an out?" At the bottom of the fourth inning I quietly announced I needed fresh air. I returned a few minutes later and informed her that that the third truck had yet to return.

"How long should we wait?" she asked.

"Until all of the trucks are inside and the place is locked up tight, probably sometime during the dark side of midnight."

"That sounds fanciful."

"My dad, when I was a kid, he would warn that nothing good ever happened after midnight. The dark side, he called it—stay away from the dark side. I was a *Star Wars* fan. It made perfect sense to me."

"Speaking of the dark side."

I followed Josie's gaze to a woman who was loitering at the front entrance. She stood alone, a woman built to be of service to men, drawing long gazes from male and female patrons alike, soaking in the awareness like a solar panel—it seemed to energize her. She swung her body as she walked the length of the bar. She expected the audience to follow her, expected to be gawked at.

"Hey, Josie," she said when she reached us. Her short skirt slid up to there when she hoisted herself onto a stool and crossed her legs. Her legs were made for crossing. Being a gentleman, McKenzie would have averted his eyes. Dyson was no gentleman. "Seen Brian?"

"It's not my turn to watch him," Josie answered. There was a chill in her voice that I had not heard before.

"I thought he'd be around," the woman said. She motioned for the bartender, ordered a beer, and asked that he pour it in a glass. At the same time, she slid a pack of Marlboro Lights out of her bag.

"No smoking," the bartender said.

"Shit," the woman replied.

"Not working tonight?" Josie asked.

"I was, but the place is pretty dead, so I only did one show."

Up close I could see that the woman had large brown eyes that looked a little sad, the way that all large brown eyes do, and that her strawberry hair was tinged with gray at the roots. Her smile was warm, although her teeth were dingy from tobacco.

"You're Dyson, aren't you?" she said.

"Hmm, Dyson?" I replied.

She reached past Josie and patted my hand. "It's okay. I won't tell anyone."

I glared at Josie.

"Dyson, this is Claire de Lune," she said. "Claire is Jimmy's fiancée."

"He told me everything about you," Claire said. "From what he said, I thought you'd be taller."

"Pleased to meet you," I said. I shook Claire's hand. It was stronger than you might expect. "I hope you can keep a secret better than Jimmy."

She turned her attention toward the other customers in the bar even as she spoke. "Jimmy and me don't keep secrets."

"I do."

"Don't worry. I know how to keep my mouth shut."

A glance into Josie's eyes told me that it was an opinion not widely shared. "I hope . . ."

Claire gestured contemptuously as if the topic were undeserving of any further consideration and continued gazing around the bar. "I thought for sure that Brian would be here," she said.

"Claire de Lune is a very pretty name," I said. "It means 'moonlight' in French, doesn't it?"

"I guess."

"It's also the name of a piano solo by Claude Debussy."

"I'll be right back."

Claire took a cell phone from her purse and headed for the restroom.

"Lovely woman," I told Josie. "Very gregarious."

"She's an exotic dancer."

"You mean a stripper?"

"Jimmy says exotic dancer."

"No kidding? She's a little old for that line of work, isn't she?"

"How should I know? I only know she's a decade older than Jimmy. Her real name is Sandra Dawson, but I guess that didn't have any marquee value."

"How did she and Jimmy—"

"How did they meet? They met in a strip club, of course. Jimmy saw her and . . ." She paused and shook her head as if the words necessary to finish the sentence were too dismal to speak. "That's not even the half of it. Claire got pregnant and told Jimmy he was the father. Jimmy agreed to marry her. The family demanded that she take a paternity test. Turned out the child wasn't Jimmy's. He insists on marrying her anyway. Actually put money down on a townhouse. I begged him not to. He did it anyway. He's already underwater and they haven't even closed yet."

"Who's Brian?"

"Brian T. Fenelon. Her manager, boyfriend, pimp, I don't know what, except that he's a creep. Why?"

"I think he's headed this way."

Josie turned in her stool to see a short man with thin hair wearing a rumpled sports jacket over a colored T-shirt as if he were channeling *Miami Vice* reruns. He moved toward us with the swagger of an athlete who had let himself go, who believed he could still play the game despite the fat that settled around his middle. Claire was a head taller than he was, yet she draped herself on his arm in a way that made me regard her planned marriage to Jimmy as wishful thinking on his part.

"You Dyson?" he asked. His voice reminded me of the high-pitched yap of a fox terrier. "I thought you'd be taller."

"How the hell does everyone know I'm here?"

"Shhhh," Josie said.

I glared at her. "Why? Someone's maiden aunt in International Falls hasn't heard yet?"

"Whoa, big fella," Fenelon said.

He rested his hand on my shoulder. I didn't know if it was meant to be friendly or intimidating. I jerked my shoulder free and gave him my best "don't touch" scowl just the same. He swiveled his head and decided that too many people were watching.

"Let's grab a booth."

We sat, Claire and he on one side of the wooden booth, Josie and I on the other. I finished my Sam Adams and set the empty bottle on the table in front of me. Fenelon spit on his hands and rubbed them together before leaning forward across the table.

"I don't want to waste your time," he said.

"I appreciate that," I told him.

"I know what you're planning. I want in."

"Sorry, I don't know what you're talking about."

"Don't be like that. I can help you."

"Help me what?"

Fenelon leaned in closer and whispered. "Help you rob an armored truck."

I glared at Josie again. "We need another meeting," I told her.

"I know everybody in the county," Fenelon added. "Everybody. I can be a big help to you." He glanced around to see if anyone was listening before whispering some more. "You and me, we could run this town."

"Isn't that what the Emperor told Darth Vader before they started building the Death Star?"

"What?"

"Sorry, I've had *Star Wars* on the brain lately. Listen. Brian, your name's Brian? I don't know what you've heard—"

"Jimmy told us everything, and I'm telling you, whatever you need, I can get it for you."

"Whatever Jimmy told you, it's just talk. It doesn't amount to anything."

"Then why are you still in town where anyone who knows your name could drop a dime on you?"

"That sounds like a threat." I turned to Josie. "Does that sound like a threat to you?" I turned back to Fenelon. "Did you really mean to threaten me, Brian?"

"No, no, no, of course not. I'm just saying, I can help you—or I can hurt you."

"Ahh, you can hurt me. As long as we have that settled."

"Brian," Josie said. She didn't have the chance to finish her thought before Fenelon cut her off.

"Shut the fuck up, bitch," he said. "No one is talking to you."

I picked up the beer bottle by the neck and smacked Fenelon on his balding head. I hit him hard. Not hard enough to kill him, just hard enough to demonstrate my displeasure— the bottle didn't even shatter. There was a satisfying thud against his skull that sounded like a rock landing in soft dirt, and Fenelon jerked back against the wall of the booth before slipping out onto the floor. His falling out of the booth was what caused people to stare. I carefully set the bottle back on the table. Josie's eyes widened as if she had just discovered that one of the Seven Wonders of the Ancient World was parked in her front yard.

"He was harshing my mellow," I said in my defense.

Surprisingly—at least it was a surprise to me—Josie showed more concern for Fenelon than his girlfriend did. Claire watched him fall out of the booth without saying a word, took a deep drag of the cigarette she wasn't supposed to be smoking, and swung her impressive legs over the edge of the wooden bench like she was about to stand, but didn't. Instead, she looked down on her boyfriend's sprawling body and shook her head slowly as if it were a sight she had seen so often that she had grown bored with it.

I slipped out of the booth and knelt next to Fenelon. His hand was massaging his injury. His eyes glazed over.

"What?" he said. "What?"

I leaned in and whispered. "You're right. I need you. I need someone who knows his way around. No one can know we're working together, though, especially Josie and her people. Call me names. Tell everyone you hate my guts and you're going to get me. I'll contact you through Claire and tell you what I need in a couple of days. Don't let me down."

"You bastard," he said. I helped him up and he pushed me away, one hand still massaging the spot on his head where I hit him. There was a big red knot, but the skin was unbroken. "You sonuvabitch, I'm going to get you. I'm going to fuck you up."

The bartender came to the booth in a hurry. "What's going on here?" he asked.

"Fucker suckered me," Fenelon said. "Hit me with a bottle."

"I didn't like the way he talked to Josie," I said.

"What did he say?" the bartender asked. I told him. Apparently the bartender didn't like it, either. He turned Fenelon around and shoved him toward the door. "I told you I didn't want any more trouble from you. Now get out." Claire followed dutifully. I trailed behind, listening to Fenelon's loud albeit wholly unimaginative litany of epitaphs and threats. Outside the bar he turned on me.

"I'm not finished with you," he shouted. It was an impressive performance. You couldn't even tell he was acting, but then Fenelon was just playing himself, wasn't he? I gave him the thumbs-up sign in a way that only he could see it and stood watching while he retreated to his car. Across the county road I noticed that the third armored truck had been returned to the terminal, the other vehicles had disappeared, and the enclosure was now locked tight. After watching Fenelon spin his wheels on the loose gravel and drive off, I went back inside.

Josie had returned to our original stools at the bar. I joined her there. She looked at me as if she didn't know whether she should be impressed or angry. After a few silent moments, she asked, "Did you do that for me, hit Brian for insulting me?"

"Yes."

"I don't believe you."

"There's no reason why you should."

"What if he calls the police?"

"He won't," I said.

"What will he do?"

"Whatever I tell him."

"How do you know?"

"Greed. The only thing that makes a man act more stupidly than a beautiful woman is greed."

Josie studied me for a long moment and then motioned to the bartender and ordered another vodka Collins.

———

I waited until the ball game was over, about twenty after twelve, before settling the tab and leading Josie outside. She was unsteady on her feet. I poured her into the passenger seat of the Ford Taurus, went to the driver's side, and proceeded to activate the GPS loggers.

"I can't figure you out, Dyson," Josie told me. "You're such a nice guy and then you're such a shit. I can't figure that out. You can't be both. How can you be both?"

"Practice," I said. "Stay here."

"I want to help."

"Stay in the car."

"Dyson?"

"What?"

Josie took my face in both of her hands, kissed me hard on the mouth, drew back, giggled, and brought her hand to her lips.

"Oh, no," she said. "Oh, no. I didn't mean to do that. You should go. You should go right now."

"Stay here," I told her again.

I crossed the country blacktop after making sure there were no vehicles coming that might catch me in their headlights. I opened my padlock and took it off the chain, being sure to lock it again so there would be no confusion later. Once inside the enclosure, I tagged the bottom of the back bumper of each of the three armored trucks with the magnetic boxes containing the GPS loggers. I returned to the gate and rechained and locked it using Mesabi's padlock. Less than five minutes passed before I was once again settled behind the wheel of the Taurus. Josie was slumped against the passenger door, snoring softly.

Josie stirred, sighed, and mumbled something incoherent as I lifted her from the passenger seat. Her head lolled against my chest, and I carried her to her home. She was not heavy. Still, her body was slack, and that made it difficult, especially when I had to unlock the front door and haul her across the threshold. I carried her upstairs and laid her gently on the bed. As I looked down on her body, a lot of things came to mind that I could do, all in the guise of making her more comfortable. I did none of them except remove her shoes and drape a quilt over her. I went downstairs to her living room and settled on the sofa—I knew how to get to her home from Buckman's but not to the lake cabin, so I was there for the duration.

Life shifts, doesn't it, I told myself, as the days pass and circumstances change. If I had remained in St. Paul with Nina, my life would have continued unaltered. I would never have given Josie so much as a passing glance, much less a thought. Yet I came up here at the behest of the ATF and now I found myself thinking of her affectionately, thinking of her in ways that invited disaster.

You've got to get the hell outta here, my inner voice warned me. *Get out before you do something that you'll have to keep secret for the rest of your life.*

EIGHT

I woke early, went upstairs, and cleaned up as best I could in the bathroom without disturbing Josie, then snuck back downstairs again. I found the ingredients and made coffee. While it was brewing, I rummaged through Josie's refrigerator, where I found eggs and shredded Swiss cheese in a plastic pouch. There were hash browns and breakfast sausage in the freezer and onions in the cupboard. I chopped the onions and sausage and fried them up. When the sausage was no longer pink, I added the browns, seasoned them with salt and pepper, and cooked them until they were heated through. I took the mixture off the heat, added the shredded cheese, and stirred the ingredients together until the cheese melted. I poured the mixture into a brownie pan and made four indentations with a spoon. I cracked open the eggs and poured them into the indentations without breaking the yolks. Afterward, I put the pan into the refrigerator.

While I waited, I explored Josie's home. It was neat and tidy, or at least neater and tidier than my place. For someone who claimed she didn't read, Josie had a surprising number of books, including a volume of poetry by Carol Connolly, the poet laureate of St. Paul. She had a lot of framed photographs and posters on her wall, too, most of them of Paris.

I heard Josie stirring upstairs, so I preheated the oven. When it reached 350 degrees, I popped the egg dish inside. Twenty minutes later I called to her. Josie came into the kitchen wearing a pale blue terrycloth robe and nothing else that I could see. Her face had been washed, but not her hair, which stuck out at odd angles.

"What are you doing here?" she asked. She didn't seem surprised by my presence, just annoyed.

"I didn't know how to get back to the cabin, so I slept on your sofa."

"Oh. Sorry."

I filled a coffee mug and set it on the table. She sat down across from it and took a sip. "This is good," she said.

"Of course it is."

She drank it with both hands. "Last night—did we?" she asked.

I fought the impulse to tease her. "No," I said.

"I didn't think so."

I carved out a square of the egg dish with a spatula, slipped it onto a plate, and slid in front of her.

"What's this?" she asked.

"Breakfast."

"I'm not hungry."

"Try it."

"I said I'm not hungry."

"I need you to eat."

"Oh, you need me to eat, do you? Like suddenly that's the most important thing in your world."

"I need you to feel better than you do now."

"Why?"

"If we're going to spend the day together I don't want you to be all cranky because you have a hangover. Now eat."

She did, reluctantly taking a forkful and then another. "Dammit, Dyson," she said. "This is delicious. You cook better than I do; you make better coffee . . ."

"I'm practically perfect in every way," I said. I was quoting *Mary Poppins*, but Josie didn't catch the reference.

Nina would have, my inner voice said. *She wouldn't have a hangover, either—she knows how to drink. And if she did have a hangover, she'd still look terrific. She doesn't even own terrycloth.*

Don't you forget it, I told myself.

We ate together in silence. To break it, I mentioned the photos and posters of Paris on the walls.

"The one of the Eiffel Tower is my favorite," she said.

"It looks even better at night," I said.

"You've been to Paris?"

"Yes."

"When?"

"Couple years ago."

"Did you like it?"

"Very much. I didn't really see that much of it, though. Just the tourist stuff."

"Can you speak French?"

"A little. I'm better with Spanish."

"I want to go to Paris so bad. After this is over . . . Have you ever thought about going back?"

"Many times."

Josie drank her coffee and ate her breakfast. The air vibrated with all the words she left unsaid.

You have got to get out of here, my inner voice told me yet again.

It took Josie an hour to get dressed. It was an hour well spent, I decided but didn't say aloud. Twenty minutes later we returned to the cabin on Lake Carl. We found the old man sitting at the picnic table on the deck. An impressive display of empty beer cans was already arrayed in front of him despite the early hour, and the way he kept adding to it, you'd have thought his stomach was on fire.

"Where the hell have you been?" he wanted to know.

He was speaking to Josie, not me. She attempted to explain, but the old man stopped her when she got to the part where I spent the night at her place.

"He did what?" he said.

"Dad, nothing happened."

I reached for one of the old man's beers. He slapped at my hand and I pulled it back.

"You spent the night with my daughter?" Technically, it was a question, yet the old man made it sound like a damning accusation.

"Nothing happened," Josie repeated. "After he put me to bed—"

"He put you to bed?"

"He slept on the sofa in my living room."

"And you let him? You let him?"

Josie's face expressed a silent apology to me. I smiled it away. Parents, more often than not, must take responsibility for their children, must take much of the credit or blame for the way they turn out. Children, on the other hand, cannot be held accountable for their parents. After all, they have no choice in the matter.

"I had thought about ravishing her defenseless body," I said, "but I knew you wouldn't like it."

The old man's eyes narrowed. "Are you making fun of me?" he asked.

"Yes, I am. Listen, Dad—has your daughter ever done anything that made you ashamed of her?"

"No." He didn't even pause to think about it.

"Well, then." I reached for a beer. This time he let me take it. I popped it open and took a sip. "Moving on."

"I can't stay here," Josie said. "I have work, such as it is. Do you need me for anything, Dyson?"

"Not until tonight."

That caught the old man's attention. His eyes swept from his daughter to me and back again.

"The dark side of midnight," Josie said.

"Exactly so," I said.

She was gone a moment later. I sat at the table across from the old man. I asked one question—"How's it going?" His answer was surprisingly long and illuminating. I suspect the beer had something to do with it. Up until that moment I had dismissed him as being little more than an aging hippie. Still, we are all rarely just one thing, and Josie's father was also a weathered, callused, tired old man, the kind that had worked hard his entire life with every expectation of having something to show for it at the end. Only the paper mill he had given his life to closed, taking the hard-earned pension he had been promised with it—the owners had looted the fund to pay for their own salaries and bonuses. When he heard the news, the old man's best friend of nearly sixty years put a shotgun in his mouth and pulled the trigger.

"He thought his life was all behind him," the old man said. "Couldn't see no way of going forward. Didn't have much of a family, no one to help him out, no Iron Range Bandits. It broke my heart what he did, yet I've thought about doing it once or twice myself."

"Except you have a family that cares about you."

He nodded and drank more beer. His eyes glazed over, and for a moment I thought he might start weeping.

"I shoulda done better," he said. "Taken care of my family. I shoulda done better. They shouldn't be worrying about me now, taking care of me. That's not the way it's supposed to work."

"Sure it is," I said. The reason I had quit the St. Paul cops to take the reward on the embezzler was to give my father a rich and carefree retirement. Unfortunately, he died six months later.

"Would they be doin' what they're doin' if not for me?" the old man asked.

"I don't know."

"Dyson, you gotta do me a favor."

"If I can."

"Will you promise?"

"If I can."

"Take care of my JoEllen. David, too. All of 'em. Take care of all of 'em. Don't let nothing bad happen. Promise?"

"I promise."

I meant it when I said it. I just didn't know how I was going to manage to keep Josie and the Bandits from harm and still do the job I had been sent there to do.

Dave Skarda emerged from the cabin. He stood in the center of the deck wearing nothing but a thin pair of shorts that were far too tight for him. Back when I played ball, my friends and I would have called them "crowd pleasers."

"What's all the noise?" he asked.

"He walks, he talks, he wiggles his belly like a reptile," the old man said. "It's about time you got up."

"Why? Is there somewhere I need to be?" Skarda moved to the picnic table, picked up the old man's beer can, and took a chug. He returned the can and sat down. "Another day in paradise."

"Get dressed," I said. "We need to sneak over to your place."

"What for?"

"So I can steal some of your clothes and other supplies."

"Buy your own shit. You've got more money than I do."

"I spent most of the money from the Silver Bay job," I said. I explained what I spent it on and why.

"That worked?" Skarda asked. "Just switching locks?"

I looked over at the old man. "He seems impressed," I said.

"You are a caution, Dyson. Won't that be dangerous, though, going over t' Dave's place?"

"Danger is my middle name. 'Course, my first name is Avoid, and At All Costs is my last name, so . . . Anyway, I don't think the cops are looking for us that hard. Considering how many people know we're here, they could have scooped Dave and me up with a butterfly net by now."

"In that case, bring back some more beer, will ya?"

Skarda did not live in anything a city boy would call a neighborhood. It was just a string of houses between the county road and the forest. We parked the Jeep Cherokee in his driveway. Skarda's place had a woman's decorative touch, yet there was no sign that a woman actually lived there. He opened some windows and went to the refrigerator. He found a couple of Leinenkugels. It wasn't Summit Ale; still, it was a damn sight better than the swill the old man drank. Skarda led me to the deck on the back of his house that had a nice view of a stream that cut through the forest.

While we drank the Leinies, Skarda told me his story. It wasn't particularly original. He was merely another casualty of the housing crisis. His company laid off ten percent of its workforce. Then another ten. Then another, until his seniority could no longer protect him. He had a couple of weeks' salary coming, plus what seemed at the time to be a generous severance package. Then there was unemployment. However, Skarda also had mortgage payments, car payments, credit card bills, health care payments he now had to make himself because he lost his coverage when he lost his job, plus gas, oil, and insurance for the car, phone, cable, trash collection, utilities, electricity, and groceries.

"When we needed a new car, I got credit," Skarda said. "Never had no trouble getting credit for anything, and when we reached the limit on our credit cards the company just raised the limit. Then came the depression—don't fucking tell me it's just a recession.

"Liz was wonderful," Skarda said. "She never got depressed, at least not that I ever saw. Not even when we were wondering how we were going to pay this bill or that bill. She figured it would all work out somehow. Gradually, though, as things became more serious, more precarious, and I was spending more and more time going out with Roy and Jimmy, going out to the bars and the strip club, watching Claire perform, getting drunk—it was all my fault, I know that. One day Liz up and left. Walked out of the house. Didn't pack. Didn't say anything. Just walked out. I called her parents and spoke to her over the phone. I begged her to come back. She said it would be better for both of us, easier if we went our separate ways for a while. Not a divorce. Just—it was just until things got better, she said."

"Do you think things will get better if you steal?" I asked.

"Money was our only problem. The lack of money. I get money, she'll come back."

I didn't know what to say to that, so I said nothing. Instead, I asked to borrow Skarda's facilities. We went upstairs, found clothes and bathroom supplies, and packed them in suitcases. I laid out a change of clothes on Skarda's bed. Afterward, he went downstairs while I took a shower. I'm told that aboard U.S. naval vessels sailors are allotted only two minutes of fresh water. Anything beyond that is considered a "Hollywood shower." I showered like I was a three-time Oscar winner, long and lavishly.

While I rinsed my hair, I made plans that would get me on the road by tomorrow afternoon. Afterward, I dressed and made myself look pretty. I left the bedroom and walked to the carpeted staircase. It was while descending the staircase that I saw Skarda. His back was to the sliding doors that led to his deck. His hands were up. There was a frightened expression on his face. I didn't blame him for the expression. A man was standing in front of him and pointing a handgun at his heart. I would have been afraid, too.

I crept down the staircase as quietly as possible. To his everlasting credit Skarda did not look at me, did not speak. He just stood there listening as the man said, "I'm sorry, Dave. I really am. I need the reward money."

I crossed the living room, coming up behind the shooter. Along the way, I picked up a long-nose lighter that Skarda had used to start the logs in his fireplace.

"You know how things are," the shooter said.

I grabbed a fistful of his hair and yanked backward. At the same time, I jammed the working end of the lighter against his throat.

"Drop the gun," I said. I gave him an extra-hard poke. "Drop it."

He dropped the gun. It bounced against the carpet. I shoved him hard away. His knee hit the edge of a chair and he fell. I picked up the gun, a double-action, 9 mm SIG Sauer. Nice.

"Oh no," the man said. "Oh no."

It was the first time I got a good look at him. It was the bartender I had met at Buckman's roadhouse the night before. Skarda came close and shouted a few obscenities at the bartender. I thought he might kick him a few times while he was down, but he didn't.

"I'm sorry," the bartender said.

"Yes, you are," I said.

"He was going to turn me in," Skarda said. "He was watching the place hoping I'd show up so he could turn me in."

"Yeah, I gathered that. I don't know why, though."

"For the reward."

"There is no reward, Dave. The Minnesota Department of Corrections has over two hundred and seventy fugitives in the wind, and they haven't offered a reward for any of them. The only people who offer rewards are bail bondsmen looking to protect their investment. Have you posted bond?"

"I never got the chance."

"So there is no reward."

I tossed the lighter in the bartender's lap so he'd know what a putz he'd been.

"Oh no," he said.

"Turning on your own people for money—tsk, tsk, tsk. What would Josie say?"

"I was hoping she'd never know it was me."

I checked the SIG. It was loaded, all right. I parked in the chair next to the bartender. He looked at me, the gun, then back at me again.

"What are we going to do with him?" Skarda asked.

"Shoot him and bury his body in the woods behind your house," I said.

"No." Skarda and the bartender spoke the word in unison.

"Are you sure, Dave? I know why this guy doesn't like the idea . . ."

"No," Skarda repeated.

I turned to the bartender. "Listen—what's your name, anyway?"

"Scott," the bartender said.

"Listen, Scott—how much money do you need?"

"Only five thousand dollars . . ."

"Only five thousand dollars," Skarda repeated.

"It's the tourist season, and I always do well. I just need some money to tide me over, to pay my suppliers. I'm COD with some of 'em. Five thousand and I'll be good."

"All right. I'll pay you the money, but you're going to earn it."

Scott gazed into Skarda's eyes for a few beats. They both seemed confused.

"What do I need to do?" the bartender asked.

"Whatever I tell you, when I tell you. You can start by getting some Summit Ale in that dive you own. I'll be in later tonight."

"When—when will I get the money?"

"When the job is over."

"What job?"

"The other thing you can do is keep your ears open. I want to know the gossip. I want to know what people are talking about, especially Brian Fenelon and what's-her-name, Claire de Lune."

"You're not going to tell me what the job is?"

"I could, Scott, but then I really would have to kill you."

From his expression, he didn't like that idea at all. He kept looking at Skarda as if he expected Dave to help him. As usual, Skarda just looked confused.

I stood and offered the bartender my hand. He took it and I helped him up. "See you later," I said.

He watched my eyes for a second. "When I leave—when I leave," the bartender said, "you're going to shoot me in the back."

"Don't worry. If I shoot you, you'll see it coming. Now get out of here. And don't forget; when I call, you had better do exactly what I say. Okay?"

He nodded, then looked over at Skarda. "Sorry, Dave," he said. The bartender started for the door, then stopped and turned around. "Please don't tell Josie."

"I'll think about it," I said.

"Can I have my gun back?"

"No."

The bartender left the house in a hurry.

"Why did you let him go?" Skarda asked.

"Because you didn't want to shoot him. What else were we going to do? Chain him to a post in your basement? Besides, there's an old saying—keep your friends close and your enemies closer."

"Who said that?"

"Al Pacino in *Godfather Part II*."

We returned to the cabin on Lake Carl about a half hour later. The old man was asleep on one of the sofas, and we tried not to wake him. I had rarely seen a man go through a day so quickly—it wasn't even one in the afternoon yet. There was a stack of old paperbacks on the floor next to him and I sorted through them. They were all romance novels written by authors I had never heard of—Helen Carter, Violet Winspear, Catherine Coulter, Heidi Strasser, Roumelia Lane . . .

"The old man reads these?" I asked.

"He likes 'em," Skarda said. "He's been getting sentimental as he grows older."

"From the moment actress Marla Travis begins reading the lead role in Alexander Stratis's new play, she feels something vibrantly compelling about him—a restrained mascu-

linity that fires her blood, a sensitivity to the deep mysteries of life that stirs her soul! Her impassioned reading convinces him to produce his play; but Marla's wary of rushing into more . . . convinced that her life of bright lights and applause can never mesh with Alex's faith in family and tradition. Then, in a sun-baked Greek village, she experiences a moment of shattering insight . . . and realizes that her elemental need for this dynamic man outstrips all else!"

After reading the book description, I set Carter's *Change of Heart* on top of the pile. "I don't know about sentiment," I said. "There sure seems to be a lot of exclamation points, though."

"Only ten percent of all the books that have ever been written are worth reading," Skarda said. "But it's a different ten percent for everybody."

Skarda busied himself filling the refrigerator with Leinies while I went onto the deck, leaned against the railing, and watched the lake glistening in the sun. There was no TV in the cabin, no ESPN, so when lake watching got old I went looking for a book to read and found only the old man's romance novels. I gave *Bad Karma* by Theresa Weir a try. It wasn't enough to convert me into a Harlequin Harlot, yet it did make me reevaluate my prejudices. I even made Josie wait a half hour when she returned to the cabin so I could finish reading the book before heading off to Buckman's.

After switching the padlocks again, we sat on the same stools at the end of the bar as the previous night and watched the Twins play the Angels. About the only difference was the starting pitchers. The bartender served us, just not with a smile. I ordered Summit Ale, only he didn't have it. He was very apologetic; claimed he had searched far and wide only to come up empty. I didn't believe him, but let it slide. Josie wondered why Scott would have gone to the trouble of chasing my favorite beer.

"Apparently I'm a celebrity up here," I said.

Josie ordered the same drink as the evening before, only fewer of them. Around the third inning she noticed that the bartender was keeping his distance.

"Scott doesn't seem to be himself tonight," she said.

"He's probably jealous because I'm sitting here with you."

"Why would he be?"

I remembered what he said at Dave's place—*Please, don't tell Josie*—yet shrugged and said nothing.

"Do you have a girlfriend, Dyson?"

I flashed on Shelby Dunston, which I found inexplicable, and then refocused on Nina Truhler.

"No," I said.

"Have you ever been involved with a woman?"

"Frequently."

"I meant with someone you cared about."

"I cared about them all or I wouldn't have become involved. That's just the way I'm wired."

"Yet none of them lasted."

"I'm a professional thief, remember?"

"There are plenty of women who like bad boys."

"I'm not a bad boy."

"What are you?"

"Misunderstood. What about you?" I didn't really want to know, yet I was desperate to change the subject.

"What about me?" Josie asked.

"Whose little girl are you?"

"No one's."

"Not ever?"

"I've known my share of wrong men."

"Anyone lately?"

"Besides you?"

There it was, I told myself. Josie was making her move. I couldn't allow it. I couldn't do that to Nina. I couldn't do it to Josie, either, not if there was even the slightest chance that I might be responsible for sending her to jail.

"We're not involved," I said. I spoke firmly. Decisively.

"What are we?"

"Co-conspirators. I'm here for the money. Once I get it, I'm out the door and down the street. I'll be going alone and I won't be coming back. I'd prefer not to leave any misunderstandings behind."

"Such as?"

"Josie, I'm not taking you to Paris."

"Who asked you to?"

"We can't have this conversation. We can't even think about it. You can't look across the table at me and think 'Mmm, mmm, mmm, how I'd like me a slice of Dyson pie . . .'"

"Dyson pie? Does that come à la mode?"

"Someone will read your thoughts and all hell will break loose. Do you understand?"

Josie started laughing at me. She paused only long enough to whisper, "Dyson, you moron. I'm gay."

I must have had the dumbest expression on my face, because she shook my shoulder with one hand and laughed even harder, laughed until a quarter of the people in the bar, including Scott, started laughing, too, even though none of them could tell you what was so damn funny.

First Jenness Crawford and now Josie, my inner voice said. *How can you not know these things? McKenzie, you are a moron.*

"You thought I was hitting on you, didn't you?" Josie said.

"I kinda talked myself into it, yeah."

"Oh, that's wonderful."

Josie clapped her hands and laughed some more. I had been more embarrassed, but not since high school.

"All right, all right," I said. "C'mon, now. It was an honest mistake. After all, you did kiss me last night. Your old man did get bent out of shape when he thought we spent the night. And, and, and what about all this 'I've known my share of wrong men' stuff?"

Josie leaned in and lowered her voice.

"First of all," she said, "my father doesn't know. Only Dave knows, nobody else. Not up here, anyway. I've dated men, some because I enjoyed their company and some because— most people think I'm high-maintenance, they think I haven't married because I have impossible standards. I like it that they think that. This is small-town America, Dyson. You get politicians and pundits, people talking about small-town values as if they were something to emulate, and sometimes they are, but small towns, this is where bigotry and intolerance hold sway. Discrimination. This is where the militias live. And the Klan. So, please, please, I beg you to keep my secret."

"Only if you promise not to tell anyone what a nitwit I am."

"Agreed."

"Wait a minute. You still haven't explained the kiss."

"What can I say? Pour enough vodka into a girl and even you will look good."

"Thanks," I said. "That makes me feel so much better."

Sometime during the dark side of midnight, we left the tavern and went to Josie's Ford Taurus. A few patrons followed us out, and we sat in the car until they left the parking lot. While we were waiting, Josie leaned across the seat. "Should we pretend to make out?" she asked.

"You're an evil woman."

"You'd think it was because my parents didn't love me, but actually they loved me a great deal."

As soon as we were alone, I crept across the county road, opened the padlock, entered the enclosure, reclaimed the GPS loggers, locked the gate, and returned to the car. Josie started it up, and a few moments later we were on the county road heading for Lake Carl. Somewhere along the way I started thinking about Jenness Crawford and the fact that I had known her almost as long as I had known Nina without having any idea that she was gay. Or bi-gay. Or whatever they call it. I found myself shaking my head at my own confusion.

"What?" Josie said.

"There's something I never thought I'd say to a woman."

"What's that?"

"I know a girl that would be perfect for you."

NINE

The next morning, Jimmy walked into the cabin carrying a map stretched out on a sheet of plywood the size of a high school chalkboard—the City of Krueger was nearly actual size in his blow-up. He probably knew what I was going to say, because before I could open my mouth he reminded me, "You said a big map."

He propped the board on the back of a sofa in the living room. He knelt on the cushion below it and proudly indicated a series of red numbers inside circles. Each number corresponded with a cash-intensive business that he had identified in a three-ring binder.

"I stopped after I got to eighty-seven," he said.

"Fair enough," I told him. I gave him the three GPS loggers. "These will tell you the routes the three trucks took yesterday. Track the movements on your map. Pay close attention to where the trucks stopped, when, and for how long."

Jimmy produced a PC from a black carrying case and proceeded to connect it to a phone jack. I moved to the cabin door. I was dressed in a pair of Skarda's swim trunks and carrying a towel. He asked me where I was going. I thought it was obvious, yet I told him just the same.

"There's no beach," Jimmy said. "If I were you, I'd take the pontoon out in the middle of the lake and anchor it. You won't be bothered by weeds out there."

"Sounds like a plan."

"What about Dave and the old man?"

"They're still asleep," I said. "From what I've seen of their habits, I don't expect to see either of them until noon."

"I should have this all worked out by then."

"You're a good man, James."

He smiled and then quickly looked away, as if he felt it was unmanly to be pleased by the compliment. As I descended the wooden staircase to the dock, I thought what a complete louse I was for putting him and his family in the jackpot.

I anchored the pontoon as Jimmy suggested and swam around it a half-dozen times, loosening my muscles and clearing my head. My plan was simple and nearly complete. I'd return to the cabin in a little bit. Together, the Bandits and I would pick a target, I'd make an argument for the need for enhanced firepower, Roy would name his gunrunners, I'd sneak away and call Bullert, and then I would drive home. With luck, I'd be at Rickie's in time for happy hour. Simple. Yeah, right.

The pontoon boat had a number of cushions arrayed on top of lockers that contained all manner of life jackets, ropes, a couple of paddles, fishing equipment, and suntan lotion. I slathered a palmful of the lotion over my body after I took my swim and stretched out across the back cushion. I was only going to rest my eyes. Instead I slept for over an hour. I was so concerned I would get sunburned that I rolled over on my stomach and slept for another half hour. Afterward, I swam a few more laps. Just for fun I slowly circled the lake in the pontoon. There was only one other cabin that I could see. I returned to the dock, tied off the boat, and climbed the stairs to the deck. A woman stepped out of the cabin carrying a tray of hamburger patties for the grill. She was a healthy-looking girl and so stereotypically Minnesotan with her pale skin, short blond hair, and blue eyes that she could have posed for the brochures extolling the state's scenic wonders that the tourism office sends out.

"Hi," she said. "You must be Dyson. Dave told me about you, although—I thought you'd be taller."

"Dave?"

"I'm Elizabeth Skarda, Dave's wife. Call me Liz."

"Liz, what are you doing here?"

The question seemed to surprise her. She set the tray on top of the picnic table. "Dave said I could come over . . ."

"Did he tell you what we're planning to do?"

"Yes. It sounds very exciting."

"Who did you tell?"

"What do you mean?"

I turned toward the door. "Dave," I shouted. I walked across the deck and went inside the cabin. Dave was standing next to Roy, who was standing next to the old man. The three of them were watching as Jimmy put the finishing touches on his map.

Skarda turned to look at me. Before I could speak again a pretty voice interrupted. "Dyson," it said. "There you are."

Jill was standing at the kitchen table with a knife in her hand. She was using it to slice wedges of pie and lift them from the tin onto paper plates. Josie was behind her, opening plastic bags filled with hamburger buns.

"Did you enjoy your swim?" Jill asked.

She was wearing sandals and a short yellow sundress with

a khaki scarf tied around her thin waist. She looked like a million bucks. Hell, she looked like the gross national product of Venezuela. Her smile was so bright that it hurt my eyes to watch her.

"Fine," I said. I was confused. What did Jill have to be so gloriously happy about all of a sudden?

"Have some strawberry-rhubarb pie," she said. "We brought it down from the Chocolate Moose in Ely. Roy and I went there together for brunch after church." She repeated the word— "together"—speaking it the way some people say "love."

I took the pie from her outstretched hands and ate a forkful. It was mighty tasty. While I chewed, she sidled up to me and spoke softly. "May I speak to you for a moment?" she asked. "In private?"

"Sure."

I set the remnants of the pie on the table and followed her into the master bedroom. I could see Roy watching us out of the corner of my eye, and my internal alarm systems climbed to Defcon Three. We stepped into the room, and Jillian closed the door. She leaned against it, her hands behind her back. I sat down on the bed, thought better of it, and stood again, circling the bed until it was between us.

"I want to thank you," she said. Listening to her voice—it was the most I'd heard her speak since I arrived, and I noticed for the first time that it had a sweet, rhythmic quality that reminded me of woodwinds.

"For what?" I asked.

"For beating some sense into Roy."

"Excuse me?"

"He told me what you did. He told me what you said. He told me that he loved me more than his own life and that he was so very sorry it took you punching him in the mouth for him to realize it. He said he was glad that you punched him and said the things you said, too, because it reminded him that I was the only person in the whole world that he cared about and that we were a team and that he would never hurt me again, not ever. He said it was me and him against the world and while he might get angry at the world, he would never again get angry at me."

"I'm happy to hear that," I said.

"Anyway, I just wanted to thank you because, well, you kinda saved my marriage."

No, no, no, my inner voice chanted. *Don't tell me that.*

"It doesn't work this way, you know," I said aloud. "Roy might be contrite now, but he'll fall back into his old habits. They always do."

"You're wrong, Dyson."

"I don't think so."

"You don't know anything about love, do you, Dyson? Love is unconditional."

No, it isn't, my inner voice insisted.

Jill replied as if she had read my mind. "My love is unconditional," she said. "I'm going to tell you a secret. I've never told anyone else because I was afraid they would laugh at me. You won't laugh, though, will you, Dyson?"

"Not even if I thought it was funny."

"When I was a little girl—and I mean little, three, four, something like that. When I was a little girl my parents took me to the Science Museum in St. Paul, and they were showing this film, this film about insects on the giant Omnitheater movie screen. They showed this extreme close-up of a butterfly, the butterfly's face, and I thought it was the most horrible thing I had ever seen in the world. It terrified me, made me cry. My parents had to take me out of the theater. I've been afraid of butterflies ever since. What it taught me, this experience, it taught me to take things for what they seem and not look too closely, especially at the things that I find beautiful."

"I don't agree that's a good idea."

"That's because you're cynical." She waved at the people behind the closed door. "All of you are."

"I suppose . . ."

"Should I tell you how we met? Roy and I? It was during the Ely Winter Festival just before I graduated from high school. First at the Spaghetti Feed and then later at the Polar Bear Dance. Roy had been discharged from the army, only he was still wearing his dress uniform with his medals on his chest, and when I saw him—saw him from across a crowded room, isn't that how the song goes?—I knew he was the one. He didn't come after me; I went after him. He doesn't remember it that way, though, because guys are all like, 'Hey baby, want to see the bruise where the puck hit me?' and women are way more subtle than that.

"We didn't spend time together around here because people —so many people knew us—you can't date in a small town without everyone knowing your business. Instead, we went to Virginia or Hibbing or Tower or even Duluth. Then, after I graduated, well, then we made it official. I know what you're thinking, Dyson. You're thinking he's too old for me. Everyone thought that at first. Roy did, too. Only then he told me after we were seeing each other for a while, he said how being with me, it made him feel young. He said that I reminded him that he was over forty years old but he had never been twenty because of the army, you see. Maybe I should have looked closer. I've told myself that the last couple of weeks. I didn't, though, and I'm not going to start now. Anyway, I just wanted to thank you."

"Jill, get out of here," I said. "Bad things are going to happen. I don't want you involved in them. I don't want you hurt."

I don't know where the words came from or why I said them out loud. I only know I meant them with every fiber of my being. Unfortunately, nothing I said registered. Instead, a smile started in her eyes and spread across her face—you have never seen a smile like that—and she whacked me on the shoulder.

"Oh, you," Jill said. "You're nothing but a big softy. Just like Roy."

A moment later, she was out the door and heading back to the kitchen. I joined her a moment later, retrieved my plate of strawberry-rhubarb pie, and stepped into the living room. I stood in front of Jimmy's map next to Roy while I ate. Roy leaned in and whispered.

"Did Jill thank you for slugging me?"

"As a matter of fact, she did."

"She said she was going to. What else did she say?"

"She said you were a big softy."

"Women. Listen, I need to tell you something. In private."

You, too? my inner voice asked.

"Sure," I said aloud.

We retreated to the same bedroom and closed the door. This time I brought my pie with me.

"What?" I asked.

"Brian Fenelon."

"What about him?"

Roy glanced around the room as if he were afraid someone was watching. "He's the man I bought the guns from. He's the one who sold me the AKs. I didn't tell you before, tell anyone before, because—because I didn't want Jill to know."

"Know what?"

This time Roy lowered his voice as if he were afraid someone was listening at the door. "I didn't want her to know—I met Fenelon in a strip joint; the strip joint where Claire was working, Jimmy's girl. I didn't want Jill to know I went to those places, that I watched Claire. She can be—she can be so young."

Seriously? my inner voice asked. *You abuse your wife but you don't want her to know that you ogle strippers?*

"Your secret is safe with me," I said, "although it would have been nice if you told me before I hit Fenelon over the head with a beer bottle."

"You did what?"

"Never mind. Spilled milk. Did Fenelon tell you where he got the guns?"

"He mentioned something about Mexicans. He was being very cagey about it, though. Fenelon likes people to think he's connected, you know; like he's some kind of crime czar."

"Yeah, there's a lot of that going around. Thanks, Roy."

Roy nodded his head, and we both returned to the living room. The burgers had been grilled, and Josie and Liz were handing them out.

"Do you want cheese on yours?" Josie asked.

I waved my fork at her. "In a minute," I said.

So that's that, I told myself while I finished my pie. *You have what you came for. It's time to go home.*

A few minutes later the old man pointed his half-eaten cheeseburger at the map. "Do you have it all figured out yet?" he asked.

I shrugged.

"Let me show you what I have," Jimmy said.

He knelt on the cushions below the plywood and explained it to me. According to the GPS trackers, trucks A and B both left the terminal in Krueger at about the same time, 10:00 A.M. They went to a spot marked in blue near Lake Vermilion, where they stayed for about thirty minutes each. Truck A went east and north across the Arrowhead region, stopping a half-dozen times along the way—never lingering for more than fifteen minutes—until it arrived in Grand Portage in the corner of the state where Minnesota, Canada, and Lake Superior met. It made frequent stops after that in Grand Marais, Lutsen, Tofte, and Silver Bay as it followed the lake south; each stop was also marked in blue, most of them corresponding to Jimmy's red circles. It turned northwest again, making several stops in Ely before returning to Lake Vermilion. It rested there for half an hour before driving south to the Krueger terminal, arriving at 7:21 P.M.

Meanwhile, Truck B went northwest from Lake Vermilion, driving nonstop to Baudette, a city near the center of Minnesota located on the U.S. side of the Rainy River. It then worked its way to International Falls, Littlefork, Big Falls, Effie, Cook, and Tower before returning to Lake Vermilion and finally Krueger at 7:27 P.M.

Truck C, on the other hand, did not leave the terminal until 1:00 P.M. It also went first to Lake Vermilion before backtracking south, stopping in Aurora, Biwabik, McKinley, Mountain Iron, and Virginia—there were plenty of stops in Virginia. It returned to Lake Vermilion, waited nearly forty-five minutes, and drove all the way to Duluth. It did not return to the Krueger terminal until almost three hours after the other trucks.

While Jimmy was able to identify every stop—there were bank branches, department stores, grocery stores, you name it—he could not identify the location near Lake Vermilion.

"That's the Fortune Bay Casino," Roy said.

"No," Jimmy said. He tapped a spot on the map several miles away. "The casino is over here on the west side of Pike Bay, and none of the Mesabi Security trucks drive there. We're over here on the east side of the bay."

"Then what is it?" Skarda asked.

"I don't know. It doesn't have an address. There's a road leading to it here off Highway 1, but this is where the maps, the satellite pictures, stop. I can't get up the road."

I stood in front of the map, staring at the blue dot Jimmy had drawn there. I actually felt a thrill of excitement ripple through my body as I thought of it.

"What do you think?" Roy asked.

I handed him my empty plate and fork. "I have to get dressed. You kids play quietly while I'm away."

The old man made a production out of popping open a beer can using only his middle finger.

"I saw that," I said.

I retreated into the bathroom, where I took my time making myself presentable, all the while thinking, now's the time—jump in the Jeep Cherokee and get the hell out before you cause any more damage. I tapped the left pocket of my jeans where the cell phone was and the right pocket where I carried the car key.

While I was dressing, I heard a commotion from the cabin, voices raised in greeting, yet did not understand what was said. When I emerged from the bathroom, I found Claire de Lune eating a cheeseburger in the kitchen while chatting with Jill and Josie. Liz was sitting on the sofa with Skarda in the living room—they were holding hands and talking quietly. Roy and the old man were behaving like long-lost army buddies, and Jimmy was sitting on the second sofa and tossing an infant in the air and catching him in the way that I found alarming, although both he and the child seemed to be having a wonderful time. It was just one big happy family sharing a pleasant Sunday afternoon together. Watching them, listening to them, it occurred to me how absurd it all was—ridiculous, simple-minded, self-aggrandizing, and brain-dead stupid. We lost our jobs, so let's rob an armored car. If that doesn't work, we can rob a bank. Then what, I wondered. Live happily ever after?

Time to say good-bye, my inner voice said.

"What's wrong with this picture?" I said aloud. I liked the sound of the words so much that I repeated them, this time tossing in a few expletives. That silenced the room.

"Are you people crazy?" I shouted for good measure.

"What is it?" Skarda asked.

"What is it? You brought your ex-wife to the hideout where you're planning to commit a federal crime."

"She's not my ex-wife—"

"You"—I was talking to Jimmy now—"you bring a child, you bring a woman who's connected to the local punk?"

"Claire is my fiancée," Jimmy protested. "This is my son."

"He's not your son," Josie said.

"I don't care," I said. "Geezus, people—no wonder Fenelon knows what we're doing. Even the frickin' bartender at Buckman's knows what we're doing. God knows who they told. And you, you're no better." I stepped close to Josie and glared into her eyes. "Giving out chunks of cash in a public place the day after you pull a job like you're frickin' Robin Hood? You must all be suicidal. Everyone in the county has to know you're the Iron Range Bandits. The fact the sheriff hasn't already scooped you up is astonishing to me. Now this. We're going to rob an armored truck. What better reason to throw a party?"

"Now, now, Dyson," the old man said. "Let's not get carried away."

"Hey, pal, you're the one who's going to get carried away—straight into federal prison for twenty goddamn years. Tell me something. If by some miracle you pull this off, what are you going to do with the money? Do you think you can walk into a bank and pay off your mortgage with cash—pay your power, your cable, your utility bills with cash—and not make people suspicious?"

"Brian can help you launder the money," Claire said. She was perfectly sincere.

I threw up my hands.

"I can't work like this," I said. "Listen. You're all good people at heart. You have no business doing this shit. Robbing grocery stores, robbing armored trucks—you're not wired for it. You have a chance, though; a chance to get out clean if you just quit. Quit now before the cops get wise to you. Get rid of the guns." I waved at the map. "Get rid of all of this. Stop thieving. Stop pretending that armed robbery is going to solve all of your problems." I was staring at Skarda when I said that last line. "If you do that, you can go on enjoying Sundays like you're enjoying this one. If you don't, every damn one of you will be spending your best years in prison. Some of you might even die there." I was speaking to the old man when I said that. The expression on his face suggested that he had thought about it before.

"As for me," I said, "I'm going to Canada."

That's how I left them.

I actually felt proud as I fired up the Jeep Cherokee, shoved it in gear, and headed down the long access road. This under-cover gig—not so tough, I told myself. I had discovered the name the ATF wanted, and I could give it to them without implicating the Iron Range Bandits. Maybe the county sheriff would come for them now and the law—if not justice—would take its course. If it did, though, it wouldn't be because of me. I would not be the agent of their destruction. I might even be able to help them out, give them G. K. Bonalay's name; maybe take care of some of their legal fees. After all, they did open their house to me. Actually, it was a house owned by the dead stockbroker from Chicago; still . . .

I halted the SUV at the end of the access road where it met the county blacktop, pulled out the cell phone, and called Bullert.

"Brian T. Fenelon," I told him after he answered. "Roy Cepek bought the AKs from a local punk named Brian T. Fenelon. Roy told me that Fenelon said he got them from some Mexicans. I met Fenelon. He'd rat out his own mother if you make it worth his while."

"What reason would we have to arrest him?" Bullert asked.

"I'm sorry, Chad. Am I missing something?"

"You say he'd talk if we put pressure on him. Okay, what do we have to pressure him with?"

"Gee, I don't know. What's the going rate for selling illegal weapons these days?"

"Were you there when he sold the weapons? Have you seen him with the weapons?"

"No."

"I see . . ."

"I see, what? Give me a name, you said. Don't worry about arresting anyone, just give me a name."

"And a location," Bullert said.

"Look up his address in the goddamn phone book."

"We have no evidence that Fenelon is running guns. You telling me what Roy told you, that's hearsay, inadmissible. If we arrest Fenelon on that alone, c'mon, McKenzie, even a third-year law student would go screaming to a judge claiming we violated the man's rights. Fenelon would be free in thirty-six hours. By then the Mexicans—if there are Mexicans—will be gone."

"Then turn the case over to Homeland Security. They don't give a shit about judicial rights."

"McKenzie . . ."

"A name, you said. Remember? You have no idea what I went through to get that."

"Enlighten me," he said.

So I did.

"Whoa, whoa, whoa, whoa—whoa," Bullert chanted. "Wait a minute. You did what?"

"Convinced them to rob an armored truck."

"Are you insane?"

"The point was to keep the Bandits from robbing any more grocery stores—"

"I appreciate that."

"And to supply a reason for them to need the guns, for them to set up a meeting with their supplier to get the guns."

"Everything you've done is illegal."

"What are you talking about?"

"Conspiracy, trespassing, breaking and entering, burglary, assault, felony assault with a car, for God's sake."

"Well, if you're going to nitpick . . ."

"Just—just let me think about this for a second."

Bullert paused for so many seconds that I thought I had dropped the call. Finally, "Actually, you know what," he said. "It's just crazy enough to work."

"Tell me you didn't say that."

"Your plan . . ."

"My plan? My plan is finished. Get a name, you said."

"If the Bandits are convinced you're actually going to rob an armored truck . . ."

"Chad."

"This Fenelon will be convinced, too."

"Chad."

"You can set up a buy with Fenelon, bring us in, we take him with the guns in his possession, convince him to lead us up the chain . . ."

"Chad."

"I like it."

"Hell no, Chad."

"You've taken it this far, McKenzie. It's just one more step."

"This is the part of the program where I admit to you, I like these people. I don't want to see them get hurt."

"There won't be any charges stemming from the armored truck robbery. We won't even cite them for conspiracy. It is entrapment, after all. You have to know, though, McKenzie—they're going to be hurt whether you continue to help us or not. They're wanted. They're armed robbers. Skarda is an escaped prisoner."

"I know."

"Look, the ATF has no interest in the Iron Range Bandits, and the FBI, Harry, he'll tell you the same thing. The county sheriff, the local cops—that's a different matter. We won't intercede, not to help, not to impede. On the other hand, helping us take the guns off the border no matter how indirectly, that might be useful at their trials. You could even testify on their behalf. An ATF operative, that might carry some weight."

"You would allow me to do that, call myself an ATF operative in open court?"

"Sure. Why not?"

"I can think of lots of reasons."

"McKenzie, if we can get those guns off the Canadian border without any innocent people getting hurt, you can call yourself any damn thing you want. You can be His Holiness the Fourteenth Dalai Lama from Tibet for all I care."

"I can take your word on that?"

"Of course you can. I work for the federal government."

I parked the Jeep Cherokee behind Josie's car and climbed back onto the deck. There were voices raised in heated debate inside the cabin, and I paused outside the door to listen. What I heard filled me with sadness. I had hoped my words earlier would scare them straight, only I was mistaken.

"Truck C," Skarda said. "It's gotta have the most money because it goes to the biggest cities. We can rob it here." There was a loud tapping sound. "Rob it here on Highway 135."

"No, no, no," said the old man. "Just because it goes to Virginia . . . Look, Truck A stops at the casino up here in Grand Portage." There was more tapping. "That's gotta have the most money."

"Why?"

"It's a casino."

"You're not listening to me," Jimmy said. "Why not rob all of them?"

"All three?" Josie said. "That's crazy talk."

"I've been doing research. It's not all that hard to rob an armored truck." I heard the flipping of sheets of paper, and I knew he was thumbing through his three-ring binder. "In New York, in the Bronx, two men pepper-sprayed a guard who was delivering a bag of money to a check-cashing center and took off with the money. In St. Louis, a group of robbers overpowered a guard who was leaving a bank with a sack containing nine hundred thousand dollars. In Rochester, some men took a guard hostage who was getting fast food and forced him and his partner to drive to a secluded spot where they transferred the money into a van. Eleven million dollars. Eleven million."

Better put a stop to this right now, my inner voice said.

I walked into the cabin. The Bandits all turned to look at me.

"Jimmy," I said. "In your research, how many robbery attempts failed? How many of the thieves were caught? How many people were shot? How many killed?"

He didn't answer.

"That's not a rhetorical question," I said. "You said you did the research. How many jobs went to hell in a handbasket?"

"A lot." He spoke just above a whisper.

"How many?"

This time he answered loudly. "A lot."

"You're an ambitious kid, I appreciate that. One job at a time, though. Let's keep this thing manageable. Okay?"

"Okay."

"Don't think for a second it's going to be easy, either. It won't be. Our job, if we're going to get away with it, is to make it look easy. Okay?"

"Okay."

I glanced at Josie. She was smiling at me. They were all smiling. I had no idea why.

"You're back," Josie said.

"So it would appear."

"What changed your mind?"

"I got halfway to the county road and realized I didn't have enough money to fill the gas tank."

"Then you're in the same boat as the rest of us," the old man said.

"I want fifty thousand dollars off the top," I said. "That's what I came here for. That's all I came here for. More than enough to hide on until I can get to my own money. You can split the rest however you see fit. Don't be surprised if it's less than you expect. This is the Iron Range, not downtown Manhattan."

"What if it's more than fifty thousand?" Skarda asked. "The split, I mean. What if our share is more than that?"

"It won't matter as long as I get my fifty."

"What do you want us to do?" Roy asked.

I moved deeper into the living room and pointed at him. Jill was in the kitchen, my back to her, so I could only guess at her expression when I said, "Go home and make love to your wife." I pointed at Skarda. "You, too." He smiled; Elizabeth frowned. I pointed at Claire. "Since you're reporting everything to your boyfriend anyway, tell Fenelon I want to meet."

"What about?" Claire asked.

"He's not her boyfriend," Jimmy said.

I ignored them both and pointed at Josie. "You come with me," I said.

"Any place in particular?"

I went to the map and tapped the blue dot Jimmy had drawn near Lake Vermilion.

"You know what it is, don't you Dyson?" Josie asked.

"I think so."

"What?"

"The mother lode."

TEN

"In the 1940's the National Geographic Society declared Lake Vermilion one of the top ten most scenic lakes in the United States. And it still is today. With its 40,000 acres of water, 365 islands and 1200 miles of shoreline, it stretches 40 miles across the heart of Minnesota's Arrowhead Region." Or so it says on the lake's official Web site. To reach it, Josie and I followed Minnesota Highway 1 west of Ely through the tiny town of Tower, the oldest Minnesota city north of Duluth, population 479, which owes its existence to the long-closed Soudan Iron Mine. Its current claim to fame is that it holds the state record for the coldest temperature on a single day at minus sixty degrees. All that's on the Internet, too. What isn't is the name of the road Jimmy found that jutted north off of Highway 1 just outside of town.

Josie drove while I followed our progress on a state road map. We drove west away from Tower and then east back toward town. It was while driving east that I discovered the road. There was no street sign, fire department address marker, or road reflector. If I hadn't already known it was there, I would not have seen it.

Josie drove north at a slow speed. The road was hard-packed dirt and wide enough for only a single vehicle to pass. It was flanked on both sides by tall trees that kept the road in shadows. One tree in particular was both wide and tall enough to be mistaken for one of those sequoias in California. The road curved around it.

We followed the road until it came to a huge clearing. In the center of the clearing was a large, white, windowless, one-story cinder-block building that reminded me of a warehouse. The bright sun made the walls shine like alabaster. There were no signs identifying it. A gray metal door had been built into the south wall of the building. A half-dozen vehicles were parked on either side of it, their bumpers nearly kissing the wall. In the center of the east wall was a metal garage door big enough for an armored truck to fit through. Well-worn tire tracks veering off the main driveway told me the trucks drove into the warehouse through that door and came out of a door in back that I couldn't see, circling the building until they met the driveway again.

A tall cyclone fence with razor wire strung along the top surrounded the clearing, not unlike at the truck terminal in Krueger. There were no trees or brush for fifty yards around the building inside the fence and nothing but flat ground for twenty yards between the fence and the tree line outside of it. We stopped just short of the gate. It had one of those long arms that you see in parking ramps that was controlled with an electronic keypad. The arm was down. There was a small gatehouse next to the opening; however, it was empty. I counted at least three cameras without turning my head.

"Get out of the car," I said.

"Why?"

"I want them to get a look at us."

"Is that a good idea?"

I slid out of the passenger side of the Ford Taurus. I spread the map over the hood of the car and bent to it as if I were lost—certainly that was the impression I wanted to convey. Josie left the car without shutting her door. Instead of looking at the map, she looked at the building, the gatehouse, and the fence. I shouted at her and waved my arms.

"You've seen what there is to see, now pay attention to me."

She did, a concerned expression on her face. "Why are you shouting?" Josie asked.

"I want the guards to think that I'm commenting on your lousy driving."

"What guards?"

"Don't look now, but there are at least four cameras pointed at us." I had spotted one more after I left the Taurus.

"What cameras?" She turned away and started searching for them.

"I said don't look. Dammit, Josie."

She turned back and waved her arms at me. "Sorry," she said.

"You're a terrible actress, too."

"Why are you being so mean?"

I folded up the map and circled the front of the car. "That's enough," I said. "I'll drive."

"Why?"

"So the scene has a dramatic and satisfying conclusion."

"Who are you? Martin Scorsese?"

"Get in the car."

Josie quickly moved to the passenger door and slid inside. While she buckled her seat belt, I maneuvered the car through a series of Y-turns until we were back on the narrow road and heading for the highway. Josie glanced through the rear window even though there was only empty road and trees behind us.

"What is that place?" she asked.

"It's a remote vault. It's where the bank—the bank Mesabi Security works for—it's where it processes its largest transactions with its most cash-intensive customers in the region. The Mesabi Security trucks roll in early in the morning to get cassettes loaded with money that they'll insert into ATM machines along their routes. Later in the day, they return with deposits—canvas bags filled with currency from the bank's largest depositors—the casinos, check-cashing stores, bank branches, and grocery stores that we talked about before. Inside the building there's a huge processing room with cafeteria-style tables. The cash is dumped out on the tables, and a small army of bank employees count it. Afterward, two of the armored trucks will return to Krueger. The third will take the deposits to the bank's vault in Duluth."

"You've seen this—what did you call it, a remote vault? Have you seen this before?"

"Yes, I have."

"Have you ever robbed one?"

"No."

Josie didn't have anything to say to that. Neither did I, although I was thinking as I hit the intersection of Highway 1, robbing a remote vault, damn, that would be something. The thought lasted only a moment before my inner voice started screaming, *Are you out of your frickin' mind?* Still, the thought was there.

We drove east through Tower and back toward Ely. Traffic was light. WELY-FM, which promoted itself as "end of the road radio," was playing an eclectic song list that included Bob Dylan, Elvis Costello, Mos Def, Bob Marley, Tom Waits, Janis Joplin, the White Stripes, Kool and the Gang, and Alberta Cross, plus a poem read by Noël Coward. It reminded me of "The Current," a public radio station back home. I wasn't listening that closely, though. Mostly I was wondering how I was going to get back home.

The problem—or the solution, depending on how you looked at it—was Claire de Lune. I would use her to get close to Fenelon, eliminating the need to involve Roy or any of the other Iron Range Bandits. I'd place my order and then make sure the ATF was on hand when Fenelon delivered the weapons. 'Course, since Claire was so close to the operation, it meant I would need to continue my preparations to rob the remote vault right up until Bullert and the badge boys bagged Brian.

Bullert and the badge boys bagged Brian, my inner voice repeated. *Nice alliteration.*

Thank you, I told myself.

I couldn't really blame Jimmy for telling Claire everything. Well, yes I could. As Harry would testify, I was in the habit of spilling my guts to Nina. On the other hand, there was plenty that I kept to myself. For example, I knew I would never tell Nina about the woman who was sitting next to me in the Ford Taurus. Our relationship was complicated enough.

It was because I was thinking about Nina while half listening to a remix of "Sympathy for the Devil" by Fatboy Slim that I didn't see the county sheriff's department cruiser until its lightbar started flashing in my rearview mirror.

"What?" Josie saw me gazing into the mirror and turned her head to look out the rear window. "Oh, shit."

I leaned forward in the seat, reached behind me, and slipped the 9 mm SIG Sauer out from beneath my shirt. "Take this," I said. "Put it in the glove compartment."

Josie took the gun reluctantly, holding it by her fingertips as if it were something she wanted to flush down the toilet.

"Where did you get the gun?" she asked.

"If I told you, you wouldn't like the bartender at Buckman's anymore. Put it away."

Josie slipped the handgun into the glove compartment. As soon as she did, I pulled over onto the shoulder of the highway. By then the deputy had hit his siren. I stopped the Ford and engaged the emergency flashers.

"Whatever happens, do nothing," I told Josie. "Say nothing. Don't even think of touching the gun."

Josie nodded in reply.

I sat in the car and waited. There were two deputies in the cruiser. One tall and fat, the other shorter and thin. I recognized them instantly. The tall deputy approached from the driver's side of the car, the short deputy approached from the passenger side. Both of them had hands resting on the butts of their holstered guns.

"This just keeps getting better and better," I said.

I made a production out of placing both of my hands on top of the steering wheel. Deputy James seemed to like that. He smiled when he said, "Roll down your window," and smiled some more when I returned my hand to the steering wheel afterward and said, "Is there a problem, Deputy?"

"He wants to know if there's a problem," James said.

Deputy Williams was leaning against the passenger door of the Taurus. Josie's window was rolled down, and he was looking across her at me.

"I don't have a problem," he said. "Do you have a problem?"

"I don't have a problem unless Dyson gives me one."

"Hmm, Dyson?" I said. "Who's he?"

"Oh, dang," James said. "Now we have a problem."

"Here I was hoping for a problem-free day."

"Just goes to show." James took a step backward and rested his hand back on the butt of his gun. "Outta the car, Dyson."

I reached down for the door latch. When I opened the door, Josie turned to do the same. Williams put an arm through the window, covered her breast with his hand, and pushed her back against the seat.

"Don't move, honey," he said. He gave her breast a squeeze. "Mmm, nice."

Josie squirmed under his touch and tried to push his hand away. Williams grinned at her.

"Atta girl," he said. "Now, stay put."

He removed his hand, stepped back from the window, and made his way to the rear bumper. I was already standing there, facing James.

"This will go much easier if you just admit that you're Nicholas Dyson, escaped criminal," he said.

"Who?" I asked.

Williams drove his fist deep into my stomach. I lost my breath, doubled up, and went to my knees. It took me a few moments to regain my composure. While I did, I noticed the shiny bands of chrome-plated steel wrapped around the fingers of his right hand. *No wonder he hit so hard,* my inner voice said. I used the bumper and trunk lid to pull myself upright again.

"Brass knuckles," I said. "I thought that went out with Polaroid cameras."

"We're traditionalists," Williams said. "Something works for us, we stick with it."

"Let's talk, Dyson," James said.

"My name isn't Dyson."

Williams hit me again and again I went down. Loose gravel dug into my knees. To alleviate the pain, I fell backward into a sitting position, propping myself up with one hand while clutching my tender stomach with the other.

"We can do this all day," James said.

"We?" asked Williams.

"I'll take a turn. Do you want me to take a turn?"

"That's up to Dyson here." Williams nudged me with his toe. "Whaddaya say, Dyson?"

"You can call me anything you want," I said.

"We can call him anything we want," Williams said.

"How 'bout dipshit?" James asked.

"That, too," I said.

James squatted next to me. "You're a smart guy, aren't you, dipshit?" he said.

" 'Course he's smart," Williams said. "He's from the big city. Way smarter than us good ol' country boys." He nudged me with his toe again. "Ain't that right?"

I continued to clutch my stomach. "I don't feel smarter," I said.

"He doesn't feel smarter," Williams said.

"Don't know why," James said. "Big-time criminal mastermind like him." He circled a beefy hand under my arm and pulled me upright. "You are a big-time criminal mastermind, aren't ya?"

"No, actually, I'm not," I said.

"He's not a criminal mastermind," Williams said.

"We've been misled," James said.

"Wouldn't be the first time."

"So, here's what we're thinking," James said. His fingers dug into my shoulder and pain shot down through my arm, numbing my fingertips. "We slap the cuffs on you, drag you down to Duluth, we're heroes. Might even get a commendation out of it."

"But then we'd have to make statements," Williams said. "Explain how we caught you. Probably testify in court . . ."

"All that paperwork."

"We hate paperwork."

"Actually, most everything is done on computers now, but you get the gist of it."

"Typing," Williams said. "Ewww."

"We hate typing." James held up both index fingers for me to see. "Never did get the hang of it."

"It is skilled labor," I said.

Williams rapped the side of my head with the brass knuckles. The blow wasn't hard enough to break the skin, yet it made me regret the remark just the same.

"The point is, we end up wasting all those man-hours in the office when we could be out here chasing real criminals," James said.

"Like the father of the honey you got in the car," Williams said. "Have you done her yet, Dyson?"

I ignored the question. "Is there an alternative?" I said.

"Funny you should ask," James said. "Don't you think it's funny?"

"Hysterical," Williams said.

James gave my shoulder another squeeze, and I fought back a groan. "What we're thinking, Dyson, is instead of paying your debt to society to, well, society, you should pay it to us," he said.

"That way you're punished for your grievous crimes . . ." Williams began.

"Grievous," said James.

"Society is spared the bother and expense of supporting yet another freeloader through the prison system."

"And we avoid all that typing."

"We don't like typing."

"I gathered that," I said. "How exactly would this work? I mean, what would be the amount of my fine?"

"We're not greedy," James said.

"Oh, no," said Williams. "We want a lot less than the courts would take."

"How much?" I asked.

"Half."

"Half of what?"

Williams punched me yet again. I doubled over and fell like a small tree toppled by straight-line winds, landing first on my knees and then sprawling forward on my shoulder. I gripped my solar plexus. This time I thought he might have done some real damage.

James squatted next to me. "We know all about your plans to rob an armored truck," he said. "One belonging to Mesabi Security."

"Geez," I moaned. Not because of what Deputy James said, but because of the pain. Williams saw it as a form of capitulation, though.

"See, us country boys, we know a thing or two," he said.

"I won't ask how you know," I said.

"He won't ask how we know," Williams said.

"Told you he was a criminal mastermind," James said.

"When are you going to make your move?" Williams asked.

"Haven't decided," I told him.

Williams brought his foot back and up like he was preparing to stomp me.

"No kidding. We're still working out the details."

Williams set his foot back on the pavement.

"Don't wait too long," James said.

"We're not patient types," Williams said.

"How would I get ahold of you once I decide?"

"Oh, we'll be around—partner," James said.

"I don't suppose you'd recommend which armored truck to take," I said.

"Us?" Williams said.

"Us?" James repeated. "You're not asking us for help, are you, Dyson?"

"Oh, no, we can't help you," Williams added. "That would be illegal."

"I thought we were partners now," I said.

"Think of us as silent partners," James said.

A few moments later, the deputies were back in their cruiser and heading down Highway 1. I sat behind the Ford Taurus and nursed my stomach. Several vehicles passed while I did. The drivers and passengers all stared at me intently, yet did not stop. Josie knelt at my side.

"Are you all right?" she asked.

"I've been better."

"Can you stand?"

"Yes," I said and then I proved it, although without her assistance I would have toppled over into the roadside ditch.

"You drive," I said.

Josie helped me to the passenger seat, circled the car, and slid in behind the steering wheel. She started the Taurus, yet did not put it into gear. Her eyes were moist and her voice was hoarse as if she were fighting back a good cry.

"Bastard put his hands on me," she said. "He, he—he put his hands on me."

"Don't worry about it," I said.

"That's easy for you to say. All he did was hit you. What he did to me—I hate him so much. I want to get him, Dyson."

While she spoke I opened the glove compartment and removed the SIG Sauer.

"That's the part I don't want you to worry about," I said.

The only vehicle parked near the cabin on Lake Carl when we returned was my Jeep Cherokee. I thought the place was deserted until Josie helped me through the cabin door.

"What happened to you?" the old man asked. He was sitting at the kitchen table and nursing a beer. He stood while I shuffled to the sofa across from Jimmy's map and sat down, still clutching my stomach.

"Occupational hazard," I said. "Where's Roy?"

"Lying in a coffin filled with his native earth. Or is that too much to hope for?"

"Dissension in the ranks? We haven't even started yet."

"What happened?" Josie asked.

"Jimmy," the old man said. "After you left, he wanted to know why you told Claire to set up a meeting with Fenelon, why you would even want to talk to Fenelon. Claire said she didn't know. Jimmy accused her of lying. He also accused Claire of still seeing Fenelon even though she had promised she wouldn't. Claire said she had to keep seeing Fenelon because Fenelon was her business manager. It went back and forth like that for a while until Jimmy said if Dyson—you—wanted to see Fenelon so bad, you should have Roy set it up. That's when Jill said that Roy didn't even know who Fenelon was. Jimmy told her Roy and Fenelon sure seemed like pals the way they would huddle together whenever they, meaning Jimmy, Roy, and Dave, would go to the strip club to watch Claire dance. Before he could even finish, though, Jill was all over Roy. How could he, she wanted to know, how could he go to a stripper joint, which was bad enough, but then sit there and watch Claire dancing naked, which was worse, and Claire going, 'What's wrong with what I do?' Meanwhile Liz, Dave's wife, she starts shouting at Dave about spending time with whores when they were having problems holding their marriage together and Dave claiming that he never actually looked, which causes Jimmy to ask who the hell was Liz calling a whore and why wouldn't Dave look. That's when Jill said she—meaning Liz—was calling Claire a whore. Jimmy then called Jill a whore for sleeping with Roy while she was still in high school, a man old enough to be her father, who did she think she was kidding. Jill slapped Jimmy. Jimmy made like he was going to hit her back, only Roy hit him first, just wham, puts him on the floor. Then Jill screams at Roy for hurting her brother . . ."

My head was starting to ache almost as badly as my stomach, but the old man wasn't finished.

"Liz said she wasn't going to spend any more time in a cabin with someone like Claire. She leaves, slamming the door behind her, and Dave follows her out, trying to calm her down. Claire announces that she's tired of being insulted by a bunch of sanctimonious hypocrites, which was the word she used— sanctimonious. Said whatever we thought about what she did for a living, it was a whole lot better than holding up liquor stores. So she grabs the kid and leaves—slams the door, too— which causes Jimmy to start chasing after her. That leaves Jill screaming at Roy for being no kind of man because one, he punched her brother and two, he went to see that whore Claire dancing naked. Finally she leaves and Roy follows her out, saying how sorry he is."

"Okay," I said. "Only why single out Roy? From what you said when I came in . . ."

"Before he left he pointed at me, pointed a finger right in my face, and said everyone in my family was crazy. I don't take that from anybody."

"Old man, everybody in your family is crazy." I gestured at Josie. "You most of all."

"You're just out of sorts right now," she said. "You'll feel better in the morning."

"Do you have your cell?"

"Yes."

"Let me talk to Roy."

Josie dialed her phone and handed it to me. It was answered by Jill. I asked her how she was.

"Just fabulous," she said.

"Really? I heard you and Roy were on the outs again."

"Dyson, do you know what's the best kind of sex? Make-up sex."

"Way too much information, Jillian. Let me speak to your husband."

A moment later Roy was on the phone.

"Did you do any recon work while you were in uniform?" I asked him.

"Some."

"Tomorrow starting early, you and I are going to do an all-day surveillance of the building Jimmy found near Lake Vermilion."

"Tomorrow?"

"Yes."

"Not tonight?"

"No."

"Good," he said, and hung up.

I handed the phone back to Josie. "Looks like everyone is getting lucky tonight but us."

"Speak for yourself, big boy," she said, and patted my knee. "Dad, I have to go down to Virginia tonight. Need a lift home before I leave?"

It turned out he did. Twenty minutes later I was alone in the cabin with Jimmy's map still perched on the back of the sofa. I stared at it for a while, went to the refrigerator for a

Leinenkugel, returned to my seat, and stared at it some more, while I wondered what to do next—it's what I call multitasking. Half a beer later I removed the secret cell phone from my pocket, called directory assistance, and had them connect me with Buckman's roadhouse. When the bartender answered the phone I said, "This is Mc— Dyson."

"Who?"

"Nick Dyson," I answered.

Dammit, you nearly used your real name, my inner voice reminded me. *Focus.*

"Yeah, what do you need?" the bartender asked.

"Got a minute to talk?"

"Yeah, a minute."

"Hear anything about Fenelon? Has he been around?"

"Yeah, he's been in. He was talking to—well, I guess that would be interesting."

"What?"

"He was real chummy with John Brand?"

"Who's he?"

"He's kind of a gangster."

"Oh, God, not another one."

"Up here, he's like, he's into a lot of things. He's on the Ely City Council and he owns a couple of businesses, a couple of outfitters, the strip club where Fenelon's girl works, Claire de Lune. They say he used to control all the gambling in the region right up until the Indians opened the casino at Fortune Bay and took most of the profit outta it. Now they say anyone up here dealing drugs or sellin' girls, he gets a piece. At least that's what they say. Don't know for sure. I do know he got busted a while back, got busted for running stolen car parts across the border and launderin' the profits through his businesses. Only right after the charges were filed they went away and nothing came of it, so I guess up here he's the closest thing we got to a gangster."

"What were he and Fenelon talking about?"

"Couldn't say, cuz they, whenever I got close to the table to serve 'em their drinks, they'd stop talking. Heard 'em say only one thing, don't know how interesting it is."

"What?"

"Brand—he's into everything, like I say, and people say, they say he always wants to put his 'brand' on everything, you know what I mean?"

"What did he say?"

"He said, 'My toys, my rules.' "

"I can see how he might take that attitude. Anything else?"

The bartender said nothing came to mind. I finished our conversation by telling him to keep his ears open and promising that he would see some money, soon. Afterward, I punched LUNATIC into the keypad of my cell—the word seemed to become more and more appropriate as we went along. Chad Bullert answered on the fourth ring. I gave him a quick update on my plans. He seemed pleased, although not for long.

"I need twenty-five hundred in cash," I told him.

"Why?"

"Down payment on an informant," I explained, and then gave him the details. He agreed to have someone stash the money at the Chocolate Moose, where I could pick it up the next evening, but not before chiding, "You're pretty free with the government's money."

"Do you know how much I pay in taxes?"

"Yeah, yeah, yeah . . . Do you think John Brand is connected to the guns?"

"More likely him than Fenelon. The bit about smuggling car parts across the border intrigues me."

"What else do you know about him?"

"He has political connections."

"So do we. I'll look into it."

"You might also want to look at a couple of bent sheriff deputies named Eugene James and Allen Williams while you're at it."

"Why?"

I explained.

"They know who you are," Bullert said. "At least they know you're Dyson."

"Yep."

"They know what you're planning. They even knew you would be out on Highway 1—pulling you over the way they did, that wasn't a coincidence."

"Nope."

"McKenzie, you have a spy in your crew."

"Uh-huh."

There was a long pause, and for the second time that day I was afraid I had dropped his call. Finally Bullert asked, "What are you going to do?"

"I know what I'd like to do."

"Yes, but what are you *going* to do?"

"If Brand really is Fenelon's gun connection, I doubt he'll wait for my call. He'll come to me at a time and place of his own choosing. He'll make sure he has the advantage."

"And then what?"

"And then I'll call you."

Bullert paused for a moment before saying something I didn't expect. "I really appreciate everything you're doing, McKenzie. I know it's not easy. I just want to say thank you."

"Stop it, Chad. I'm starting to get misty-eyed over here."

"Harry was right. You are a pain in the ass."

ELEVEN

Roy and I never walked "around" the white building. Instead, we would creep up to the edge of the clearing, take our photographs, then edge straight back until we melted into the thick forest. After we were comfortably out of sight, we would move to our left forty or fifty yards and do it again, crawling on our forearms, knees, and the inside of our feet in a straight line while always being careful to keep our asses down. The first time we did it, I moved all the way up to the line where the field met the trees. Roy cursed under his breath and grabbed my leg, dragging me backward on my stomach until I was about five yards deep in the woods. "Relax," I told him as I rolled on my back and started working the camera from its case. Roy leaned over and whacked me on the top of the head.

"Stop moving," he hissed—actually hissed. He stole the camera case from my hands and motioned for me to follow him—on hands and knees and stomach—back down the trail. Once he determined we were safe, he spoke low and harshly.

"You don't move," he said. "You don't wave arms and legs and camera cases in the air. Movement is what catches the eye. Movement is how the enemy sees you. Haven't you ever been hunting?"

I assured him that I had. I don't think he believed me.

"You're a real desperado, aren't you, Dyson? Fucking amateur is what you are; don't even know how to walk in the goddamn woods without being seen. You think you know my business? You don't know shit. Now you're going to do exactly what I tell you exactly when I tell you or I'm going to leave you here."

He didn't like the smile on my face, but I couldn't help myself, his lecture was so similar to the one I had given him in the cabin before the Silver Bay raid.

"You've been holding that in for quite a while, haven't you?" I said.

"A little bit, yeah," he said. Now he was smiling, too.

"Tell me what to do."

"Get your camera out now," he said. "Be ready by the time we're in position. No sudden movements of any kind, I don't care if a horsefly the size of an Apache gunship parks in your ear. Don't even take deep breaths. No talking."

"Yes, sir."

I followed Roy back toward the clearing. He spent as much time looking behind him as he did looking forward. We found a position with an unobstructed view of both the gate and the front and side of the remote vault. From there I was able to take photos of all the cars that entered the compound, emphasis on their license plates. Assorted vehicles started arriving at 8:00 A.M. They'd roll up to the gatehouse, the drivers would lean out the window and punch a code into the keypad, the arm would rise, and they would motor down to the building, parking with their front bumpers nearly kissing the white brick. Afterward, the drivers would move to the gray metal door and punch a code into another keypad, wait a moment, then yank the door open. Three of the drivers were outfitted in crisp, clean guard uniforms. The others dressed as if they were planning on cleaning out their garages.

"It's dirty work handling money," I whispered. It was the first time I'd spoken since Roy's lecture and I was surprised he didn't whack me on the head again. Maybe he didn't hear. "These people, there should be several containers of baby wipes on the tables where they count the money so they can clean off the black, waxy film that covers their fingers. It's the reason bank tellers take so many sick days; they get ill from all the germs on the money they handle."

"Huh," Roy grunted.

I guess he did hear me.

An armored truck arrived at exactly 9:03 A.M. I wrote down the time in a small notebook. It had the name Mesabi Security printed on the side, except unlike the other trucks I had seen, this one was all shiny and new. It rolled up the gate and paused. The arm rose without the driver punching a code into the keypad. The truck followed the road leading to the remote vault, veered off near the end, circled the white building, and came to a stop in front of the large metal garage door. The door rolled up slowly; the truck went through it and stopped. I could see the rear bumper as the door slowly closed.

"Bandit trap," I whispered. "Series of rooms. Impossible to open a door to the room in front of you without locking the door behind you first. Digital cameras cover each of the traps. If a door is left open for more than twenty seconds or so, alarms go off."

"Hmm," Roy said.

At 9:29, the armored truck exited the building from a door on the far side of the remote vault, circled the building till it reached the road, and drove toward the gate. The arm went up before the truck reached it. The truck didn't even slow down, and it soon disappeared down the narrow dirt road. At 10:33, the first of the armored trucks from the Krueger terminal arrived, followed by the second truck at 10:38.

"The money handlers are loading cassettes with twenty-dollar bills that they took from the first armored truck," I said. "The guards in these trucks will take the cassettes and load them into ATM machines along their route."

This time Roy didn't even grunt.

Both of the Mesabi Security trucks were gone by 11:15 A.M. Fifteen minutes later, half of the employees working in the remote vault left, too. They drifted back at about noon, and the other half left. Everyone was on hand at 1:30 P.M. when the third armored truck arrived. That truck departed at about 2:05, and a few minutes later, most of the employees left, too. We remained in our position, unmoving, until 3:00 P.M. Afterward, we slowly and cautiously worked our way around the white building, approaching it from different angles, taking several photographs. When we reached the backside of the building, I was surprised to see what appeared to be a narrow abandoned road that moved from the forest right up to the cyclone fence. Yet there was no opening in the fence.

"Probably used it when they were building the place," Roy said.

"For what?"

To find out, we carefully followed the road—without actually stepping on it—to the banks of what I thought was a river. Roy explained my mistake.

"More like a creek," he said. "I don't even think it has a name. It winds down from Lake Vermilion."

It was about twenty feet wide.

"How deep is it?" I asked.

Roy didn't know, so I walked into it. The creek was knee-deep near the bank and sloped until it came to my waist at the center; the water saturated the hem of the dark blue Minnesota Timberwolves sweatshirt I had borrowed from Dave Skarda. I cursed silently when I realized I had forgotten the cell phone in my pocket. Unfortunately, there was nothing I could do about it without Roy seeing. I followed the creek toward Lake Vermilion. There were no obstructions that I could find. I stood at the mouth of the creek where it opened onto Pike Bay. Beyond the bay, the forty-mile-long lake with its 365 islands beckoned.

"What do you see?" Roy asked.

"A lot of places to hide."

He didn't know what I was talking about, and I didn't elaborate, mostly because I wasn't sure I knew what I was talking about, either. We made our way back to the remote vault, eventually returning to the perch where we had hidden earlier. The sun was warm; however, the shadows of the trees kept my jeans and shoes from drying. I was as uncomfortable as hell yet said nothing for fear Roy would make fun of me. My biggest concern was for the cell phone.

Most of the employees were back in place by 6:00 P.M. At 6:25, the first armored truck returned from its rounds, joined by the second truck ten minutes later. They both departed, one after another, at about 7:00 P.M. We waited until the third truck arrived at 7:20 P.M. It lingered almost forty-five minutes before leaving. I put all that in my notebook, too. A few minutes later, the place was deserted. The sun set at 9:03 by my watch. We waited until 9:30 before leaving. It was while I was lying on the ground in the forest waiting for night to fall that my inner voice began talking to me, as it often did.

You're out of your mind, it told me. *Do you seriously think you could pull this off?*

Of course not, I told myself. Robbing a bank—that would be wrong. On the other hand . . .

What?

Nothing. Forget it.

Spit it out.

I know how it could be done.

You're certifiable.

A short time later, Roy led me through the woods until we reached his car, parked discreetly off Glenmare Drive. It wasn't until we were safely in the car and making our way toward Tower that he asked, "How the hell are we going to get in there?"

"Getting in isn't the problem," I told him. "It's getting out that worries me."

We passed through Tower and quickly approached Ely. The Chocolate Moose wasn't far from the intersection where we turned south toward Krueger, and I told Roy to stop.

"What for?"

"So I can use the restroom and you can buy your wife a strawberry-rhubarb pie."

He thought that was a helluva good idea. "Jill's still a little miffed at me," he said.

"Can't say I blame her."

We parked on Sheridan Street. The Chocolate Moose was inside a building made to look like a lakeside cabin and was surrounded on two sides by a wide porch. We climbed the wooden stairs and went inside. Roy stepped up to the counter to place his order. I was directed to the restroom the restaurant shared with Piragis Northwoods Company, a camping outfitter. I locked myself inside the restroom and removed the top of the toilet tank. A sealed plastic bag was taped to the bottom of the cover. It contained $2,500 in cash. Next, I checked the cell phone and sighed audibly in relief when I discovered that it still worked. I took the cell and the bag and stashed both in my pocket. After finishing my business—my pants were still damp and my legs were chilled—I returned to the Chocolate Moose. Roy was waiting for me. The pie was in a box that he held with both hands.

"Now where?" he asked.

"Let's stop at Buckman's Roadhouse for a quick beer before heading back to the cabin."

Roy liked that idea, too.

It was 10:40 P.M. when we arrived, and Buckman's was surprisingly busy—at least I was surprised, given what the bartender told me about his business earlier. We sat at the bar and ordered Sam Adams because the bartender still hadn't laid in a supply of Summit Ale. Halfway through the beer, Roy excused himself as I had hoped he would, and I waved the bartender over. He asked me what I wanted, and I answered by slipping him the plastic bag filled with cash as unobtrusively as I could. His eyes bulged a little in his head.

"What's this?" he asked.

"Half of what I promised. You'll get the rest later."

He pushed the money down deep into his pocket and produced a couple of fresh beers. "On the house," he said.

"Anything going on I should know about?"

"I haven't heard anything," the bartender said. "Fenelon was in earlier. He waited until Brand arrived, and then they left together. Brand might have had someone else with him, only I can't be sure. That was a couple hours ago."

"Okay," I said.

By then Roy had returned from the restroom. We finished the fresh beers and headed out.

"It's getting late," I said. "Jill will probably be upset."

"It's okay as long as I'm with you and not with . . . Well, you know."

"Claire. What does Jimmy see in her, anyway?"

"Tits, ass, and legs, not necessarily in that order, what do you think? Weren't you ever twenty-two years old, Dyson?"

"Yeah, I was—just never that dumb." I stopped on the passenger side of the car and waited for Roy to unlock the driver's-side door. While he did, I surfed my memory of that heady year after I graduated from college and all the women I was fortunate—and unfortunate—enough to hook up with. "Actually, I guess I was that dumb."

"Me, too," Roy said. "Not now, though."

"Oh no," I agreed. "We're way smart, now."

Roy took me back to Lake Carl. He had intended to drop me off and drive away, but all the lights were on inside the cabin and the yard was littered with cars, so he decided to stop to see what was going on. He went through the cabin door first and was hit by a big man who used the butt of a handgun to put Roy on his knees. A woman screamed. It was Jill, and she crossed the living room to Roy's side. Roy covered the back of his head with his hand. I could see blood seeping between his fingers. The man quickly turned his full attention on me, pivoting so that the gun was pointed at my throat. He was shorter by a half-dozen inches yet didn't seem to have a complex about it. My eyes traveled from the muzzle of the gun to his face. I did not recognize him. He was smiling, so I smiled back, although I sure as hell wasn't getting any pleasure out of the experience.

"Be careful with that," I said. "You might hurt someone."

He snorted his contempt at my bravado. At the same time, Roy pushed Jill away and managed to regain his feet. He spun toward the gunman, fully intent on charging him, gun or no gun. I stepped between them and wrapped Roy in my arms.

"No, no, no, no, no," I chanted. "That's just his way of saying hello."

I pushed Roy backward three steps, not an easy feat, believe me. He glared at the big man while I surveyed our surroundings. Everyone was huddled in the living room—Josie, the old man, Dave, Liz, Jimmy, and Claire; Jill was on her knees. They were all frightened. Only Jill was looking at us. The rest were staring at something past us in the kitchen. I followed their eyes. Fenelon was standing near the refrigerator, his hands behind his back, and leaning against the counter. A second man was sitting at the rickety table. He had the vaguely bored expression of someone that had ordered a beer in a bar and was waiting for the waitress to deliver it.

"What's this?" I asked. "A party? You should have told me. I would have worn a nicer sweatshirt."

"Thank God you're here," said Josie.

"Bastard's kept us prisoner for hours," Jimmy said.

"Tell your friends to shut up," the man said. He spoke loudly, like he was giving a lecture on self-improvement to a full auditorium.

"You tell 'em," I said. "You're the one with the guns."

"Sit down, Dyson."

"Everyone seems to know my name, and yet I've tried so hard to remain incognito."

He spread his hands wide as if he were as baffled by the phenomenon as I was. His hair was short, brown, and curly, except for a bald patch the size of a tennis ball at the back. He was wearing a charcoal suit jacket over a wine-colored shirt that was open at the collar and slacks that matched the jacket—easily the best-dressed man I'd seen since I arrived in the northland. There was a small-caliber wheel gun shoved under his belt just above his left hip, ideally positioned for a right-handed man to cross-draw while sitting down.

"Kinda late, though, isn't it, John?" I asked. "After all, tomorrow's a school day."

"You know who I am?" He continued to speak loudly, even though I was less than ten feet away. At the same time, his voice was as smooth as a combination lock.

"Of course I know who you are. I've been expecting you."

I was still holding on to Roy and whispered in his ear. "Sit next to Jill. When I call your name, stand up—slowly." He nodded imperceptibly. I released him, and he bent to Jill. He helped her up by the shoulders and eased her onto the corner of the sofa farthest from the door. He sat next to her, and although he took hold of Jill's hand, his eyes never left the big man standing at the door.

I moved into the kitchen. Brand shifted in his seat.

"So, John, how's it going?" I said. "You don't mind that I call you John, do you?"

"I prefer Mr. Brand."

"When I was a kid, I wanted everyone to call me Deadeye, Deadeye Dyson, but no one ever did." I pulled a chair out and slowly sat while keeping both hands on the edge of the table. The big man leaned against the closed cabin door, his hands crossed in front of him, the gun pointed at the floor, and watched. Fenelon watched, too.

"You said you were expecting me," Brand said.

"I figured you'd turn up eventually, just not in the middle of the night like a sneak thief." The insult registered on his face, yet Brand said nothing in reply. "Has everybody been properly frightened?" I gestured toward the living room. "Have you and your pet thug made all the threats you care to make?"

"You're cutting it pretty thin, Dyson."

"John." I spread my hands wide, then set them back on the

edge of the lightweight kitchen table again. "You came here to negotiate. You brought Fenelon and your muscle in the middle of the night so you could negotiate from a position of power. That's cool. I understand that. Let's talk. Here's what I want you to do . . ."

"What you want me to do?"

"Well, you're big man on campus, aren't you? The man who runs everything." I gestured with my chin at Fenelon. "No matter what Brian has to say."

Fenelon stiffened at my words yet said nothing.

"What did Brian have to say?" Brand asked.

"He said he and I could run this town. I'm sure he was exaggerating."

Brand smiled at me. "You're deliberately attempting to induce a quarrel between me and my associates, aren't you, Dyson?"

"Why would I do that? After all, I don't think I've made it a secret that I'm just passing thorough on my way to Canada."

"Yet you intend to stay long enough to conduct a little business before you leave." Brand tapped his chest. "In my town. You don't do business in my town without I get a taste."

"Yeah, I know. You're nothing new to me, John. You're no different than the guys in the Cities or San Francisco or Chicago or any other place I've worked except that you're small market. You were here first so you think you deserve a little extra consideration. Fine. When in Rome, right? Now, John, what I want you to do . . ."

"Mr. Brand," he said. His voice confirmed his growing frustration.

Good, my inner voice said. *Angry people make mistakes.*

I sighed dramatically. "Mr. Brand," I said. "Are you happy now?"

I heard Fenelon whisper "Jesus" under his breath.

(199)

Brand pointed a finger at me. "You're a funny guy, Dyson. A real comedian. Funny's gonna cost ya."

"Cost me what?"

"Half. I want half."

"Half of what?"

"Half of everything."

"That kind of steep, isn't it, John—excuse me, Mr. Brand?"

"Do you know what kind of heat robbing an armored car will bring"—he tapped his chest again—"to my town?"

"More than you think."

"What's that supposed to mean?"

"I'm not going to rob a single armored car. I'm going to rob them all."

"All?" Josie asked from the living room.

"No," Jill said.

"Yes," Jimmy said.

"What is he talking about?" Liz asked.

"Shhh," said Dave.

"People, please," I said. "Contain yourselves."

Brand stared at me as if he didn't know if I was crazy or just joking with him. "Would you care to explain yourself?" he asked.

"Yes, yes I would. I would care a great deal. I believe you already know too much about my business."

"Your business?" Brand was shouting now. He tapped his chest yet again. "In my town, it's my business."

"Yeah, well, I'm not going to argue with you, John—"

"Mr. Brand."

"Whatever. If you want a full share, you're gonna have to earn it."

"A share?"

"I'll need at least three AK-47s, eight magazines fully loaded, four Kevlar vests, half a block of Semtex 10, two blasting caps—"

"A share?"

"How long is it going to take you to get all that together?"

"A share? Do you think you can pull a job in my town and dictate terms to me?"

"You keep saying your town, but the borders seem kinda loose. Where does it begin, where does it end?"

"It's whatever I say it is."

"Where are you going to get the guns? Brian said something about Mexicans." Brand gave Fenelon a look that could have powdered concrete. "Personally, I don't know what Mexicans are doing on the Canadian border . . ."

"That's none of your business," Brand said.

"If we're going to be partners . . ."

"Partners?" Brand slapped the top of the kitchen table with such force I thought it might collapse. He rose quickly to his feet. That was bad. I needed him sitting down for what I had in mind. "Who do you think you're talking to?"

"Why the attitude, John? I'm trying to let you in on a very good thing here and you're giving me attitude. Hey, man, you came to me, remember? Look, if you want in, you're in, if you want out, you're out. The AKs and plastic explosives, hell, I can pick that up almost anywhere."

"This is my town."

"There you go again."

Fenelon cleared his throat. "Maybe we should—"

"Shut up, Brian," Brand said.

"Yeah, Brian," I said. "John and I are talking here."

"Don't call me John," Brand said.

I let my shoulders sag as if I were conceding the point. "Mr. Brand, please." I gestured toward his chair. He sat down and made himself comfortable.

No time like the present, my inner voice told me.

"Roy," I said.

Roy rose slowly from the sofa.

The big man standing at the door spun toward him, his back to me. "Don't be stupid," he said, although he did not raise his gun.

Brand was also watching. "You heard him," he said. "Sit down."

I stood quickly, pulling the kitchen table up with me and pushing it forward. The edge of the table hit Brand in the center of his chest. I kept pushing until Brand, his chair, and the table toppled over. He landed backward hard against the floor and I used the table to pin him there. Someone screamed. I reached down and yanked the wheel gun out of his slacks. The big man was pivoting toward me, still holding the gun low. I was quicker. I brought the revolver up and snapped a shot toward him. Someone screamed again. The round drilled a surprisingly large hole in the wooden cabin door. Splinters from it tore into the big man's cheek and ear, and I thought, damn, that was closer than I intended. I nearly shot him in the face.

Oh, well, my inner voice said.

"Drop it," I said aloud.

He hesitated. Blood dripped down his temple and cheek and stained his shirt collar.

"Do I look like I'm playing?"

The big man stooped slowly forward and carefully set the gun on the floor. He stood, again moving slowly, and put his hands behind his head without being asked to. Not once did he touch his face to inspect the wounds, which impressed the hell out of me. Most people would have been whimpering in pain by now, myself included.

"Roy," I said again.

He crossed the living room, took up the handgun, and whipped the big man across the jaw with it. The big man fell to his knees in the same way Roy had and cradled his face in his hands. Jill screamed Roy's name—I didn't know if it was she who made all the noise earlier or not. Roy was going to hit the big man again. I asked him not to.

"An eye for an eye," I said.

"What?" he asked.

"Enough already."

I turned my attention back to Brand, who had managed to ease the table off of his chest. I gestured at Fenelon, and he helped me put the table upright. Before that he hadn't moved a muscle. I suspected Brand would both remember and comment on that, later. Still, Fenelon did have the presence of mind to help lift Brand back into his chair. I sat across from him.

"Shoot him," the old man said from the living room. "Shoot the bastard."

"Now, now, now," I said. I began to spin the wheel gun around by the trigger guard in front of me, acting as indifferent as I could manage. "Let's not get crazy."

Brand's eyes went from the handgun to my face. He smiled. "Why don't you shoot me?" he asked.

I wasn't impressed by his nonchalance. After all, I had done the same thing myself when the big man threw down on me earlier. I stopped spinning the gun, making sure the muzzle was pointed at Brand.

"We're businessmen conducting negotiations," I said. "No one actually intended to shoot anybody. Am I right? The guns are all for show."

Brand shrugged. He and I believed it, although a quick glance around the room told us that nobody else did.

"Now, Mr. Brand," I said, emphasizing the "Mr." "Three AK-47s, eight magazines, four Kevlar vests, eight ounces of Semtex 10—I'll settle for C-4 if that's all you have. What else? Two blasting caps."

"Detonators?" he asked.

"I'll make my own."

"How resourceful of you."

"Can you get all that or not?"

"I can get it."

"When?"

"I won't know until I make a call."

"Fair enough. Are there really Mexicans on the Canadian border?"

"Why not? It's a free country. Canada, I mean."

"I expect you to front for us."

"Oh, you do, do you."

"You pay for the merchandise. In return, you get a full share of the take."

"How much is that?"

"That's hard to say."

"Guess."

"A quarter of a million dollars."

Brand was not impressed by the figure. He glanced at the people sitting in the living room as if he were counting bodies. "How many shares will there be?" he asked.

"Does it matter?"

"I want a quarter of a million dollars," he said, "plus expenses."

"Agreed. Something else. It's been my experience that no criminal enterprise of any magnitude can prevail in a community without at least the tacit approval of the local population, starting with the police."

"What's that supposed to mean?"

"Deputies James and Williams. They rousted me the other day for purposes of extortion. Like you, they wanted half of our profits. How they knew what my plans were . . ."

"What do you want me to do about it?"

"Get them off my back."

"How am I supposed to do that?"

"How do you keep them off your back?"

Brand thought about it for about five seconds. "It'll cost you," he said.

"How much?"

"They're very greedy men, Dyson. Very greedy. And you have no leverage. If they wanted to pick you up, they wouldn't need to pretend they found a lid of grass on your seat during a routine traffic stop, would they?"

"Bastards," I heard the old man mutter from the living room.

I sighed dramatically, again—I was getting good at it. "I'll give you a third," I said. "Not half. A full third. You can disperse it anyway you see fit."

"How much is a third?"

"Will you settle for a conservative estimate? One million dollars."

Brand sat there thinking it over, his eyes never leaving my face as if he could see the answers to all of his questions written there.

"Okay," he said. He smiled some more as he reached across the kitchen table. I shook his hand, very much aware that the third was probably what he was willing to settle for all along. He held my hand for a few beats.

"A third plus expenses," he said.

"Now who's being greedy?" He continued to hold my hand. "All right, I'll pay your expenses. I intend to inspect the merchandise before we accept delivery."

"The Mexicans might not like that."

"I don't care."

"Agreed," Brand said.

He released my hand and settled back into his chair. I slid the wheel gun across the table to him. He caught it before it hit his chest. He was surprised by the gesture. From the intake of breath coming from the living room, so were a few other people.

"I won't pretend that we're friends, Mr. Brand, or that we trust each other," I said. "You shouldn't, either. However, if we can treat each other with the respect we both deserve, it is unlikely either of us will engage in a more profitable relationship."

Brand took up the wheel gun—this time I held my breath—and shoved it down into his pocket.

"I believe, Mr. Dyson," he said, "that we have an understanding."

I nodded in approval, and he nodded back.

"There is one more thing," I said. "It might give you an idea of what I have in mind."

I left the kitchen table and gestured for Brand to follow me. I moved to the living room. The big man lowered his hands and stepped forward.

"I'd like my gun back," he said. He might have been asking for the correct time for all the emotion he displayed.

"Roy," I said.

Roy jettisoned the magazine from the butt of the automatic and made a big production out of thumbing all the rounds onto the cabin floor. He slammed the magazine home, ejected the round that was in the chamber, and tossed the now-empty gun to the big man. The big man shoved it into a holster hidden under his jacket. If he was upset by Roy's behavior, he didn't show it.

Everyone was standing now, and I shooed them out of the way so that Brand and I had an unobstructed view of Jimmy's map still propped on the back of the sofa. I tapped the red dot next to Lake Vermilion.

"There's a building here," I said. "No address, no street name, no satellite images, but it's there, and if it's there, that means the planning and zoning department had to approve its construction."

"So?"

"I presume you have contacts in county government."

"One or two."

"I need the blueprints."

Afterward, Brand made some conciliatory remarks about how we all needed to put our differences aside and work together for the greater good—he reminded me of my old bantam hockey coach. He apologized to Roy, apologized to Roy's wife, and shook a few hands. Before he left I told him not to be a stranger since he now knew where I lived. He promised he'd see me again, and soon. The vehicle holding him, Fenelon, and the thug disappeared down the road before anyone in the cabin spoke.

"That went well," Josie said.

"A third?" the old man asked. "A third? You're giving him a third while we do all the work? Couldn't you Jew him down a little?"

"I doubt I could even Christian him down a little."

The old man heard the annoyance in my voice. "Don't mean nothing," he said. "Just the way people talk."

"No, it isn't. Anyway, if he gets the guns and the blueprints, he'll be earning his share."

"I don't trust him," Dave said.

"He doesn't trust us."

"I don't understand any of this," Liz said.

"Shhh, honey," Dave told her.

"Don't shush me," she said. "A criminal points a gun at me for two hours and you shush me?"

"We're all criminals," Josie said.

"I'm not."

Jill opened her mouth as if she were going to say something only to slowly close it again without speaking.

"What's your plan?" Jimmy wanted to know. "Do you have a plan?"

"I'm going to drink one of the old man's cheap beers—" I said.

"Cheap?" he said.

"Then go to bed. The rest of you can do whatever you want."

"But what about the plan?" Jimmy asked.

"I have some details to work out. We'll talk in a couple of days." I looked Claire de Lune directly in the eye. "We'll talk after we get the guns."

Jimmy's head swiveled from me to her and back again. "What are you talking to her for?" he asked.

"Dyson doesn't trust me," Claire answered.

"She's my girl," Jimmy told me.

"She's Fenelon's girl," Josie said.

"Is not." Jimmy turned to Claire for confirmation. "Is not," he said again.

"I love you, not him," she said.

"Oh, puhleez," the old man said.

I remembered the family feud the old man described the day earlier and decided this was the beginning of round two and quite honestly, I wasn't in the mood. I had phone calls to make.

"You kids work it out on your own," I said. "Preferably somewhere else."

"But—" Josie said.

"But nothing. I'm tired, Josie. In the words of a very wise and wonderful bar owner of my acquaintance—you don't have to go home, but you can't stay here."

"Must you always call so late?" Bullert asked.

"I forgot. Government work is strictly nine-to-five."

"You're a funny guy, McKenzie."

"You know what, you're the second person who told me that tonight."

"Talk to me."

"We're getting close."

"How close."

My explanation included an almost verbatim account of my conversation with John Brand.

"I can get my people in place in just a few hours," Bullert said.

"The fewer hours the better. When this happens, I think it'll happen in a hurry."

Bullert explained exactly what he wanted me to do once I received the call from Brand.

"No problem," I said. "Except . . ."

"Except what?"

"Brand can't be trusted."

"Kinda goes without saying, doesn't it?"

"What I mean is, we should have a Plan B."

"What do you have in mind?"

"You're not going to like it."

"Tell me."

I did—in glorious detail. I was right. He didn't like it.

"Not a chance," Bullert asked.

"Before you say no, talk to Finny."

"Who?"

"Assistant U.S. Attorney James R. Finnegan."

"You and your nicknames. Fine. I'll talk to him in the morning. I guarantee, he's not going to like it any more than I do."

"You're probably right."

"Just for argument's sake, though—what will you need from us to make this happen?"

"Besides immunity? You're not going to like that, either."

TWELVE

My eyes snapped open the way they do when you hear a noise that shouldn't be there, and I reached under the pillow for the SIG Sauer. My hands were closing around the butt when I heard her voice.

"I'm sorry, did I startle you?"

I released the gun.

"Dammit, Josie. What are you doing here?"

Josie sat on the foot of the bed. I rolled on my back and looked up at her. After I had shooed everyone out of the cabin the previous night, I retired to the master bedroom. Now a bright sun was shining through the window, giving her face a near-beatific aura, and it occurred to me that when we first met I didn't think she was particularly attractive.

You must have caught her in the wrong light, my inner voice said.

"We need to talk," she said.

I grabbed a fistful of sheet and blanket and pulled them up around my chest. "What time is it?" I asked.

"Little before eight."

"In the morning? Josie, one of the reasons a guy might turn to a life of crime is so he doesn't have to get up early."

"Eight o'clock is early?"

"What do you want?"

"I'm worried."

"Suddenly you're worried . . ."

"Are you awake?"

"What? Yes, I'm awake."

"You sound cranky."

"JoEllen . . ."

"I like that you call me that. Almost no one ever does."

"I have a gun. I will shoot you."

"Are you one of those people that need a cup of coffee before they can start the day? I'll make it."

"No, no, no," I said. "I'll make it." I swung my legs off the edge of the bed even while gathering the sheet and blanket around my waist. "Give me a minute to take a shower and get dressed."

"If you're going to do that, I'm going to go jump in the lake."

"Yeah, you do that."

Josie stood and started pulling off her scoop-neck shirt to reveal a bikini top. I averted my eyes but not before I noticed that her face wasn't the only place that had freckles. All the while my inner voice chanted, *She plays ball in a different league, she plays ball in a different league . . .*

Forty-five minutes later I was clean, shaved, and dressed. Josie was sitting at the kitchen table. Her hair was damp and clung to her neck and shoulders; her bottom was wrapped in a beach towel, but her top was exposed. Again I tried not to stare. She took a sip from her coffee mug.

"How do you make such good coffee?" she asked. "You use the same ingredients I do, yet your coffee tastes so much better than mine."

"It's a gift," I said. I filled my own mug and joined her at the table. "I'm awake, I'm dressed, my gun's in the bedroom—what worries you, JoEllen?"

"John Brand worries me."

"As well he should."

"You don't trust him, do you?"

"About as far as I could throw this cabin."

"Are you really going to give him a million dollars."

"I didn't promise him a million dollars. I promised him a third of the take. I expect it to be closer to half a million."

"Oh."

"No need to tell him that, though, is there?"

"No. No, I guess not. What if . . ."

"He tries to rip us off?"

"Yes."

"Don't worry about it. I have it covered."

"Something else."

"Hmm?"

"The sheriff deputies—Dyson, how did they know where we would be when they pulled us over the other day? You don't think it was a coincidence, do you?"

"I don't believe in coincidences. On the other hand, they do happen. They happen all the time."

"What does that mean?"

"Don't be paranoid."

"There's a spy, Dyson. Someone in my family. Or Claire—I don't think of her as a member of the family. Someone, anyway, someone who was in the cabin when we left. Someone who—"

"That's what I mean by paranoid."

"Are you saying it's not true?"

"Sweetie, even the bartender at Buckman's knows I'm here. You don't think the deputies knew? They probably were on the lookout for me, waiting for a chance to have a private conversation." I quoted the word "private" with my fingers. "If they rousted me in front of witnesses, they'd have to bring me in, and they didn't want to do that. Too much paperwork. They saw us on the road, and there you go. Simple."

"Are you sure?"

Hell no, my inner voice said. I wasn't sure—nowhere close to it. The very last thing I needed, though, was for the Iron Range Bandits to start pointing fingers at each other. When the time came, I would do all the pointing that was necessary.

"Yes, I am," I said aloud.

She stared at her coffee mug for a few beats. "Don't call me sweetie," she said.

"My mistake."

"I like that you call me JoEllen, though."

"So you said."

"You shouldn't—you should be careful about calling me that when other people are around."

"Why, if you like it?"

"That's what my ex-fiancé sometimes called me, and people might get the wrong impression."

"Are you afraid they might think that you and I are . . . Wait a minute. Ex-fiancé?" I saw it then, the look in her eyes. It was like when you catch someone watching you at a party and they quickly look away, pretending that they weren't watching at all. "You lied to me. You're not gay. Or even bi, for that matter. Are you?"

"No."

"What the hell?"

"You were getting all anxious and concerned and, I don't know, guyish."

"Guyish?"

"You know what I mean, the way guys behave when they're around women."

"Oh, for God's sake."

"Admit it, you were being guyish."

"I don't admit it, and even if I was—so?"

"I thought it would be best if I took it off the table, given the stakes and everything."

"Tell me—given the stakes and everything, why are you putting it back on the table now?" She didn't answer the question, so I did. "You're the one behaving guyish, girlish, whatever, not me."

"Am I?"

"Put your shirt back on."

She glanced down at her chest and back up at me. "Why?"

"You know damn well why."

"Explain it to me."

"No. No. This is not happening. This cannot happen. Remember what I told you before? Double it."

"You mean about wanting a slice of Dyson pie?"

I was standing next to the door of the cabin with no idea how I had gotten there. "Stop it," I said. "C'mon, now."

"I like you, Dyson. It's as simple as that. Do you like me?"

"No."

"For a macho professional thief, you sure are a terrible liar."

"JoEllen . . ."

She smiled at the sound of her own name. "Nick," she said. "We're both adults."

"Who says?"

"We could take the pontoon out on the lake—"

The noise of heavy footsteps on the steps of the deck outside cut her short. I stepped away from the door. A few moments later Skarda walked in.

"Hi, Dave," Josie said. She was standing next to the coffeemaker. She was now wearing her shirt; the towel was still wrapped around her hips. "Do you want some coffee?"

"No."

"Dyson made it."

"Maybe a half a cup, then."

I was standing in front of Jimmy's map. "What brings you here?" I asked.

"I had nowhere else to go," Skarda said.

"Liz?"

"Liz wonders what's going to happen afterward. She wonders—I'm an escaped fugitive and she wonders what's going to happen to us."

You're going to prison, I told myself. As soon as the ATF gets the guns off the border every law enforcement agency in the region is going to swoop down on you and the other bandits—and there's nothing I can do about it. The thought made me feel low. I turned my attention back to the map so I wouldn't have to look at him or his sister.

"One problem at a time," I said.

"I could go to Canada with you," Skarda said.

"No," Josie said. She moved to the living room and handed Skarda his cup of coffee. "You can go to Canada, but not with him. Isn't that right, Dyson? You told me yourself, you're here for the money, and once you get it, you're out the door and down the street and you won't be coming back."

"Something like that," I said.

"And you prefer not to leave any misunderstandings behind."

"None."

Josie lifted both of her hands the way some people do when they're about to ask a question and then let them fall to her sides. "I need to get dressed," she said. A moment later she disappeared into the bedroom.

"What's with her?" Skarda asked.

"She's wondering what's going to happen the day after, too."

"What is going to happen?"

I wanted to tell him; wanted to tell them both. Sit them down on the deck and explain who I was and what I was doing there—screw Bullert, screw Finnegan, screw the ATF, the FBI, and all the rest. I had come there because I thought I might be able to do some good and because I thought it might be fun.

What do you think about the idea now? my inner voice asked.

I ignored Skarda's question as well as my own and turned my attention back to the map.

After that, it was the three of us hanging around doing nothing. I decided it was a good idea to let them see me preparing my plans for the heist, so I retrieved the camera I had used the day before. I plugged it into the PC that Jimmy had left at the cabin and started surfing the photos I had taken at the remote vault. I studied the white building from all angles, the fence, the trail, the creek, everything. The more I did, the more sure I was that I could actually rob the place. The thought excited me even as my inner voice chanted, *Don't be an ass.* I dismissed it—as I often had before doing something stupid— and started carefully jotting down all of the license plate numbers of the vehicles I had photographed. Josie wanted to know why. "Looking for a key," I told her. When I finished, I came *this*close to pulling out my cell and calling Chad Bullert before catching myself.

"I need a phone," I said. Josie gave me hers. I stopped myself again.

Okay, now what? my inner voice asked. *You can't call Bullert directly. What if Josie or one of the other bandits traced the phone number? It was an easy thing to do these days with the Internet.*

What else can I do, I asked myself. We had not worked this

out in advance, setting up a go-between to whom I could clandestinely pass information. 'Course, I had expected to be home long before now. I'm sure Bullert expected the same. I could have gone for a hike alone in the woods or taken the pontoon out on the lake, made my calls where there was no one to hear. I was afraid of how Josie and Skarda might react, though. I had no fear that they would guess I was a police spy, but rather that they would imagine I was betraying them to Brand or the deputies or both.

I decided I had to use the cell in front of them. The problem—whom could I call? Several people came to mind, only I couldn't remember any of their phone numbers. They had all been listed alphabetically by first name on the contact log of my cell phone; I would just click on them. I had memorized only one phone number in my entire life—a number I had called perhaps a dozen times a week since I was in kindergarten.

I inputted it on the keypad of Josie's cell. A few moments later a woman answered. "Hello," she said. I paused so long that she said "Hello" again before I replied.

"Hey, sweetie," I said. "It's good to hear your voice. This is Nick Dyson."

"Who?"

"I'm sorry it's been so long since I've been in touch. How's your mom?"

"Oh. My. God. McKenzie."

"Yes." I deliberately smiled when I spoke, partly for Josie and Skarda's benefit and partly because I was hoping Shelby would hear it in my voice.

"Are people listening?" Shelby asked. "Do you want me to call you Dyson?"

"Yeah, but you know, I move around a lot."

"You're still undercover and you need my help?"

"I am so happy for you, honestly."

"Bobby is going to go crazy."

I started laughing. "I imagine he will," I said. "Tell me, sweetie, do you still work for Driver and Vehicle Services?"

"Ahhh . . ."

"How about your friend, Harry?"

"Harry? Harry from the FBI, that Harry?"

"Just goes to show, once you become a member of what's the name of the union—American Federation of State, County, and Municipal Employees—once you become a member, it's impossible to get fired."

"You're going to tell me something and you want me to pass it on to Harry," Shelby said.

"You're too smart to be that pretty. Or is it the other way around?"

"Let me get a pencil."

I heard Shelby set down the handset. I covered the cell's microphone and found Josie and Skarda. Josie was watching me, but Skarda was staring out the window.

"She went to get a pencil," I said.

"Who is she?" Josie asked.

"Just a girl. Knew her when we were kids."

"Uh-huh."

A moment later, Shelby was back on the phone. "Shoot," she said.

"I'm going to give you a list of license plate numbers." I recited them slowly and carefully, although, in the big scheme of things, they didn't really matter. "Got 'em?"

"Got 'em," Shelby said. "Now what?"

"I need whatever information you can give me about the drivers."

"Does Harry know why?"

"Harry has a friend named Chad—remember him?"

"No."

"Chad is the IT guy."

"I have no idea what that means."

Think it through, my inner voice said.

"I'm hoping you'll get Harry to ask Chad to give me the name of someone off the list who might be able to help me out on something I have going."

I looked at Josie again and made a motion with my hand that suggested Shelby was ditzy.

"You want me to call Harry and tell him to call Chad, whoever he is," Shelby said. "Somehow they'll know what you're talking about."

"That would be perfect."

"This is better than *NCIS*."

"I'm glad you think so."

"Then what? Do you want Harry to call you back?"

I was staring at Josie when I answered. "That would not be a good idea. How 'bout I meet you? You can pass on the information yourself."

"Me? Fun. When? Where?"

"Rice Park. In front of the fountain." I glanced at my watch. It was 11:53 A.M. "Would six o'clock work?"

"How should I know?"

"If you're not there I'll assume something went wrong."

"Wait till I tell Bobby."

"I would prefer that you didn't. Boyfriends don't like me very much."

Josie snorted when she heard that.

"I feel just like Veronica Lake in *This Gun for Hire*," Shelby said, "lying to Robert Preston in order to help Alan Ladd."

"Good-bye, sweetie. See you soon."

I hung up and glanced at Josie.

"Sweetie?" she asked.

"I need to drive to St. Paul," I said.

"I'm going with."

"I thought you might."

"I want to meet this trollop you're dealing with."

"What do you want me to do?" Skarda asked.

"If you were Brian Fenelon, where would you be?" I asked.

If not for the sign, I wouldn't have known it was a strip joint. A brown, two-story clapboard building with white trim surrounded by a gravel parking lot—driving at fifty-five miles per hour on the county road, I nearly passed it without notice, probably would have if Josie hadn't cleared her throat and motioned toward the sign. DANGEROUS LIAISONS GENTLEMAN'S CLUB OVER 21 WELCOME. There were only four cars in the lot, and I parked next to them. A wooden staircase and a long, narrow handicap ramp led to the entrance.

"Coming?" I asked.

"I think I'll sit this one out," Josie said.

A few moments later I was opening the door. Another sign told me Happy Hour Mon.–Thurs., Live Dancing Mon.–Sat., Wed. is Lingerie Nite! The first thing I noticed when I entered the building was a surprisingly large stage with two poles. A dozen stools abutted the stage, and a dozen small tables with two stools each bordered them. Booths large enough to accommodate private dances lined the walls. A large-screen TV hung above the bar. The bartender, his back turned to me, was watching a Spanish-language soap opera. The TV was the brightest light in the room.

"Excuse me," I said. He didn't answer, so I tried again in Spanish. "Con permiso."

He turned quickly toward me. The way his mouth curled

downward suggested that he was surprised that I spoke the language and none too happy about it, like a chess player who had just lost an important piece.

"¿Qué pasa?" he asked.

"Perdone que lo interrumpa."

"¿Qué quieres? Los bailes no comienzan hasta las cuatro." In case I didn't get it, the bartender gestured at a table tent on the bar that announced that the dances began at 4 P.M.

"Estoy buscando a Brian Fenelon," I told him.

He pointed toward a booth next to an open doorway. The neon sign above the door flashed VIP ROOM.

"Gracias," I said.

"Fenelon speaks lousy Spanish," the bartender said.

"I'll talk slowly, then."

Fenelon sat in the center of the booth. There were two empty shot glasses in front of him and a half-filled beer mug. He held a third shot glass filled with bourbon between his fingers and turned it slowly, expanding a circle of condensation on the tabletop.

"Hi, Brian," I said.

He looked up at me. I could see the cut lip and the bruised chin even in the joint's dim light.

"What do you want?" he asked.

"Looks like you had a long night."

"Fuck you."

I sat down without being asked. "I'm guessing you and your boss had a falling-out."

"Why couldn't you keep your big mouth shut? Why did you have to tell him what I said?"

"So he wouldn't think I was conspiring with you to screw him over."

Fenelon brought the shot glass to his lips but did not drink.

Instead, he set the glass back on the table and fixed my eyes with his. "What the hell is that supposed to mean?" he asked.

"Let me tell you what's going to happen. After I risk life and limb to rob three armored trucks, Brand is going to rip me off. He'll give me the guns as promised. When it comes time to divvy up the swag, though, he's going to take it all for himself. Then he'll have Deputies James and Williams arrest Dave Skarda and me on fugitive warrants so he won't have to worry about retaliation. As far as Jimmy and Josie and the rest are concerned, there won't be a helluva lot they'll be able to do about it, will there?"

"I don't know why you don't just get the fuck outta here. Go up to Canada like you said."

"Good question. I have one for you. Do you like it here, Brian?"

"Whaddaya mean?"

"Do you like it here? Up here in the frickin' nowhere northland. Would you rather be in the Cities? Chicago? New York? Would you like to take Claire somewhere nice? Get her away from that nitwit Jimmy?"

"She loves him."

"Seriously?"

"You sound surprised."

"I am surprised. I thought—"

"You thought she was my girl like everyone else. Well, she's not and she never was."

"You sound unhappy about that." The hard glare in his eyes told me he was *very* unhappy about that. "I know what he sees in her. What does she see in him?"

"Who knows?" Fenelon said. "Her own lost youth, maybe. Stability for her kid. How the hell should I know?"

I shrugged at that because I didn't know what else to do.

"Why are you here, Dyson?"

"I want nothing to do with John Brand. You're the one who brought him in on this. By the way, you shouldn't have done that. When I whacked you, remember, I said I needed someone who knew his way around. I meant you, not him."

"You got it wrong, Dyson. I didn't tell Brand anything. If I had told him"—he tilted his face to give me a good look at it in the dim light—"do you think he would have done this? Brand's the one brought me to the cabin, not the other way 'round. He didn't know we talked, that we were working together, until you told him last night."

"Dammit. I thought . . ."

"You thought I ratted you out."

"Yeah."

"Well, I didn't. Now I'm paying the price for it. Way to go, Dyson. Doubt Brand will ever trust me again."

"I'm sorry."

"Fine, you're sorry. That means a whole helluva lot."

Fenelon closed his eyes and rested his head against the back of the booth. He looked utterly defeated. I called his name, and his eyes snapped open again.

"That's another reason to get out of Dodge," I said.

"What are you talking about, Dyson?"

"How much of the money is Brand going to give you? James and Williams will get a nice taste. What about you?"

"I doubt I'll get anything."

"A quarter of a million dollars, Brian. How far do you think you can go on a quarter of a million dollars?"

Brand had not been impressed when I dropped that number on the table the night before. Fenelon clearly was.

"You're gonna give me two hundred and fifty thousand dollars?"

"Yes, I am."

"What would I have to do?" Before I could answer, Fenelon held up his hand. "I won't go up against Brand. I'm not that stupid."

"No, I wouldn't put you on the spot like that."

"What are you talking about, then? The Mexicans?"

"What the hell do I care about the Mexicans? I want James and Williams."

A smile crept slowly over Fenelon's face. "What do you have in mind?" he asked.

"If I take them off the board, Brand is likely to be more reasonable with the split, don't you think?"

"I don't know about that. I'd love to see those assholes in the jackpot, though. They're bent worse than a paper clip."

"What I need is evidence so strong that even a crooked county attorney couldn't cover it up."

"I'm not testifying . . ."

"I'm not looking for testimony. That's just he said, she said stuff. Besides, it'll put you in trouble with your boss, and we don't want him to know what we're doing, do we?"

"Uh-uh."

"What I need is something you can hold in your hand."

Fenelon drank some of his bourbon and followed it up with a sip of beer. "They don't just take cash payoffs," he said. "Not that much cash around these days, you know? Sometimes they take merchandise. People's ATVs and boats and shit. They get Brand to fence it for them sometimes—that's how I know. Brand'll have me move it for 'im, get it to the right people in exchange for envelopes filled with money."

Fenelon finished first his bourbon and then his beer.

"Go on," I said.

"I know where they store the shit."

———

A few minutes later I opened the passenger door of Josie's Ford Taurus. She turned in the seat and looked up at me. "Is he on our side now?" Josie asked.

"Brian is on Brian's side. Don't ever forget it."

"Oh, I won't."

"Do you know where a small lake, might not even be a lake—they call it Cody. Do you know where it is?"

"Yes. I sold some property over there a couple of years ago."

"You drive."

Josie had to backtrack toward Krueger and then turned east. That made it easier for me to memorize the route, knowing I'd have to drive it myself later, probably in the dark. We eventually turned down a dirt road that led to the lake. Josie slowed, not because it was hard to drive, but because we were looking for a little-used track that veered off of it. We found it easily and followed it to a clearing just big enough to turn around a car and trailer. On the edge of the clearing was a prefabricated pole barn. We left the car to take a closer look. There were no windows. A single door large enough for a small SUV to pass through was sealed with a cheap combination lock like the kind you find on high school lockers.

"This shouldn't be too difficult," I said.

"How are you going to open it?" Josie asked. "Listen to the tumblers like a safecracker?"

"I need a can. A pop can. Beer can."

When Josie saw me searching the clearing, she did the same, eventually finding an empty beer can that had been lying in the tall grass so long that its logo had faded. I asked if she had a knife. She did, handing me a pocketknife with the emblem of the Swiss Army on the handle that she carried in her glove compartment. I used the knife to cut a 1½-inch square of aluminum out of the can and then trimmed the square until it resembled the block letter *M*. I folded the top of the *M* down and the legs of the letter up to create a sturdy shim. I slid the shim in the space between the shackle and the body of the lock and pulled upward. The lock popped open easily.

"Ta-da," I said.

"Where did you learn that?" Josie wanted to know.

"Public school."

I dropped the shim where I could easily find it again, removed the lock, and swung open the large door. I stepped inside the barn. It was crowded with a bass boat and trailer, an ATV, a big-screen TV, some PCs, a couple of sets of tools, and a lot of boxes that I didn't bother to open.

"I bet they don't have receipts for any of this crap," I said.

"What do we do now?" Josie asked.

I closed the door and relocked it. "Head to St. Paul," I said. "I'll drive."

Josie stood there, her hands on her hips, and watched as I circled the Taurus and opened the driver's-side door.

"What?" I asked.

"Aren't you going to tell me what you're up to?"

"Plausible deniability."

"What's that mean?"

"You can't testify about what you don't know. Are you coming?"

THIRTEEN

I parked Josie on one of the cobblestone streets surrounding Rice Park and went on alone. The park was created in 1849, the same year St. Paul was named capital of the Minnesota Territory, and was flanked by the Romanesque Revivalist jewel that is the Landmark Center, the luxurious crescent-shaped St. Paul Hotel, the Renaissance-style Central Public Library, and the opulent Ordway Center for the Performing Arts—each building as rich in history as the park itself. It was a prime lounging area for the city's downtown worker bees, who were drawn there by the period streetlamps, benches, and honest-to-God grass, trees, and flower gardens. There were ice sculptures and trees laced with webs of light in the winter, and music, mostly jazz and blues, in the summer, and nearly every day of the year there was a vendor on the corner happy to sell you soft drinks, coffee, soft pretzels, hot dogs, and juicy Polish sausages from his umbrella-covered cart.

At the center of the park was a large round fountain. I didn't see Shelby, so I sat on the low brick wall containing the fountain and waited. The clock on the Landmark Center told me it was 6:07 P.M. I started tapping the face of my watch, or rather the watch I had borrowed from Skarda. There was a bronze figure of F. Scott Fitzgerald near the street vendor and a clutch of statues depicting the Peanuts characters created by Charles M. Schulz, both St. Paul natives. I was debating which author had the greater cultural impact when I saw her zigging and zagging her way through what remained of the rush-hour crowd. Shelby was hurrying the way some women do when they're inexcusably late, eyes staring straight ahead, chin up, chest out, walking with quick steps just this side of a trot. I had never seen a man walk like that no matter how late he was. She was carrying a black bag by a strap draped over her shoulder and a manila envelope that she clutched to her chest. Her dress was black, low cut, and inexplicably tight and ended half a dozen inches above her knees. I had seen the dress before—on Nina Truhler.

When she reached the fountain, I said, "What the hell, Shelby?"

"Sorry I'm late."

"I don't mean about that. I mean the dress."

"Do you like it? It's Nina's."

"I know it's Nina's. Why are you wearing it?"

"I'm the mother of two teenage girls. I don't have any femme fatale outfits."

"You're not supposed to look like a femme fatale. You're supposed to look like you work for the DVS. Wearing that dress, every man and most of the women within a three-mile radius are watching you this very moment."

"You think so?" Her face brightened like someone impressed by the prize she found in her Cracker Jack box. "Are you being watched?"

"Not anymore."

"I should sit down."

"No," I said, only Shelby wasn't listening. She nestled next to me on the stone wall, her skirt riding dangerously up her thighs. I averted my eyes, fixing them on the street vendor.

"Bobby is going to kill me," I said.

"Oh, yeah. He promised that was going to happen. Right after Nina gets through with you."

"You told him?"

"Of course I did. I tell Bobby everything."

"Nina, too? Why did you involve her?"

"Because I needed to borrow a dress. She wants to know why you didn't call her, by the way. So does Bobby."

"I couldn't remember her phone number."

Shelby began to laugh. She laughed so hard and vigorously that I was afraid she'd fall backward into the fountain.

"Oh, that's wonderful," she said.

"All right, all right . . ."

"I want to be there when you tell her."

"Is that envelope for me?"

"Take a good look, McKenzie. You are never going to see this dress again."

"This is what comes from trying to be a good citizen."

"I'm going to have them carve that on your tombstone. Honest to God, McKenzie . . ."

Shelby handed me the envelope. It was unsealed. I reached inside and pulled a sheaf of documents halfway out and looked them over.

"Chad, the guy from the ATF, he said the report with the paper clip in the center is the one you want." I found it, studied it without separating the pages from the others. "If you think Bobby and Nina are miffed—those guys, Chad and Harry, oh my."

"You spoke to them?"

"They were both there when Chad gave me the envelope.

Mostly I listened as they shouted at each other. Chad kept saying everything would be fine. Harry was pretty sure it wouldn't be. He kept saying, 'It's McKenzie, it's McKenzie,' as if that alone should warn Chad how bad things can get."

"Harry's just cranky because the FBI moved its headquarters from downtown Minneapolis to Brooklyn Center. A lot of crime in Brooklyn Center—150 percent above the state average, something like that."

"Chad said if things go badly, they'll blame Finnegan since he's the one who approved your plan. Is he the U.S. attorney who signed the letters you showed us?"

"Yes. Assistant U.S. Attorney James Finnegan, but they're wrong. Blame almost always filters down. Rarely does it go upward. Doesn't matter, though." I turned to look at her, making sure my eyes were locked on her eyes and not looking somewhere else. "Everything *will* be fine," I said.

"Famous last words."

We sat like that for a few more beats, staring into each other's eyes. Shelby smiled brightly. I found myself smiling back.

"You want to look at the dress again, don't you?" she said. "Go 'head. Do I look as good in it as Nina?"

"Stop it, now."

"What are you going to do about her?"

"Apologize profusely, beg forgiveness, and buy her something both tasteful and expensive."

"Then what?"

"What do you mean?"

"I mean—how long have you two been dating?"

"I don't know. I've known her for nearly five years, but we've been monogamous for only what, three and a half years? Four?"

Shelby continued to stare.

"What?" I said.

"Don't you think it's time to take the next step?"

"I've proposed to Nina three times. Each time she changed the subject, blew me off. The lady doesn't want to get married again. I met her ex-husband. I don't blame her."

"She doesn't want to get married because you don't want to get married. You have commitment issues, McKenzie, you know you do."

"How can you say that? I proposed. Actually got down on one knee."

"What would you have done if she said yes?"

"I would have . . ."

"You would have run for the hills. Nina knows it, too."

"I haven't got time for this, Shel. In case you haven't heard, I'm working undercover as a dangerous and unpredictable armed felon."

"A lot of our friends, and I'm including Nina, they all think that you want to marry me—and because you can't you're not going to marry anyone. Only two people know that's nonsense—me and Bobby, probably because we've known you the longest. If I suddenly became free you'd find a way to sabotage the relationship just like you did with Kirsten, just like you did with Jillian DeMarais."

"You didn't like either of them."

"You did—for a while."

"I don't understand women." I took Shelby's chin in my hand and kissed her lips. It was a short kiss. I knew my boundaries. I stood up and started moving away from the fountain. "My best to the family," I said.

When she saw me coming, Josie scooted behind the steering wheel of the Ford Taurus, which was fine with me. I opened the passenger door and settled into the seat.

"Home, JoEllen," I said.

"The woman, she was your contact?"

"Yes."

"She's lovely."

"I hadn't noticed."

"Kinda slutty looking, though, in that black dress."

Before she could say more, I directed her to I-94, through Spaghetti Junction, and north onto I-35E. It wasn't difficult. The roads were still congested, and the slow-moving rush-hour traffic gave us plenty of time to switch lanes safely.

"This is awful," Josie said. She said it more than once. "I can't imagine having to deal with traffic like this every single day."

"Me, neither," I said. "That's one reason why I don't work nine-to-five."

It took us thirty minutes to travel from downtown St. Paul past the I-694 interchange, a trip that should have taken less than ten. Josie was increasingly annoyed by the delay. I added to it by dialing up KBEM-FM on the radio, which played "that music." Maryann Sullivan was subbing for Kevin O'Connor, and she liked playing local jazz talent. I was able to hear Debbie Duncan, Hall Brothers, Doug Haining Quintet, Christine Rosholt, Fantastic Merlins, Mouldy Figs, and Connie Evingson—perhaps my favorite vocalist, channeling Django Reinhardt on "You and the Night and the Music"— one right after another. While I listened, I thought about what Shelby had said and wondered if she was right.

Commitment issues? How can I have commitment issues? I had proposed three times—on bended knee, no less—and not once did I hope the lady would say no; actually felt a jolt of pain when she didn't say yes. Not to mention, a lot of women have slid in and out of my life in the past four years, and I've kept them all at a distance, including the one sitting

next to me in the car. That has to say something about com-
mitment, right? Besides, so what if we weren't married? A lot
of people commit to each other for a lifetime without the ben-
efit of marriage. 'Course, they actually live together and Nina
and I don't, but that's mostly because she wants to set a good
example for her teenage daughter, Erica, who isn't actually a
teenager anymore, she's an undergrad at Tulane University.
Still, we have spent many a long weekend at each other's
homes. I have plenty of stuff at her place and she has a lot of
personal items at mine, including a slinky black number that
she has never worn for more than a few minutes at a time in
my presence. That says commitment, too, doesn't it? Well,
doesn't it?

Just this side of Harris, we lost KBEM's signal. Josie switched off the radio. "Finally," she said. "How can you listen to that stuff?"

"Jazz, my dear, is the only music God approves of."

"Is that right?"

"It is a music in which it's impossible to speak a mean or hurtful thing. Wynton Marsalis once said it's 'an art form that cannot be limited by enforced trends or bad taste.'"

"Who's he?"

"Never mind."

"The woman back there at the park, does she listen to jazz?"

"I have no idea."

"Have you slept with her?"

"What? No."

"Why not? The way she fills out that dress . . ."

"Ahh, geez . . ."

"Don't you want to sleep with her?"

"Of course I do."

What are you saying? my inner voice shouted. *Talk about your Freudian slips.*

It's not a Freudian slip, I told myself. I'm pretending to be someone else, remember? Of course Dyson would want to sleep with Shelby. That doesn't mean McKenzie would.

"Then why haven't you slept with her?" Josie asked.

"Let's just say the opportunity never presented itself; let it go at that."

"Are you sure you're not the one who's gay?"

Instead of answering, I turned the radio back on.

"Let me guess," Josie said. "This is your way of telling me to shut up."

I found a station that was broadcasting the Minnesota Twins game and turned up the volume.

"C'mon, Dyson. We're going to listen to this now?"

"Baseball, my dear, is the only sport God approves of."

"Is that right? Jazz and baseball. What else does he approve of in your unchallenged opinion?"

"Chili dogs."

"Apparently God has peculiar tastes," Josie said.

We were fifty miles down the road and approaching the Cloquet exit before she spoke again. "I've been thinking."

"Uh-oh," I said.

"You're not that difficult to figure out, Dyson. In fact, I have a theory. Want to hear it?"

"Not particularly."

"The reason you haven't slept with the woman in the park is the same reason you haven't slept with me. Despite your choice of careers, at the end of the day, Dyson, you're a nice guy."

"What a terrible thing to say."

"You pretend to be this dangerous individual, and I suppose you are from what I've seen. You also care about people. You care about Jill, and you barely know her."

"She's easy to care about."

"You care about Dave, too. And Roy and Jimmy and the old man. And me."

"I wouldn't go that far."

"You're loyal to your friends."

I turned my head to stare out the passenger window, a sign to Josie that I didn't want to talk anymore. My brain shifted from thoughts of Shelby and Nina and whatnot to the Iron Range Bandits.

Nice guy? my inner voice asked. *Who says?*

Once again I was faced with the question—why? Here I was, leading Josie and her family merrily by the hand toward catastrophe. Why? To save a government bureaucracy from its own hubris?

"You should get out," I said. I didn't know why I said it. The words spilled out just as they had when I spoke to Jill, to hell with the ATF and the FBI and all the other initialized so-and-sos intent on making the world safe for the American Dream, whatever the hell that was. Or maybe it was my sub-conscious showing a commitment to Josie. "When we get to Krueger, you should pack your things and leave. Go to Duluth. Go to the Cities. Go anywhere. Just get out of here. Start over someplace else. What we're planning, even if it works out, you're going to be running for the rest of your life, afraid of everyone you meet, jumping at every unexplained noise, scared to use your own name. If not that, then the crime spree you and the rest of the Bandits have embarked on is going to put you in prison or worse. Give it up while you can."

"Why don't you?"

Stay in character, stay in character, my inner voice chanted.

"I have nowhere else to go," I said aloud. "You do. Right now, this minute, you can go anywhere and do anything with-out a worry—"

"Except how to pay for it."

"In a few days you won't have that option."

"Why are you telling me this?"

"Because you're right. I like you. I don't want you and your family to end up like me, hoping to make a big score so you'll have money enough to hide on."

"I'm not going to hide. Once I get my share, I'm going to live."

Well, you tried.

"Call your father," I said. "Tell him we're on our way back. Tell him that we're going to stop at Buckman's for a quick beer before we go home."

"Why?"

"So he doesn't get bent out of shape like he did the last time I kept you out late."

Josie fluttered her long eyelashes at me. "Are you going to keep me out late?" she asked.

"I liked you better when I thought you were gay."

Despite the best efforts of daylight savings time to keep it at bay, night engulfed us long before we approached Buckman's, which made the lightbar on the sheriff's department cruiser all the more brilliant.

Josie saw the lights at the same moment I did. "What should I do?" she asked.

"Pull over slowly, put the car in park—they'll see your taillights and know what you're doing. Keep your hands on top of the steering wheel. No sudden movements. The cruiser has a high-powered spotlight, so the deputies can see everything. Don't look directly into it. Don't speak, not even when spoken to."

Josie did what I told her. A moment later Deputies James

and Williams approached exactly as they had before. Because of the spot, they were half bathed in light and half lost to darkness. James leaned against the car and looked through the open driver's window. Williams was on the passenger side, looking back. They spoke to each other across the front seat of the car.

"Beautiful evening, isn't it?" James said.

"Certainly is," Williams said. "I'm surprised that the honey is driving, though. Kinda hard to have her head in your lap if she's behind the wheel, ain't it?"

"You kiss your mother with that mouth, Deputy?" I said.

Williams didn't like the remark. He abruptly pulled open the car door; the dome light flicked on, giving me a good look at the half of his angry face that wasn't illuminated by the spotlight. I was wondering if he had his brass knuckles when James intervened.

"Personally, I didn't have a mother," he said. "We were too poor."

"That's sad," Williams said.

"I might buy one, though, with my end of the heist. What about you?"

Williams slammed the door shut. "Nah," he said. "She'd just complain that I don't call enough."

"Mr. Brand wants to see you," James said.

"I'm going to guess that you and he have come to some kind of arrangement," I said.

"That's right," Williams said.

"Kinda sucks to be you, though, doesn't it? I was going to give you half. What is Brand offering?"

"Not as much," James said.

"Seems unfair."

"Sometimes you have to make sacrifices. Go along to get along."

"Brand gave us the greater-good speech, too."

"We're all striving for Sir Thomas More's utopian society," Williams said.

The remark so surprised me that I damn near gave myself whiplash turning toward him.

"Deputy Williams," I said. "You read. I'm impressed."

Williams actually smiled, but James's laughter wiped it from his face.

"He got that offa *Jeopardy!*" James said.

"Nonetheless," I said. "Where is Brand?"

"He's waiting at Buckman's," Williams said.

"What a coincidence. We were just headed that way."

"We know," James said. "We just wanted to make sure you didn't get lost."

"We'll be right behind you," Williams said.

"That's comforting," I said.

"Think of us as guardian angels," James said.

"Or cherubim, if you prefer," Williams said.

James stared at Williams across the front seat of the Taurus. "Now you're just showing off," he said.

We waited until the deputies were back in their cruiser and the spotlight was extinguished before pulling off the shoulder and back onto the county blacktop. The deputies followed close behind. Josie spent more time watching them in the rearview mirror than the road in front of her. Her fingers grasped the steering wheel, and she was breathing hard through her nose.

"Do you have something to say?" I asked.

"What, I get to talk now?"

"Josie . . ."

"This is bullshit. No way the deputies are working with

Brand for less than half. If they're working with Brand, that means they plan to take all the money and split it between them."

"I was wrong, what I said the other day. You just might have a future in this business after all."

"Well?"

"Well, what?"

"Well, what are we going to do?"

"Nothing is going to happen, Josie, until we have the money. Until we actually have the cash in hand it's just a bunch of guys pretending they're tough."

"You're saying I shouldn't be afraid."

"Not yet."

"When?"

"I'll let you know."

Scott, the bartender at Buckman's, looked nervous. His eyes flitted all over the place, moving from me to the deputies to Brand and Fenelon seated in a booth to Brand's thug sitting at the bar and nursing a bottled beer, and then back again. I had no idea what he was thinking, yet my intuition told me he was afraid something bad was going to happen while at the same time wondering how he was going to profit off it.

I took hold of Josie's arm and whispered in her ear. "Sit at the bar, order a vodka Collins, let the boys see how pretty you are."

"What the hell . . ."

I tightened my grip on her arm. "Make sure the thug can see your hands. Whatever happens, stay out of it." Jose gave me a look as if she wanted to protest some more. "Please," I said.

She nodded and went to the rail. I marched to the booth and sat next to Fenelon across from Brand. "Gentlemen," I said. "Funny meeting you here."

Brand showed me his empty hands, which made me flash on the knights of old. Whenever they met fellow knights they didn't intend to slaughter, they would make a production out of revealing that they weren't holding weapons—that's how the handshake was developed. Funny the things that pop in your mind when you're nervous.

"We heard this was your favorite spot," Brand said. He seemed incapable of speaking softly; the words flew like bird shot from a 12-gauge, and I thought, this is supposed to be a secret meeting?

"It's the only place I know of up here, although I'm told you have a gentleman's club down the road somewhere."

I felt Fenelon's body stiffen next to mine, yet his face gave nothing away.

"It's a few miles from here on County 21," Brand said. "You should drop in sometime. I'll take care of you."

"I'll bet," I said even as my inner voice spoke to me—*He doesn't know about your conversation with Fenelon.*

"Speaking of which . . ." Brand reached into the pocket of his charcoal sports jacket. It was the same color yet a different cut from the suit coat he wore the night before. He stopped, though, when the bartender appeared at the table and set a bottle of Summit Extra Pale Ale in front of me.

"Hey," I said. "Thanks, man."

"Anything I can get you others?" Scott asked.

Both Brand and Fenelon glanced at the drinks in front of them and said no, they were fine. While Scott drifted back to the rail I took a long pull of the Summit. "I love this stuff," I said.

Brand didn't seem to care. His hand disappeared into his pocket again and reappeared with a thumb drive. He slid the device across the table.

"We scanned the blueprints you wanted," he said. "We couldn't give you the actual documents, though, could we?"

"Of course not."

"Someone might suspect we're up to no good."

I slipped the drive into my own pocket. "What about the other half?" I asked.

"Other half? Oh, yes. The . . . other half. Do you know where Crane Lake is?"

"No idea."

"Get a map," Fenelon said.

I turned in my seat to get a good look at him. His bruises seemed more pronounced than they had that morning.

"What happened to you?" I asked.

"None of your damn business."

I liked hearing the anger in his voice. It suggested that he was pissed at me instead of Brand.

On the other hand . . . my inner voice warned.

I took a long pull of the ale and contemplated the interior of Buckman's. It was half filled, and most of the patrons seemed to be having a reasonably good time. Except for the thug, who sat with his back to the rail and balanced a beer on his knee, and James and Williams, who were seated at the far end of the bar. They were watching us intently, a grim expression on their faces. Josie sat between them, sipping from a tall, frosted glass, her back to us. Yet I could see her unhappy face in the mirror behind the bar, and I knew she was watching us, too.

"Crane Lake?" I said.

"It's a U.S. Port of Entry in Voyageurs National Park near

the border," Brand said. "It mostly serves seaplane traffic. Something like five thousand takeoffs and landings each year. Do you know where Orr is? The town of Orr?"

"No, but I'll get a map."

"After you find Orr, get on 23, follow it to 24, and then go north toward Crane Lake. Go east on County Road 425. That will take you to Scotts Seaplane Base, but don't stop there. Stay on 425. You want to take the first left after you pass Rocky Road. It's an unpaved road. No sign. Follow it to the end. That will take you to a private seaplane base. Mine."

"Yours?"

"Radar follows the planes as they approach Scotts. In the last half mile, when they're below the radar, occasionally a plane will turn toward my dock."

"Doesn't the Customs and Border Patrol mind?"

"What the CBP doesn't know won't hurt them."

"Okay."

"Meet us at noon tomorrow. My Mexican associates will be present, so, Dyson, don't embarrass me by keeping us waiting."

"Okay."

"When will you make your move on the remote vault?"

"Hmm? Vault?"

"I can read a blueprint, Dyson."

"A couple of days after I have the weapons. No more than that."

Brand motioned toward the thug at the rail. "I want my man going on the job with you," he said. "Canada is only a few miles away, and I don't want anyone getting lost."

I could have told him sure, why not. After all, there wasn't actually going to be a robbery. At noon the ATF was going to bust Brand and his Mexican associates, and by this time tomorrow night I was going to be explaining to Nina why I called

Shelby instead of her. If I was going to hit the remote vault, though, I wouldn't be doing it with Brand's armed thug standing somewhere behind me, so, keeping in character, I said, "No frickin' way."

"Oh?"

"He makes me nervous."

Brand leaned in and spoke softly. It was the first time he'd used an indoor tone of voice since I met him, and I have to confess to a ripple of anxiety that rolled up my spine.

"He should make you nervous, Dyson," Brand said. "Very nervous. He's a made man. You know what that means, don't you?"

"He pulled himself up by his own bootstraps? Oh, wait, that's a self-made man."

"You're a real funny guy, Dyson. Don't you think he's funny, Brian?"

"Smart mouth," Fenelon said.

"It's like my old man used to say, just because it's important doesn't mean it's serious," I said. "In a couple of days we're all going to be rich."

"I want to be there when you divide the take," Brand said. "Me and my man."

"Imagine that."

Brand displayed his empty hands again. "Until tomorrow, then," he said.

I left the booth without saying good-bye, lingered at the bar for the length of time it took Josie and me to down what remained of our drinks, and escorted her past the deputies outside to the Ford Taurus.

"What did Brand say?" she asked when we were safely inside the car and pulling out of the parking lot.

"We're on for tomorrow noon. A place called Crane Lake."

"I'm going with."

"No, you're not, Josie, and don't even think of arguing with me."

"You're not going alone, are you?"

"No. I'll take one person with me. Someone who knows the area."

"Who?"

FOURTEEN

"Why me?" the old man wanted to know. He had been asking the same question since we boarded the Jeep Cherokee that morning and started driving toward the tiny town of Orr, population 267—yes, I looked it up. Hell, he had been asking the question since I made my choice known the evening before. All the other Bandits had asked it as well, only the old man's voice was the loudest and most strident.

"Why not take someone else?" he asked. "Any of 'em, all of 'em be better use to you than me." His hands trembled—his entire body trembled—and I knew he was desperate for a beer or a joint. I made sure he had neither. "It don't make sense to bring me."

"Perfect sense," I said.

"I don't get it."

"Remember what you said when we were on the deck that one time? Take care of my JoEllen, you said. Take care of David. Take care of all of them. That's what I'm doing."

"How? How are you doin' that?"

"Think about it."

He did, for nearly thirty seconds. "Tell me, Dyson." His voice sounded desperate, and I decided it was better to have the conversation now instead of later—we were about five miles shy of Orr.

"What we're about to do—meeting with your pals like this—someone might get hurt," I said. "If that happens, I want it to be you."

"Me? My pals? What are you talking about? What did I do?"

"You're the rat."

I spoke the last word like it was an obscenity. The old man's eyes grew wide with the sound of it. His mouth fell open yet spoke no words.

"Did you think I wouldn't find out?" I asked.

He didn't have an answer for that.

"Anyone who was in the cabin Sunday could have told James and Williams to look for Josie and me out on Highway 1, could have tipped them to what we were planning. Truth be told, I suspected it was Claire. Turns out I was wrong about her. Well, at least wrong about that. Anyway, only you, Josie, Roy, and Jill could have told Brand that Roy and I would be out of the cabin checking on the remote vault—giving him plenty of time to settle in and wait for us Monday night, taking us by surprise when we arrived. I eliminated the others when I had Josie call and tell you we were stopping at Buckman's on our way back from the Cities. Deputies James and Williams pulling us over last night, telling us they knew exactly where we were going and that Brand was waiting for our arrival—that pretty much settled it."

"No, Dyson, please."

"Only one person knew our plans. Only one."

"Dyson . . ."

"That's why you're here, old man. If something goes wrong with your friends, I'm going to make sure it goes wrong for you, too."

"Stop saying that. They're not my friends."

"If you say so."

"You don't understand."

"I understand perfectly. James and Williams scared the hell outta you. Dying in prison—you hadn't actually thought about the possibility until they pulled you over, and I believe the idea really messed with your head. The thing is, though, the thing that pisses me off, is that you didn't take the hint. You didn't quit. You didn't ask the other Iron Range Bandits to quit, either. Yeah, you're afraid of prison. You're afraid of being poor, too, afraid of ending up like the friend you told me about. So you kept thieving until this job came along and you saw a way to get what you needed for yourself even if it cost the others. That's why you made a deal with the deputies and with Brand. If I'm mistaken, tell me."

"The others wouldn't have been hurt."

I flashed on Josie's encounter with Deputy Williams. "If you say so."

"Besides, you said it was okay to look out for yourself. On the deck, you said . . ."

For the first time since I arrived in the northland, I lost my temper.

"It's your family, you sonuvabitch," I shouted. "It's your son and daughter, your niece and nephew, and all the people they love. You take care of yourself only after you take care of them. What the hell is the matter with you?"

"I couldn't think of no other way."

"Then you didn't think hard enough."

"Dyson—"

"Don't talk anymore."

"You don't know what it's like getting old and havin' nothin'."

"I'm serious, old man. Not another word."

He didn't speak, but he made a lot of breathing sounds meant to convey the emotional anguish he was suffering. I ignored him the best I could until we pulled into the parking lot of Norman's One Stop and Motel off Highway 53. It was part motel, part Clark gas station—another business built to resemble a log cabin.

"I'll be right back," I said. "Stay here. Or leave. I don't care." I made a production out of removing the key from the ignition so he knew if he left he'd be doing it on foot. "Look, old man," I said—a parting shot. "I haven't said anything to your family, and I'm not going to. I'll leave it to you to decide what's best."

I left the Cherokee, walked inside Norman's One Stop, and was immediately surrounded by bait, tackle, sweatshirts, ball caps, automotive supplies, toiletries, soft drinks, and snacks. In the center of the snack area near the ceiling-high cooler was a metal patio table with a glass top surrounded by matching chairs, all white. Seated at the table were two men dressed as if they were refugees from a fishing camp. Despite their attire, though, you could tell they were city boys.

"How's the time?" I asked.

"You should be fine," Bullert said. "County Highway 23 is just down the road. Once you reach it, it should take no more than half an hour to get to the seaplane base. I just got word. The Mexicans landed five minutes ago."

"Are your people in place?"

"They are. On land and sea. Don't look for them, McKenzie."

"I know how it works."

While we spoke, the second man rose from his chair and began to unbutton my shirt. I wasn't offended. Instead, I spread my arms wide to give him ample room. He taped a green body bug about the size of an iPod to the side of my rib cage and ran the foot-long wire antenna up my back.

"It'll pick up sound from twenty feet away," the tech said.

"What about range?"

"Don't worry, McKenzie," Bullert said. "We'll hear you fine."

"If I'm frisked?"

"We'll come to your rescue."

"In the nick of time? Just like the cavalry?"

"Just like."

"I hope so."

Bullert patted my shoulder as I finished rebuttoning my shirt. "When this is over, drinks are on me."

"You better bring plenty of cash, then, because I'm going to be thirsty."

I glanced at my watch. 11:24. I took a deep breath and let half out slowly just like I was taught on the police academy firing range. "Ain't nothing to it but to do it," I said.

It wasn't much of a prayer, yet Bullert said "Amen" just the same.

The old man was waiting for me when I returned to the Jeep Cherokee. "I want to make this right," he said even before I climbed behind the steering wheel. "There's gotta be a way to make this right." His voice was filled with both pain and determination. He had missed his chance to behave like a human being and was now seeking redemption. "What can I do?"

"Exactly what I tell you when I tell you," I said, even though I knew he didn't have a chance; there would be no redemption. When the feds swooped down to grab up Brand and the

Mexicans, they were going to take him, too. I didn't like the idea very much, but better him than any of the others.

County Highway 23 was where Bullert said it would be. I followed it northeast until we reached Buyck, pronounced "bike" according to a sign just outside of town. We passed Vermilion River Tavern, which looked like a red barn with a large liquor sign attached, and the Pumpkin Shell Gift Shop, which looked like, well, a gift shop, before catching County Highway 24 heading north. A street sign conveniently labeled it Lake Crane Road. I said the name out loud. I also spoke the names of the Sportman Last Chance Café and Facowie Lodge as we passed them as well. Each time the old man looked at me, a confused expression on his face.

"Are you nervous, Dyson?"

"What makes you say that?"

"You're talking to yourself."

I thought about it for a few miles and decided, you know what, the old man's wrong, I'm not nervous.

How is that possible? my inner voice asked.

I guess I've been doing this sort of thing far too long, I told myself.

Scotts Seaplane Base was on County Road 425 just like the map said. I passed it just as Brand had said. I ignored the turn for Rocky Road and kept following 425 until we came to a narrow channel that looked is if someone had carved it out of the woods with a plow and left it at that. I announced my turn.

"What?" the old man asked.

"We're turning down the dirt road that leads to Brand's seaplane base," I said.

"I know that."

"Just wanted to see if you're paying attention."

We drove half a mile before coming to a clearing.

"Two men carrying automatic weapons flanking each side of the road," I said. "They look Hispanic."

"I see 'em," the old man said. I could barely hear him, though, over the sound of my inner voice.

Are you nervous now?

I stopped the Cherokee in the center of the clearing and shut down the engine.

"Deputies James and Williams are here," I said softly. "They're leaning against their cruiser on my left and looking bored. There's a Chevy Malibu parked next to them. It's empty. There's a wooden shack to the right about the size of a garage. Doors are open. Looks like barrels of aviation fuel inside. There's a Subaru Forester parked in front of me near the lakeshore. There's someone inside; I can't see who. A seaplane, single engine, white with a blue racing stripe, serial number N2-something is tied up at a long wooden dock. It looks like a six-seater, but what do I know? Brand and a Mexican gentleman are standing between the dock and the SUV. Fenelon is two paces behind them like a good little serving boy."

"What are you doing?" the old man said. "Dyson, what?"

"Something bothering you, old man?"

"You are."

"Really? I'd think you'd be more concerned about the guys with the machine guns."

I got out of the Cherokee, leaving the door open, and moved toward Brand and his companion. The old man did the same. The two Hispanics holding the road came up behind us until they were even with the back bumper of the car. I wasn't particularly concerned about them. After all, money wasn't changing hands.

"Hi, John," I said. "Who's your friend?"

Brand answered by pointing to a blue and white checkered picnic blanket spread out on the ground. Carefully arranged on top of the blanket were four Kevlar vests, three Avtomat Kalashnikova obraztsa 1947 assault rifles, eight loose magazines, two blasting caps, and what looked like a block of modeling clay. I stepped over to the blanket and inspected the merchandise like I knew what I was doing.

"It's all here," I said.

"We"—Brand nudged his companion—"didn't have Semtex 10. I hope C-4 will do."

I looked at the brilliant blue lake. In the distance I could see two speedboats racing toward us, the noise of their engines still out of range.

"Just fine," I said.

"One more thing."

Brand gestured toward the Subaru. The back door opened and his thug emerged. He was holding a handgun. He pulled a woman out after him. He pressed the muzzle of the gun against her temple. In that moment I felt as if my entire body were being squeezed though a hole way too small for it.

"Hold everything, hold everything." I was nearly screaming. "Just wait." I pivoted to face Brand. "He has a hostage," I spoke softly. "You've taken Jill as a hostage," I said loudly. "What the hell, Brand, you've taken a hostage?"

"You said no one would get hurt," the old man shouted. He was in tears. "You said my family would be all right. You promised. You promised." He sank to his knees. I stepped next to him and rested a hand on his shoulder. It gave me the opportunity to gaze back out on Crane Lake. The two speedboats had veered off.

"Thank you," I whispered.

"What?" the old man asked. "What are you saying?"

"I said I didn't like taking orders," Brand said. "From now on we're doing things my way."

I spun toward Jill again. Her hair was disheveled, and the thin, short, low-cut nightgown she was wearing was soiled, yet there didn't seem to be a mark on her from what I could see. She was trembling; I didn't know if it was from fear or cold. The way she moved her bare feet, it was probably both. I stepped to the picnic blanket, grabbed two ends, and yanked it off the ground. The weapons and the rest tumbled off and clattered onto the grass and dirt. I took the blanket and walked to where Jill was standing. The thug took a step backward as I approached. The gesture was more out of respect than fear. I wrapped the blanket around Jill's shoulders and helped her close it in front.

"They came in the morning," she said. "Roy wasn't there. Roy was at the cabin with you."

"I know. I'm sorry. Are you all right? Are you hurt?" I gave that last word all the meaning I could.

"They didn't hurt me—not like that." Jill's eyes flitted to the thug, then back to me. "He said they wouldn't hurt me—like that."

How gallant of him, my inner voice said.

"I'll get you out of this," I told her. "I'll get you back home. I promise."

Jill tried to smile, only she didn't do a very good job of it. "You did warn me, didn't you, Dyson? You said I should leave. Why didn't I listen?" She smiled again, still faintly.

"It's those damn butterflies," I said.

Jill smiled some more, but the tears forming in her eyes washed it away. "I'm so scared," she said.

I hugged her; she mashed her face against my chest. The shuddering of her body shook both of us. I found the thug's eyes. There were so many things I wanted to say to him. What came out was this: "From what I've seen, you're the only pro-fessional in the room. I'm holding you personally responsible for her safety."

"It's out of my hands," he said.

"What's that supposed to mean?"

"Dyson." Brand was calling to me, waving his hand that I should join him. I released Jill, and she bowed her head, rest-ing her chin against her chest. I cupped her face with my hands and kissed her forehead, just as I had wanted to do be-fore she went on the Silver Bay raid. Yet laughter and love, I couldn't promise that no matter how much I longed to.

"Soon," I said. "I'll take you home soon."

She didn't reply.

I moved toward where Brand was standing. The two Mex-icans were still in position behind the Jeep Cherokee. My eyes went from them to James and Williams. Williams was point-ing at me as if his finger were a gun. *Why are they here?* my inner voice wondered.

The old man was still kneeling on the ground. He had his head turned away as if he were afraid Jill would see him.

"Pick up the guns," I told him as I passed. "Put everything in the back of the Cherokee."

"Dyson." His voice was the squeak of chalk on a black-board.

"It is what it is, old man. Now do what I tell you."

I went up to Brand, stopping far enough away that I wouldn't be tempted to punch his smug face. It wasn't for his safety. It was for mine. Fenelon was still behind him. He spent a lot of time staring down at his shoes. My impression was that he was even more afraid than Jill was.

I tried hard to keep my emotions in check when I spoke. "You have very bad manners, Brand. Your mother ever tell you that?"

"Now we do things my way."

"So you said."

"When you pull the job my man goes with." Brand gestured with his chin toward the thug, and my inner voice told me, *That's what he meant by Jill's safety being out of his hands.* "He's going to be with you every second of the day until you get the money. Once you do, he'll tell you where to take it. Any questions?"

"What happens after you get the money?"

"You get the girl."

"Then we all go our separate ways and no hard feelings, right?"

Brand gestured again with his chin, this time pointing it at Deputies James and Williams. "Oh, I don't think you'll get far," he said.

So that's why they're here, my inner voice said.

"The arrangement seems a bit one-sided," I said aloud. "You get the money and I get the time."

"What's the matter, Dyson? Don't you think the girl's worth it? The old man said she was your favorite."

"She's my favorite because she's not an asshole or a bitch. You're both."

"Don't call me names, Dyson. I don't like it."

All the while we spoke, I regarded the Mexican standing next to Brand. He watched me watching him. I had seen the expression on his face before. It said he was more than willing to shoot me in the face and toss my body in the nearest ditch if I pushed him into it, otherwise he'd rather not be bothered. So why was he here? The answer came to me when I looked at Brand again.

The thug is his only muscle, my inner voice told me. *Probably he was more than enough until now. Fenelon doesn't count. The deputies, they're here just for show—no way they'd let Brand dirty their hands any more than he said. That's why he needs the Mexicans. If you can keep them involved, make sure they're at the exchange . . .*

I took a chance and asked the Mexican how much Brand had promised him. "Mire, amigo, ¿cuánto le prometió ese hijo de puta? ¿La mitad?"

Brand took a step backward so he could see us both at the same time. "What are you saying?" he wanted to know.

The Mexican paused before answering. "Sí, la mitad."

Half, my inner voice translated. *Brand promised him half.*

James and Williams were still leaning against their patrol car watching the scene as if it were a bad performance of Shakespeare in the Park. I used my thumb to point at them and told the Mexican that Brand had promised the deputies who allowed him to operate in their county the same thing. "La policía le permite a Brand hacer lo que quiere en este territorio. Él les prometió la mitad también."

"¿Ah sí?"

"Stop it," Brand said. "Speak English."

"¿A quién crees que él va a engañar?" I asked.

The Mexican gazed at the deputies and then studied Brand with an expression that asked the same question—which of them was Brand planning on screwing over?

"What the hell are you talking about?" Brand wanted to know.

"Sabes que él no se está metiendo en todo este lio por nada," I said.

"Pues claro que no," the Mexican replied, agreeing that Brand wasn't likely to be doing all this for free. I offered advice.

"Si yo fuera tú, yo me iría al lugar del cambio con todas las armas y hombres que tengas."

He nodded and smiled just a tiny bit as if to say that bringing all the men and guns he had to the exchange was a good idea. But he then suggested that trying to mess with him was most decidedly not. "Puede ser que los use contra ti."

"Todo lo que quiero es esa chica sana y salva sin ningún daño," I said. "Ustedes pueden resolver el resto por su cuenta."

"Está bien," the Mexican said, yet I wasn't sure if he actually believed that I didn't care what he and Brand did with the money as long as the girl was delivered safe and sound without a scratch on her—or if he cared one way or the other.

"Dammit, speak English," Brand said. He turned toward Fenelon. "What did they say?"

Fenelon seemed confused. "I don't know exactly."

"You speak Spanish."

"Not that good, you know that."

Brand turned his attention back to the Mexican. "I don't know what deal Dyson was trying to make with you . . ."

"No deal, hombre," the Mexican said. "He warned to make sure the girl she not be harmed."

"Brian?"

"That's what I got, what I could get," Fenelon said. "Dyson said if the girl was harmed, there would be, what's the word, consequences."

"Consequences, Dyson? Are you threatening me?"

"I'll be seeing you around, John," I said.

I turned my back on Brand so he wouldn't see me smile. Both the Mexican and Fenelon were on board—at least they seemed to be—which meant the chance of rescuing Jill just improved greatly. I moved toward the Jeep Cherokee. The two Mexican sentries were clutching their rifles like they were teddy bears—very unprofessional—while watching the old man load the last of the ordnance in the back. Behind me I could hear Brand talking quickly to the Mexican gunrunner.

"Dyson's got nothing," he said. "Nobody to help him. He's all talk."

My only fear was that I overplayed my hand, that Brand would hurt Jill just to prove that he could. I tried to shake the thought from my head, but it held on too tightly.

"Get in the car," I told the old man.

He did. At the same time, Brand's thug helped Jill into the backseat of the Subaru. From where I was standing it looked like he was being gentle about it.

"You coming?" I asked.

The thug waved Fenelon over and whispered something into his ear. A moment later he walked purposely to the Jeep Cherokee, opened the back door, and slid inside. He didn't say a word.

I turned my attention back to Brand. He was speaking earnestly with the Mexican gunrunner, who seemed to be hanging onto his every syllable.

"Tomorrow," I said. "We'll pull the job tomorrow. I'll have the cash in hand by tomorrow night."

"See that you do," Brand said.

He was smirking. I refused to let it annoy me. There were so many better reasons for wanting to kill him.

I turned the Cherokee and drove down the makeshift road until we hit 425 and started backtracking toward Orr. The old man kept turning his head to look at the thug in the backseat. He wanted to talk but was afraid of being overheard. Finally he just came out with it.

"What are we going to do?" he asked.

"We're going to do what we always planned on doing," I said. "Rob the remote vault near Lake Vermilion."

"Then what?"

"Then take the money to Brand and his Mexican gunrunners and ransom Jillian."

"Just like that?" The old man was speaking, yet in the back of my mind I could see Chad Bullert. It was to him that I was actually communicating—God help us if he didn't understand what I was saying.

"This time there won't be any surprises," I said. "I'll take care of Jill, and everybody else can do what comes natural."

"I hope you know what you're doing."

"If everyone does what they're supposed to, there shouldn't be any problems." I angled my head so I could see the thug in the rearview mirror. "You got a name?"

"Daniel."

"Anyone ever call you Danny or Dann-o?"

"No."

"How did a guy like you end up in a place like this?"

"Circumstances beyond my control."

"Boy, does that sound familiar. I don't suppose you want to tell me where we're going to take the money after we steal it."

"No."

"I could make you."

"I doubt it. Anyway, it would take more time than you have."

"You're probably right. Well, in that case, Dann-o, strap on your sneakers."

Daniel grimaced at the modification of his name, which was fine with me. I wasn't talking to him anyway.

We were nearly back at Orr before the old man asked the inevitable question. "What'll we do first?"

"First, we're going to Norman's One Stop and Motel so I can take a leak," I said. I parked in the same spot as earlier that morning and shut down the Cherokee. "I'll be right back."

"I'm going with you," Daniel said.

"What? Are you my new potty pal?"

Daniel shook his head as if he had now heard everything and was disappointed by the achievement.

I pointed at the old man. "What about him?"

"I stay with you."

"It's going to be a long couple of days."

I left the Cherokee. Daniel followed. He paused only long enough to tell the old man not to do anything stupid. We entered the building, found a door in the back with a sign that read MEN, and went inside. There were two urinals and one stall. I moved to the stall, paused, said, "This is where I draw the line, Daniel," went inside and locked the door.

I didn't actually need to use the toilet, yet I went through the motions just the same. Once I was sitting down, I slowly pulled the body bug off of my ribs—I didn't know what kind of tape the ATF's tech agent used; whatever it was it hurt like crazy coming off. I hoped Daniel would attribute whatever noise I made to something else. After removing the bug, I wrapped it in paper and set it behind the base of the toilet. I would have preferred to keep the bug, but I was afraid that Daniel might discover it—God knows what fresh hell that would bring. I could only hope that Bullert and the badge boys understood the references I had made earlier and would act accordingly.

I put myself back together, flushed the toilet for dramatic effect, and stepped out of the stall. Daniel was leaning against the far wall, his arms folded across his chest and staring at his reflection, a pensive expression on his face. I've seen him before—hell, I've *been* him before—the man looking in the mirror wondering who the hell it was looking back. I went to the sink and washed my hands.

"Just out of curiosity, what did you tell Fenelon back there before we left?" I asked.

"I told him that if anything happens to the girl, it had better happen to him first."

I pulled a couple of paper towels from the dispenser and dried my hands. "You like her, too," I said.

"You should never have involved her in your schemes."

"Oh, I didn't. It was her nitwit husband."

Daniel moved his hand to the side of his face where Roy had clipped him with the handgun, and for the first time I realized that there wasn't a mark on him.

"I think I met her husband," Daniel said.

"Is there going to be a problem about that?"

"Not unless he causes it."

"Roy's a hotheaded fellow. But I need him in one piece."

"It's like you said before—I'm a professional."

"Daniel, I think we're going to get along just fine."

"I wouldn't bet my life on it if I were you."

The Iron Range Bandits didn't take the news well. There was plenty of weeping and shouting and angry sounds that reminded me of those days when I was a cop knocking on doors late at night to tell bewildered parents about their children. The language they used—the Bandits didn't say anything that you couldn't hear on HBO, yet I found the words truly shocking coming from them. Roy wanted to throw down on Daniel right then and there; Skarda and Jimmy wanted to help—I had to step between them and stay between them for the longest time. It took a lot of talking, a lot of promises, to calm the group, especially Josie, who reminded me more than once that I had claimed there would be nothing to fear until after the job, until after we had the money. I apologized profusely for the mistake, yet that did little to assuage her rage. The old man did his best to help. He kept telling Roy, told anyone who would listen, that Jill hadn't been hurt. He repeated the words like a mantra—"She's all right, she's all right." I suspected he was talking mostly to himself.

What genuinely impressed me was that no one wanted out; that every one of them wanted to help bring Jill home safely, including Claire.

"What can I do?" she asked.

"I bet you look sensational in a bikini," I said.

Claire's eyes fell on Jimmy. "So I have been told." He smiled broadly despite the context of the remark.

I pointed at Liz. "You, too."

Liz turned her eyes on Skarda, who wasn't smiling at all.

"What do you have in mind, Dyson?" Josie asked.

I led them all onto the redwood deck and pointed at the pontoon boat. "Do we have a trailer for this?"

Josie answered slowly. "The stockbroker has one in the shed out back. Why?"

"How 'bout an ATV?"

"I have one," Skarda said.

"Me, too," said Roy.

"All right," I said. "Now listen carefully. I'm going to tell you exactly what we're going to do and exactly how we're going to do it. We'll go over the plan again and again and again for the rest of the day and into the night so everyone will know what's expected of them. I don't want to hear any noes or maybes. If we're going to pull this off it's going to be yes all the time. Yes?"

There were a few spoken yeses in reply and the nodding of heads. If I were a basketball coach I would have repeated the question with the hope of a more boisterous response, except what I was planning could not remotely be considered fun and games.

Roy threw a thumb at Daniel. "What about him?" he asked.

"He gets to watch," I said.

"That's bullshit."

"Nonetheless."

"We're going to do all the work, take all the risks, for what? So that he can take the money? So he can rape my wife?"

I stepped in front of Roy just in time to keep him from attacking Daniel again. For his part, Daniel didn't move a muscle, not to defend himself, not to get out of the way. Instead, he spoke softly to Roy.

"We want the money," he said. "Make no mistake. As for your wife, taking her wasn't my idea, although I went along with it. I have since made it plain, however, to Brand and the others, that I will kill anyone who touches her."

That quieted the deck considerably. While the threat wasn't particularly original—Roy, after all, had been saying pretty much the same thing most of the afternoon—the Bandits were obviously impressed by the sincerity with which it was expressed. If I seemed less dumbfounded than the others it was probably because I had determined earlier that Daniel was a lifelong bachelor like myself, and us bachelors, damn if we don't fall in love easily.

FIFTEEN

It was a pretty day. A clear blue sky, gentle wind, and if you breathed deeply, the sweet scent of pine and fir trees, an aroma that you only get in the North Woods. We were parked on Fourteenth Avenue and East Conan Street not too far from the Dairy Queen, although in Ely, you're never too far from anything. The FOR SALE sign in front of the house gave me a nervous start at first but made perfect sense once I had time to think about it.

I kept glancing at Skarda's watch strapped to my wrist and thinking disagreeable thoughts. So many things could go wrong. Start with the sight of four guys sitting in a Jeep Cherokee on a residential side street with the windows rolled down, just begging for someone to stroll up and ask, "What's going on?" Or a deputy on a routine patrol through the neighborhood—that would be perfect, just perfect.

Is she late, my inner voice asked, *or are you early?*

I silently reviewed the schedule of comings and goings I had noted while Roy and I were watching the remote vault, even though I had gone over it ad nauseam the evening before.

The employees left the vault at about 2:15 P.M., not long after the third armored truck departed on its daily run. They were back in place at 6:00 P.M., approximately one half hour before the first and second armored trucks returned from their routes. That gave them a three-hour-plus window to do what—eat, go to the movies, go fishing, do their laundry, shack up in one of the motels along Highway 1?

I glanced at the watch face again: 2:58 P.M. with the vault only thirty minutes away if you obeyed all the traffic signs.

She is late, my inner voice said again. *Or you're in the wrong spot.*

Helluva time for second-guessing, I told myself, yet that's exactly what I was doing, reexamining in my head the sheaf of papers that I had obtained from Shelby. *The report with the paper clip in the center is the one you want,* she had said. I didn't even bother to look at the others. There was no need. I recognized the woman by her driver's license photo. Or did I?

Stop it.

I have been known to not always consider the consequences of my actions, only now I couldn't afford mistakes, none; not with Daniel studying my every move. He hadn't displayed any special interest in what I was doing—didn't so much as grunt back at the cabin when I pulled the cheap sneakers out from under the sofa and put them on—he just watched. He seemed to blink only once in a while and kind of deliberately, like an owl. I was amazed I was able to sneak out of the cabin last night and back in again without waking him. He was sitting next to me now in the Cherokee, his hands resting in his lap, perfectly relaxed. Jimmy and Roy in the backseat, not so much.

"How long are we going to sit here?" Jimmy wanted to know.

"As long as it takes," I said.

"How long is that?"

"Is this the right house?" Roy asked. "It looks kind of abandoned to me. The grass needs mowing."

"We should change the plan," Jimmy said. "I never liked the plan. I still think my idea was better."

"I like the plan," Roy said. "On the other hand, just sitting here . . ."

"How 'bout from now on no one speaks unless something actually goes wrong," I said, "and not even then."

"How much time will we have in the vault again?" Jimmy asked.

"That's what I mean."

"How much?"

"According to MapQuest, it's exactly 24.08 miles from the sheriff's department substation in Ely to the mouth of the dirt road. Get the call, get the car, get out of the city onto the highway, estimate a top speed of eighty miles per hour—think a nineteen-minute response time. Probably it's longer. Even so, we'll go with fifteen minutes. The road itself is 1.8 miles long. The average jogger will cover six miles per hour. The cops won't be jogging, though. Not with equipment, not when approaching a possible hostage-barricade situation. Their first move will be to locate and contain unless shots are fired, and we won't be shooting anyone, right? Right?"

"Right," Jimmy said. Roy mumbled something. Daniel didn't say a word.

"It's possible the cops'll camp out on the road and wait for backup, except we won't make that assumption. Instead, we're betting they'll be walking carefully up the road at approximately three miles per hour. That's another forty minutes, call it thirty to be on the safe side. We should have forty-five minutes from the moment the alarm is triggered. I plan to get in and out in half that time."

"You could have just said so," Roy told me.

"I didn't want you to think I was making this up as I went along."

"Wait a sec," Jimmy said. "Why would the police walk up the road? Why wouldn't they drive?"

I glanced at him through my rearview mirror. "Were you paying any attention at all last night?"

I repeated my admonishment that everyone should keep quiet, yet I couldn't shut up myself. Nerves, I guess. After a few moments I said, "An old piece of verse I learned in high school keeps repeating in my head. Worse than a song you can't get rid of."

"What?" Roy asked.

"Beware the Jabberwock, my son! The jaws that bite, the claws that catch!"

Daniel's smile seemed positively joyful, yet it came and went so quickly that it was almost as if it had never appeared at all.

"Shun the frumious Bandersnatch," he said.

"Words of wisdom," I told him.

"What are you talking about?" Jimmy wanted to know.

I didn't answer. Instead, I kept reviewing the plan in my head. So many details. I wanted more time, yet I could not leave Jill in Brand's hands for another night—I just couldn't. I made as many of the preparations myself as I was able, partly because it was easier than explaining it all to the others and partly to convince myself everything was done correctly. But mostly I did it because I needed to keep busy and not think too much. I was the one who put Jill in the jackpot. I could blame Bullert and the ATF all I wanted—and I did—yet I was the architect of this insanity and no one else. Jill was in danger because I wanted to play junior G-man, and the realization tied my stomach in knots. The nonstop work was because I was afraid that if I remained still even for a few minutes my growing anxiety would infect the others.

In between tasks I had briefed the Bandits relentlessly.

"Probably there will be complications," I told them.

"What complications?" Josie had asked.

"I don't know yet. That's why they're called complications. Otherwise they'd be problems, and those we can solve ahead of time."

That hadn't seemed to fill anyone with confidence. As it was, the last thing Josie said that morning before I sent her off was, "Should I be afraid now?"

"Probably," I told her.

She had hugged me and kissed my cheek, and for a brief moment I told myself, if we get out of this alive . . .

And then the woman we had been waiting for drove up the street.

"Here we go," I said.

She slowed as she approached the house, turned into the driveway, and stopped parallel to the side door. She got out of the car, pulling a large purse with her that she draped over her shoulder. Her long hair was dark, nearly black though not quite, and she wrapped it in one of those god-awful scrunchies to keep it out of her face. She was dressed as if she expected to spend the day working in her garden. She opened the trunk and heaved out two bulging paper grocery bags by the handles. After closing the trunk with her elbow, she carried the bags to the door, fumbled briefly with her keys, unlocked the door, and stepped inside the house, leaving the door open behind her.

Clever girl, my inner voice said.

"Stay here," I said. I opened the door to the Jeep Cherokee and stepped out. Daniel ignored the command and followed me. I didn't ask if maybe he wasn't being just a tad anal retentive in his compliance with Brand's orders—I didn't have the time. Instead, we crossed the street and the woman's lawn in a hurry, pulling on black ski masks as we went. I met the woman at the door. She was coming out just as I was going in. I grasped her throat with one hand and shoved backward. My other hand I filled with the bartender's SIG Sauer. I pushed the woman inside the house, pinning her against a kitchen wall. The way she gripped my wrists and fought to pull my hand away, you'd have thought I was trying to strangle her. I loosened my fingers on her throat, yet she gasped for breath just the same. I pointed the gun at her face.

"Where are your children, Ms. Rooney?"

Her eyes were large and fearful. Her voice was like the loud whisper of a stage actress. "Children?" she asked.

"Where are they?"

"At, at their grandmother's."

"Do they always stay there while you're at work?"

"Yes. Yes, I see them . . . see them . . . after."

"Do you love your children?"

"My children, yes, I love—my children—what are . . ."

"Your children are perfectly safe, Ms. Rooney. Do you want to see them again?"

"What are you saying? What do you want?"

"Do you want to see them grow up?"

"Please . . ."

"You must do as I say, Ms. Rooney."

"Don't hurt me. Please . . ."

"I will not hurt you. I will not hurt your children. Everything will be fine if you do exactly what I say. Do you understand?"

"I don't understand anything."

I tightened my fingers slightly. Rooney pulled her head up

and away as if the pressure were too much. The words came out of her mouth as if she were speaking them with her last breath.

"I'll do what you say. Anything. Please don't hurt me."

Daniel was standing inside the kitchen doorway and watching. I could see his eyes through the slits in the mask. They seemed flat and without emotion.

"Park the Cherokee in the driveway," I told him. "Bring the others in. Remember, no names."

He continued to watch me.

"What?" I said.

He turned and hurried out of the door. I released the woman's throat. She brought her hands up and massaged her neck.

"That hurt," she said.

There was much I wanted to tell her; even more that I wanted to ask. I didn't get the chance. As I led Rooney into the living room I heard movement in the kitchen—Daniel must have waved Roy and Jimmy into the driveway instead of crossing over to the Cherokee as I had hoped. I quickly became Nick Dyson again.

"I won't tell you not to worry, Ms. Rooney," I said. "There's plenty to worry about. Do what I tell you when I tell you and you'll be all right. You'll be back with your children in no time. Do you understand?"

Rooney settled into a stuffed chair and held her face in her hand.

"I understand," she said.

Time moves slowly when you're not having fun. Jimmy and Roy spent most of it arguing. Twice I was forced to intervene. Daniel sat quietly until an idea crept into his head that prompted him to explore the other rooms. When he returned, he stood in front of Rooney's chair and looked down at her.

"There aren't any personal possessions in the house, Ms. Rooney." he said. "Are you sure you live here?"

"I live with my mother," Rooney answered. "Me and my girls. I've been trying to sell the house since my divorce, only I can't get any takers. I would have moved my furniture out, but the real estate agent says it's easier to sell the house if it's furnished, if it looks like someone lives there. I only come around to make sure it's okay or when I'm—"

"When you're what?"

"Entertaining."

"You're not here every day, then?"

"No."

Daniel believed her. Hell, I believed her and I knew better. Daniel shook his head at me.

"You're so lucky," he said.

I quoted Branch Rickey, the baseball man who gave Jackie Robinson his chance: "Luck is the residue of design and desire."

"Yeah, right."

5:30 P.M. by Skarda's watch. "It's time," I said. I gestured at Rooney to stand, gave her an index card on which I wrote specific instructions, and told her to read it aloud. I made her do it three times. Afterward, I had her retrieve her cell phone and key the loudspeaker.

"Now call your boss," I said.

He answered in the middle of the fourth ring.

"Jer, this is Carolyn Rooney . . ."

"Hi, Carrie."

"Hi. I'm having trouble with my car . . ."

"What kind of trouble?"

Rooney was looking into my eyes when she said, "I have no idea."

"Do you need a ride?"

"No, Jer. I have a friend who's going to loan me his car. I'm going to be late, though—might not arrive until after seven. I'll try to get there sooner . . ."

"That's okay, Carrie. Don't worry about it. Describe the car and I'll pass it along to security."

"It's a Jeep Cherokee." Rooney read the color and license plate number directly from the card.

"Okay," Jer said. "We'll see you when we see you."

Rooney deactivated her cell. "Now what?" she asked.

6:11 P.M. and the cell phone I had borrowed from Jimmy was pressed against my ear. The Cherokee was parked on a side street just outside of Tower, Rooney behind the wheel. I was scrunched down on the passenger-side floor. I was wearing the black mask, black gloves, and Kevlar vest and cradling an AK-47 and was uncomfortable as hell. Daniel and Roy were on the floor of the backseat and fared no better. Jimmy, lying in the cargo area, probably had the worst of it, but then he was also holding a bomb.

"Hey," Jimmy said. I told him he didn't need to whisper. He kept doing it anyway. "How much longer?" I didn't answer. "Hey?" At least he remembered not to use my name.

"Not long," I said.

"You said that ten minutes ago." When I didn't respond he added, "We should have taken my car. It's bigger."

"Do you really want to leave your car at the scene of the crime?" I asked.

"Oh. Yeah." A few more minutes passed, and Jimmy asked, "Is it going to take much longer?"

Rooney gripped the steering wheel and stared straight ahead, trying hard to keep her face blank, yet her eyes wondered where the hell I found these guys.

"Would someone please shoot the kid," I said.

"If I could I would," Roy told me. "I can't even turn my head, much less point the rifle."

"Dyson." This time it was Dave Skarda speaking. He sounded excited over the cell phone.

"Talk to me," I said.

"Truck A has arrived."

"Good."

"It's way early. Do you want me to—"

"No. Just sit there and do what we talked about."

"Are you sure?"

"Yes."

"You're the boss."

Since when? my inner voice asked.

After the exchange, Rooney shook her head and spoke in a frightened single-mother voice. "You are never going to get away with this," she said.

"You are such a pessimist," I told her. "How do you even make it through the day?"

6:37 P.M. and Skarda morphed from excited to panicky.

"The second truck," he said over the cell. "Truck B. It stopped. It was turning into—and then it stopped. It's parked on the side of the highway. What are we going to do?"

"Wait," I said.

"Wait? You don't understand, the truck—okay, okay. The first truck is coming down the road, it's—okay. I get it. The second truck is waiting for the first truck to get out of the way because the road isn't wide enough for both of them. The first

(274)

truck—okay, the first truck has left, and the second truck . . ."
Skarda took a deep breath and exhaled slowly. "The second
truck is on its way. Wow. Is this what you meant by complications?"

I didn't know what to say to the man, so I said nothing.

7:02 P.M. and Skarda was now downright apoplectic. "Oh no,
oh no, oh no," he kept chanting.

"What?" I said.

"The third truck is early. It's heading up the road. The second truck—Dyson, the second truck hasn't left yet."

"It's okay."

"But Dyson?"

I glanced at my watch. If I had calculated correctly—
always an iffy proposition—we were seven minutes away from
the road. I tapped Rooney on the leg. "Let's go," I said.

"Go where?" Skarda wanted to know.

"Not you. You stay put. Watch the road."

Rooney started the Cherokee, slipped it into gear, and
accelerated down Highway 1. She had the look of someone driving to the dentist who already knew she needed a root canal.

"Hey," I said into the cell. "*This* is what I meant by complications."

7:05 P.M. "Dyson, where are you?" Skarda asked.

"What now?"

"The second truck just left. It just pulled out onto the highway. You should be passing it any second."

I couldn't help but breathe a sigh of relief. Along with the
three vault guards, an armored truck crew would be hard
enough to deal with. Two crews might have been one too many.

You are lucky, my inner voice told me.

Now, if it would only hold for a few more hours.

"We're almost there," I said.

"I see you," Skarda replied.

"Are you ready?"

"Yes."

"Don't follow too close, but . . ."

"I know. Don't follow too far behind, either."

7:10 P.M. and Rooney deftly turned the Cherokee onto the dirt road. I made her halt when we reached the huge tree that Josie and I had spotted when we first found the vault. "Pop the cargo door," I said, and she did. I jumped out of the car. My muscles ached from the uncomfortable way I had been sitting, yet I tried to ignore the pain. I circled the Cherokee to the back. Jimmy wanted to slide out of the cargo area. I told him to stay put. I rested the AK against the back bumper. Jimmy handed me the bomb. He seemed glad to be rid of it.

Late last night I had cut a hole into the frame of a cell phone, exposing its vibrator. I mounted the cell to a thin wooden board along with two metal screws, four double-A batteries, and half a block of C-4, approximately ten ounces. I ran two thin wires from the cell's vibrator, connecting one to each of the two screws. I connected the top screw to the batteries using a crocodile clip. I used other crocodile clips to connect the batteries and the bottom screw to the blasting cap that I had inserted into the C-4. Actually, I did that last bit after I nailed the bomb to the base of the tree—I mean, I'm not an idiot—and activated the cell phone.

I had built two bombs. When Skarda asked why, I told him it was in case the first didn't work. He suggested that if the bombs were identical and the first didn't explode, the second would be a dud, too. I told him to go away, he was bothering me.

After setting the IED, I locked Jimmy in the cargo area, retrieved my rifle, and squeezed back onto the floor of the Cherokee. I told Rooney to keep driving. I hadn't seen Skarda, but then, I hadn't expected to.

7:13 P.M. The Cherokee reached the unmanned gate. Rooney leaned out the window and punched the password into the keypad. The arm rose, and she drove under it, following the driveway. I took a chance and lifted my head just high enough to see over the dashboard. The armored truck was nowhere in sight, and I presumed it had driven inside the vault.

According to the blueprint Brand had stolen for me, the vault had only one bandit trap. The truck would enter through the garage door and wait. The outside garage door would close and the interior door would open. The truck would proceed into the center of the vault, where it would be unloaded and then loaded again. We would be facing the truck when we went through the gray metal employee door. The closed-circuit TV monitors and communications equipment would be arrayed against the wall to our right as we entered and manned by one guard. Cafeteria-style tables should be arranged along the near and far walls to our left. There was a platform built for a guard to stand on where he could observe the tables. There were also more cameras inside than outside—apparently Mesabi Security had a greater fear of theft by their employees then they had of an outside attack. The third guard didn't have a designated spot. I was guessing he probably wandered around the huge room or possibly kept a close eye on the armored truck crews.

When I reviewed the blueprints, it seemed to me that three

guards were not nearly enough. I wondered if the people who had built the vault thought that its location alone, so far off the beaten path, would be enough to protect it or if they had adopted that theory over a period of time. They must have had a guard stationed in the gatehouse when the place was originally constructed—why else build it? It was entirely possible, of course, that Mesabi was scamming both its clients and insurance company, showing them a well-staffed vault in order to gain business and guarantee coverage and then trimming bodies when they weren't looking. After all, it was a down economy, and a large workforce cut into profits.

I told the woman to park close to the employee entrance. When she shut off the car I said, "The money is insured, Ms. Rooney."

"I know."

"This can be a story you'll tell your children and your grandchildren or it can be a story that someone else tells your children and grandchildren. You decide."

She looked down at me. Her eyes were cold. Her voice was colder. "You're a sonuvabitch."

I came *this*close to calling it off. Screw Bullert, screw 'em all. But Jill, her lovely face, her warm smile—promises were made, some I spoke out loud, others that I had kept to myself . . .

"Everyone ready?" I didn't wait for a reply. "Okay."

7:15 P.M. Rooney left the Jeep Cherokee. She moved to the metal employee door and punched a code into the keypad next to it. She waited a moment, her hand gripping the door handle. There was a click loud enough to be heard inside the Cherokee. I opened my door just as Rooney opened hers. She hesitated just long enough for me to cover the distance between the SUV and her. I grabbed the edge of the door, flung it open, and pushed Rooney inside, pushed her harder than I probably should have. She stumbled and fell to her knees. I stood over her sighting down the barrel of the AK-47, sweeping it from one guard to the next.

"This is a stickup," I shouted. "Don't anyone move."

The words sounded so damn silly to me that I nearly laughed. No one else seemed to feel that way, though, especially the armored truck crew directly in front of me, standing next to their vehicle, drinking coffee from cardboard cups. They stared as if someone had kicked in the bathroom door, their expressions a mixture of anger and embarrassment.

Daniel, Roy, and Jimmy quickly filed in behind me. They were also wearing masks, gloves, and Kevlar and carrying the AKs Brand supplied, although Roy had his own. Roy went right and Jimmy went left. Roy leveled his rifle at the guard manning the TV monitors while Jimmy pointed his at the guard standing on top of the platform overlooking the cafeteria tables. There were several piles of cash on top of the tables, some of them neat and others not so much. A bank employee stood next to each.

"Raise your hands," Roy shouted. Jimmy yelled the same thing. The bank employees did what they were told. The vault guards already had their hands up, and I could only hope that no one noticed it but me. One of the armored truck crew let his hand fall dangerously close to his sidearm.

"I have a machine gun and a bulletproof vest," I shouted at him. "What do you have?"

His hands went up.

Daniel stepped behind me. "A little help," I told him. He went first to the armored truck crew and then the vault guards, disarming each one by one while Jimmy and I kept them covered. When he finished and stepped back, I reached down, took Rooney by the arm, and helped her to her feet. "Sorry," I muttered. She didn't reply. "Everyone over there." I gave Rooney a shove toward the far wall. Daniel, Jimmy, and I herded the rest of the building's occupants behind her. Jimmy took his position on the platform above the tables and watched them intently, the butt of his rifle pressed against his shoulder.

I was surprised by how quiet everyone was. There was none of the screaming you often hear in TV robberies, none of the threats and warnings, although one woman was weeping uncontrollably while another offered comfort, and I knew it was a sound that would stay with me for some time to come.

I turned my attention to the guard sitting in front of the monitors. Roy had disarmed him and was now giving him a good look at the AK as if he had done this sort of thing before.

"You know he must have hit a silent alarm," Roy said.

"I know. Where's our friend?"

Roy gestured toward the monitors. Looking from one to another I was able to follow Skarda's progress as he drove an ATV along the outside of the fence, circling the vault until he reached the area near the abandoned road Roy and I had found earlier. He hopped off the vehicle and started cutting a hole in the fence large enough to drive through.

I went to my watch. 7:19 P.M. I pulled the phone out of my pocket and dialed the number of the cell I had fastened to the tree. The cell was set to vibrate. The vibrator sent a low-amp charge through the wires that was boosted by the double-A batteries. It provided enough energy to trigger the blasting cap that set off the C-4. I heard the explosion through the walls of the vault, and in my mind's eye I could picture the huge tree falling across the dirt road, effectively blocking all motorized traffic.

A moment later I forced the guard to join the others at the cafeteria tables. I asked Roy to remain where he was.

"I don't expect trouble," I said. "Keep an eye on the monitors just the same. Let me know once our friend cuts through."

Daniel was standing between the captives and me. His head swiveled from one to the other, although he seemed most interested in what I was doing. I gestured for him to join me. We moved around the armored truck. The back door was open. Inside were two thick canvas bags big enough to hold a hockey player's equipment. Daniel hopped inside the truck and tried to lift a bag by the handle. He managed it, but it required both hands and a grunt.

"Damn thing must weigh eighty pounds," he said.

"I certainly hope so."

"What's that supposed to mean?"

"A bill weighs about one gram. There are four hundred and fifty-four grams in a pound. Obviously, the heavier the bags, the more cash they contain."

"Let's hope they're not all ones and fives."

"Or nickels and quarters from the casino's slot machines. Leave the bags for now. Come with me."

If Daniel disliked the way I ordered him about, he didn't show it. Instead, he followed me from the truck to the cafeteria tables. A bag identical to the two in the armored truck sat open near the platform. I turned to our prisoners. They were standing in a line against the wall. We hadn't put them in a line; it just worked out that way.

"Which one of you is Jer?" I asked. A middle-aged man reluctantly stepped forward. "Are you Jer?" He nodded. I pointed at the woman standing next to him. "Ms. Rooney." She stepped forward. "Both of you come here."

The couple moved across the vault. They were not happy to be singled out. I handed the bag to Jer.

"Fill it up," I told him.

"You're never going to get away with this," Jer said.

"So I've been told."

Jer and Rooney moved to the head of the first row of cafeteria tables, set the bag on top, and started filling it with the piles of cash, pulling the bag along the tables as they went. Jimmy kept turning his head to watch, and I had to warn him—twice—to remember where we were and what we were doing. After finishing with the first row of tables, Jer and Rooney carried the bag to the second row—it took both of them.

Roy called to me from the monitors. "The fence is down."

Jer and Rooney finished packing the bag with cash. I told them to seal it and carry the bag to the employee door—I didn't want to bother with the bandit trap. It took a lot of effort; Rooney's end sagged more than Jer's.

"Where is he?" I called.

"He's at the door," Roy answered.

"Okay. You and your friend grab the bags off the truck and bring them here." Roy and Daniel did what I asked, carrying the money bags over their shoulders like they were sacks of cement. Roy muttered something under his breath that I didn't hear. Whatever it was didn't seem to faze Daniel one bit.

I told Jer to open the door.

"The alarm will sound," he said.

"I think we're past worrying about that."

Jer opened the door and the tocsin went off—it sounded like one of those high-pitched horns the National Weather Center uses to warn people about tornadoes. Rooney covered her ears, so she probably didn't hear me when I said, "We're having some fun now, aren't we?"

I shouted at Jer, "We'll be leaving now. If this or any other door opens before we're gone, I'll assume it's because you're trying to stop us, in which case I'll spray the place with machine-gun fire. It's not your job to catch us. Let the cops do it. Understand?" He nodded. "Tell the others."

I shooed Jer back against the wall but kept Rooney near me as Roy and Daniel carried the heavy sacks of cash out the door and loaded them onto the ATV. When they finished I waved Jimmy off the platform and through the door. Once he was outside, I spoke into Rooney's ear.

"I'm sorry about all this, I really am. I didn't know what else to do." Her nod told me that she heard. "For the record, I think you're much prettier as a brunette than a blonde. Although . . ."

"Yeah?"

"I'd pay real money to see you in the short skirt and high heels you wore when you got me away from the sheriff's deputy."

"Luck," she said.

7:27 P.M. I insisted that Skarda drive slowly. I told the boys we had plenty of time, although they didn't seem to believe me. I was just as anxious as they were, yet the cautionary admonishment of my high school baseball coach kept echoing in my head—"Hurry, but don't rush"—although he was speaking about something else entirely.

We circled the building and headed for the hole Skarda had cut in the fence. Jimmy wanted to remove his mask. I told him to wait until we reached the creek. Roy walked backward, sweeping the open ground with his assault rifle, covering our rear like he had been trained. I used the cell to contact Josie. She answered in the middle of the first ring.

"Are you there?" I asked.

"Yes."

"We're on our way."

She wanted to say more, yet I ended the call before she could. It was no time for chitchat. We reached the hole in the fence and maneuvered the ATV through it and down the abandoned road. The vehicle hopped and skipped across the uneven terrain, and a couple of times I thought the money bags would slide off the back. Finally we approached the pontoon boat. The bow was up against the shore; the seat cushions had been removed, and all of the lockers were open. Three women, a brunette, redhead, and blonde, stood waiting for us at the bow all dressed in swimsuits—Josie in a one-piece and Claire and Liz in bikinis—and my inner voice said, *Minnesota girls, don't you just love them?*

We drove the ATV to the water's edge. Jimmy and Skarda hopped onto the pontoon. Daniel and I grabbed the sacks of money and heaved them aboard while Roy covered the trail. Jimmy and Skarda dragged the sacks into the center of the pontoon. They opened the bags and, with help from the girls, stashed the cash in the lockers. "Oh my God, look at all of this," Claire said. She was the only person who spoke.

I boarded the pontoon, went to the wheel, and started the engine. I called to Roy. He jumped onto the boat and stood at the bow while continuing to watch the trail. Skarda and Daniel pushed us off the shore and hopped on. I maneuvered the pontoon around and headed up the narrow channel toward Pike Bay and sprawling Lake Vermilion beyond. The Bandits finished storing away the money, closed the lockers, and returned the cushions to their proper places by the time we reached the mouth of the channel.

Another glance at the watch. 7:41 P.M. If we were lucky, the cops hadn't even arrived at the vault yet.

I stripped off the mask, gloves, and Kevlar vest and tossed them overboard along with the AK-47. Jimmy and Daniel did the same, adding the now empty money bags. Roy wanted to keep his weapon.

"We'll need it when we go to free Jill," he said. I told him I had it covered. He didn't believe me. Daniel snatched the rifle from Roy's grasp and flung it into the lake. Roy wanted to fight Daniel over that. Daniel wouldn't let him. He moved to the stern of the pontoon and sat on the back wall just above the motor while the others tried to calm down Roy.

I had expected the Bandits to be more excited by what we had just accomplished, yet Roy's outburst made it clear to me why they weren't. They hadn't just become rich off a daring raid on a remote vault. All they did was steal the ransom money they needed to buy back their wife, their sister, their cousin, their friend. They were still afraid.

As well they should be, my inner voice said.

I glanced at my watch again. 7:44 P.M. with about an hour and twenty minutes of sunlight left. By then we had all stripped down to swimsuits and T-shirts; I was still wearing Skarda's sneakers, and Jimmy's cell phone was in my pocket.

"Where's the beer?" I asked. My companions looked at me as if I were insane. "You didn't bring the beer?"

"We thought you were kidding," Liz said.

"We're supposed to be a party boat, remember?"

Josie gave me the same smile she had the morning she came into my bedroom, the one that suggested she had me all figured out. I hadn't realized she was sitting on a cooler until she stood and opened it. She removed two Leinies, twisted off the caps to both, and gave me a bottle. The others helped themselves. The pontoon had an AM/FM radio, and I dialed in WELY. It was playing Bruce Springsteen.

"I saw him once at the old Civic Center in St. Paul when I was a kid," I said. "Best rock concert ever."

"I thought you were a jazz guy," Josie said.

"We were all young once. Listen. There are two ways to do this. One is sly and sneaky. The other is loud and boisterous. Loud and boisterous is more fun."

"If you say so."

I eased the throttle forward until the pontoon boat was skimming across the lake as fast as it could. At the same time, I cranked the volume on the radio and started singing along with the Boss—*"Tramps like us, baby we were born to run . . ."*

SIXTEEN

I guided the boat across Pike Bay past the Tower Municipal Airport—Jimmy was excited to see a couple of single-engine planes land—and worked through a wide, meandering channel into the enormous main body of Lake Vermilion. The light wind died away as the sun began to set. The surface of the lake became smooth and quiet; the distant islands turned to shimmering shards of emerald. We hugged the shoreline, following it westward.

Along the way we crossed the wake of a variety of fishing boats, cruisers, and pontoons. The occupants waved at us and we waved at them because that's what people do in Minnesota. That changed when a boat sped toward us straight out of the sun. There was a badge painted on the bow. The Bandits became desperate for me to turn and run. I refused to alter course. Skarda moved to my side as if he wanted to commandeer the wheel. The boat changed course to pass us on the starboard side. The badge became the emblem of the Minnesota Department of Natural Resources. The boat driver was in uniform—tan shirt, green shorts, and aviator sunglasses.

The wind rippled his hair, and I was sure he thought he looked cool.

"Wave," I said, and the girls did, standing at the bow. The conservation officer smiled and waved back. Three attractive women in swimsuits, you would have smiled and waved, too.

I gave Skarda what I hoped was a steely glare.

"You mutinous dog," I said. He didn't respond. "Charles Laughton? *Mutiny on the Bounty*? Doesn't anybody here watch Turner Classic Movies?"

"Let me guess," Josie said. "It's the only channel God approves of."

We kept cruising west, bypassing the mouth of Everett Bay, until we reached the public boat landing near the Forest Lane Resort. The old man was sitting inside his fifteen-year-old Chevy Silverado; it was parked next to Josie's Taurus and Jimmy's old Cadillac. When he saw the pontoon, he hopped out of the cab and gave us a wave. There was another boat in front of us, so we had to wait. While we waited, I moved the nose of the pontoon close in. Roy jumped into the water, waded to the shore, and climbed into the pickup truck. The stockbroker's boat trailer was hitched to its rear bumper. When our turn came, Roy expertly maneuvered the Silverado backward until the trailer was in the lake, its wheels underwater. I manipulated the pontoon until its bow kissed the rubber rollers mounted on the rear of the trailer. Everyone left the boat; we connected it to a winch, pulled the boat onto the trailer, and drove the truck up the boat ramp until the trailer was completely out of the water. The pontoon was quickly secured.

"Now what?" the old man wanted to know.

Before I could answer, Daniel waved me toward the cab of the Silverado. "You drive," he said.

"That, I guess," I said.

"I'm coming with," Roy insisted.

"No," Daniel said.

"Listen, you . . ."

Roy grabbed his arm. Daniel spun to his right, brought his fist up, and hit the ex-soldier on the point of his jaw. Roy fell against the boat landing's concrete apron like someone had tossed him out of a second-story window. Claire was the first to reach his side. Roy was conscious but groggy. He said something; I don't know what. Claire cradled his head in her lap and screamed at Daniel, "You didn't need to do that."

I was glad Jill wasn't there to see it. On the other hand, the stripper was starting to grow on me.

The other Bandits agreed with Claire. Daniel was having none of it, though.

"You people need to go home," Daniel said. "You need to wise up. Stop pretending you're something you're not." He pointed at Roy. "I promise I'll bring his wife home safe and sound, and I always keep my promises." He pointed at me. "Now get in the goddamn truck."

We found Everett Bay Road and followed it until it became Old Highway 77. It was slow going. The Silverado was willing despite its age, yet we were asking it to lug a wide, 2,800-pound pontoon boat down the road—not to mention the weight of the motor and all that money stashed in the lockers. I couldn't get the speed up much past fifty miles per hour before the entire rig started to shudder. Several times I asked Daniel where we were going. He had nothing to say until we reached Vermilion Drive.

"Turn right," he said.

I did. By then the sun was nearly down and the world had turned to a sorrowful gray. The truck's headlights caught a sign. Vermilion Drive was the local name for County Highway 24.

"Ahh," I said. "We're heading back to Brand's seaplane base."

"You're a smart guy, Dyson . . ." Daniel said.

"You think?"

"But not smart enough." To emphasize his point, Daniel produced a small-caliber automatic and pointed it at me.

"Really?" I said. "I thought you'd wait at least until we got to Buyck before pulling on me."

"You knew I had a gun?"

" 'Course I did. I'm a smart guy. You said so yourself."

"Not smart enough," Daniel repeated. "Give me the SIG."

"Hmm? What?"

"SIG Sauer P228 nine-millimeter. It's in that little storage compartment attached to the side of the door."

I hesitated for a beat, wondering how to play it, realized there was only one way, reached down into the compartment, grabbed the SIG by the barrel, and handed it to Daniel. He opened the passenger window and tossed the gun into a ditch.

"Now the cell phone. Give it to me."

"My cell phone. Why would you want that?"

"You built two bombs. Do you actually think I'm stupid enough to believe you made the second to use as a spare?"

"Always be prepared . . ."

"You hid it in the pontoon boat, Dyson. That's why you left the cabin late last night when you thought I was asleep; you went to hide it. If things don't go your way, you intend to blow up the money, or at least threaten to. Am I right?"

"It seemed like a good idea at the time. Look, Daniel. I need leverage to make sure the girl is safe. Brand—I don't trust him. Do you?"

"I wouldn't trust Brand as far as I could throw him. He likes to fuck with people. He lies for fun."

"So you understand . . ."

"Give me the phone."

"The girl . . ."

"The girl will be fine. You have my word on that. As for you—I can't make any promises there."

"Fair enough."

"Now give it up."

I pulled Jimmy's cell phone out of my pocket and handed it to Daniel. He threw that out the window, too.

It was difficult getting the pontoon boat down the makeshift road once we reached Crane Lake. The trailer kept hopping across ruts and potholes, throwing the boat up against the trees that lined the narrow path—paint and tree bark seemed to be scraped off equally. Finally we broke into the clearing. The pickup's headlights told me that there were six men gathered around a fire pit; the flames were bright enough to illuminate their faces, yet little else. Three men were sitting in canvas chairs—Brand, Fenelon, and the Mexican. From the way they cradled their AKs, I guessed the three men who were standing belonged to the gunrunner. The seaplane was tied to the dock, its engine facing the lake. The Subaru Forester and Chevy Malibu were parked on the left side of the clearing like before. Deputies James and Williams and their cruiser were nowhere to be seen. I knew exactly what that meant.

I swung the truck and trailer in a wide arc to the right, stopping only when the trailer was settled next to the wooden shack. The shack was open like before, and I thought, that's where the canvas chairs came from. Off went the pickup's headlights and engine. I didn't realize how big and bright the moon was until I climbed out of the cab. Daniel continued to point his gun at me while we moved toward the fire.

"Do yourself a favor," I told him. "Don't stand too close."

"Oh, I won't."

"Protect the girl."

"I said I would."

The Mexican's three henchmen moved into flanking positions as we approached, one to my right and the others to my left, stopping when they found an angle that would allow them to fire on me without hitting each other. I had the distinct impression they knew exactly what they were doing.

"Veo que trajiste a tus hombres," I told the Mexican.

I heard my words echoed in English—"I see you brought your men"—something I found quite disconcerting, until I noticed Fenelon whispering into Brand's ear.

"Y bastantes armas también," the Mexican said.

"And plenty of guns, too," Fenelon repeated.

We stopped a few yards short of the fire pit. Daniel backed away while still holding his gun on me—I hadn't asked him to move for his safety, but for mine. Brand remained sitting in his canvas chair. The flames from the fire pit reflected in his face, making him look like a movie villain. All he needed was a white cat to stroke.

"I take it I'm not to be arrested, then," I said.

"You're referring to Deputies James and Williams," Brand said. "We decided not to include them in our transaction. I hope you don't mind. Their presence made my partner nervous."

The fire gave Brand's teeth an orange glow when he smiled. I glanced at the Mexican. He wasn't smiling at all.

Brand wagged a finger at me. "Trying to turn my friend against me, that was a bold move, Dyson."

"Mátenlo," the Mexican said.

"Kill him," Fenelon repeated. He leaned in when he spoke, and I could see his battered face. Someone had worked him over good and proper—the sight answered all of my questions.

"Wait, wait," Brand said—which was exactly what I was going to say. "Daniel, how did it go?"

"Perfectly. Almost too perfectly."

"The money?"

"It's hidden inside the lockers on the pontoon boat."

"How much?" asked the Mexican.

"Won't know until we count it but it's—substantial."

"I do not know that word."

"Cómo no," Fenelon said.

While they were talking I cautiously reached into the left-hand pocket of the swimsuit I was still wearing and produced my cell phone—the one I had been using ever since I arrived in the northland, the one no one else knew about.

"Now you can kill him," Brand said.

The Mexicans raised their assault rifles. I raised my hand. The light from the cell phone shone like a small flashlight.

"Are you guys in a hurry?" I was speaking loudly, almost screaming. "Do you have a bus to catch?"

"Don't," Daniel shouted. "Hold your fire, hold your fire."

The henchmen didn't lower their rifles. On the other hand, they didn't shoot, either, so I had that going for me.

"¿Qué es esto?" the Mexican asked, and then translated for himself—"What is this?"

"Daniel?" Brand asked.

"Goddamn sonuvabitch," Daniel answered.

"Daniel, what?"

"I have a bomb wired to a cell phone detonator," I said. "Any sudden moves and I'll blow up the money, the boat, that shed filled with aviation fuel, and maybe some of you. It'll be one helluva an explosion, I promise. The CBP guys at the inspection station across the lake should have no problem seeing it."

Everyone was standing now. Brand moved to Daniel's side and grabbed him by the arm. "Is this true?" he asked.

Daniel pulled his arm away. "I thought I got his cell phone."

"Two bombs, two cells," I said.

"You let him bring a bomb here?" Brand said.

"We must kill him," the Mexican said. He was speaking English so no one would misunderstand. I did, too.

"Hombre, we had a deal," I said. "The money for the girl. Bring me the girl. Do it now. You can keep the money."

No one looked like they believed me. Brand nodded his head, though, and Fenelon quickly crossed the clearing to the Subaru. A few moments later, he led Jill by the elbow to the fire. Brand intercepted him, grabbed the girl, and pushed her toward me. She stumbled. Instead of attempting to catch her I stepped away and let her fall. Brand and the Mexicans flinched like defensive linemen waiting for the ball to be snapped yet did not move.

"You sonuvabitch," Brand said.

"Don't call me names, John. I don't like it."

"You think you're getting away with something?"

Jill rose slowly from the ground and stood by my side. She was still wearing the soiled nightgown; she looked dirty and worn. I spoke to her in a low voice without taking my eyes off of Brand and the Mexican.

"How you doing, sweetie?" I asked.

"I'm okay."

"You don't sound okay."

"I bet I look worse."

A sense of humor, my inner voice said. *Amazing.*

"You got the girl like I promised," Brand said. "Now give me the phone."

"Not a chance."

"We should kill him," the Mexican said.

"All I have to do is tap the button and all that money burns."

"You will die."

"You're going to kill me anyway—you keep saying so."

"The money," Brand said. "We need to think about the money."

"You promised millions," the Mexican said.

"Yes, I did."

"In the meantime," I said, "everyone move to the fire. Do it now."

The Mexican regarded me for a long moment, then gestured for his men to gather around the fire pit. Both Brand and Daniel hesitated before joining them. When he realized he was standing alone, Fenelon joined the group, yet not before saying, "I'm sorry." I actually felt sympathy for him.

"Is this what you call a Mexican standoff?" the gunrunner asked.

"In a manner of speaking," I said. My arm was getting tired holding the cell in the air. I refused to lower it because I wanted them all to appreciate the danger; I didn't want anyone getting careless. "This is what we're going to do. You're going to give me the keys to the Malibu. Jill and I will take the car and drive away. As soon as we're gone, Daniel can disarm the bomb. He knows how. Everybody gets what they want. Simple."

"No," Brand said.

I ignored him and continued to talk to the Mexican. "You and your amigos can climb into your plane and fly back to wherever you came from with a couple hundred pounds of U.S. currency."

"No," Brand repeated.

The Mexican turned his back to me and spoke quietly to Brand. I couldn't hear exactly what he said, but his tone of voice suggested that he was questioning Brand's judgment. While they were discussing the matter, I whispered to Jill.

"In a minute, they're going to light up this clearing like

Target Field. As soon as they do, you and I are going to make a run for the dock and jump into the lake. Cannonball, don't dive—we don't know how deep the water is."

"We won't get away doing that," Jill said.

"We're not trying to get away. We're trying to get out of the line of fire."

"I don't understand."

"Once we're in the water, we'll swim under the dock and wait until it's over."

"Until what's over?"

I took Jill's hand. I had hoped to give it a reassuring squeeze, but my grip was far too tight for that.

"Dammit, Chad," I said. "They're all standing in the open in a frickin' group, no less. What the hell are you waiting for?"

"Who are you talking to?" Jill wanted to know.

"The man on the other end of the phone."

"What man?"

Daniel overheard us, although I didn't think he understood exactly what we were saying. He gripped his gun with both hands and brought it up, yet he didn't point it at us. Instead, he peered into the darkness.

"Something's wrong," he said.

Brand waved at him the way parents dismiss children who interrupt their conversations. When they finished talking, both he and the Mexican turned to face us.

"Mr. Dyson, we find your terms unacceptable," Brand said.

"I'm open to suggestions."

"I'm going to kill you."

"Ahh . . ."

"One way or the other, you're a dead man. If you want to take the money with you, that's your choice. If you give me the phone instead, I promise I'll let the girl live. Daniel will take her home. I'm not worried about her testifying because she knows what I'll do to her family if she does. If you don't give me the phone, I will kill you both."

"I'm supposed to take your word for that?"

"Not just my word, Daniel's, too. He seems to have taken a liking to her."

"I hadn't noticed."

"The money for the girl. That was our original deal."

"So it was."

"Give me the phone, Dyson. Do it now. Don't make me wait."

"Any frickin' time now, guys," I said.

"Something's wrong," Daniel repeated.

Please, please, please, my inner voice chanted.

The lights came on, five of them in an arch arranged from one end of the clearing to the other. I was right about the Target Field reference—you could play baseball under them.

"This is the ATF," a man shouted over a megaphone. "You're surrounded."

There was something else about dropping weapons and raising hands. By then I had Jill turned around and we were both running, hand in hand, toward the dock. She was in bare feet, yet that didn't seem to slow her down.

Guns were being fired. Single shots and full automatics. I heard someone shout, "Don't hit the girl."

The wooden dock groaned under our feet. We had to duck our heads to avoid being decapitated by the wing of the seaplane. When we reached the end of the dock we jumped in. The water was deep. We didn't touch bottom. I held tight to Jill's hand while I kicked my legs toward the surface. We both came up gasping for breath. I was facing the lake. In the distance I could see the lights of two boats that had not been there before. They were coming fast.

I turned toward the shore. The scene in the clearing was

chaotic. Two of the Mexicans were down. The third hench-man and his boss were standing rigid, their hands locked behind their heads. Men dressed in windbreakers embla-zoned with the initials ATF pushed them to their knees and clasped their arms behind their backs with handcuffs.

I could not see Brand and Daniel, and then I did. Somehow they had managed to reach the wooden shed. The far side of the shack was on fire—I have no idea how that happened. Brand was inside the shed; Daniel had taken cover behind the near wall. They were both firing on the ATF agents with as-sault rifles. They had attempted to escape into the woods, but the agents had blocked their path.

I pulled Jill to me, wrapped an arm under her shoulders, and swam with one hand to the end of the dock—it never even occurred to me to ask if she could swim. We grabbed hold of the piling. I positioned myself so that my body was between her and the clearing.

The fire grew until the far side of the shack was engulfed in flame. I wanted to warn the agents about the aviation fuel in-side, only I knew they wouldn't hear me—the roar from the two speedboat engines was so loud I couldn't even hear my-self. As it turned out, the agents didn't need a warning. I real-ized that when one of them jumped into the cab of the pickup truck. I whispered a "thank you" to no one in particular that I had left the key in the ignition. The agent started up the truck and drove across the clearing, pulling the trailer and pontoon boat with it.

Moving the vehicles exposed Brand and Daniel to addi-tional gunfire. Brand was the first to fall. Daniel was hit, yet he managed to keep his feet. He leaned against the wall of the shack. He looked out toward the lake. It seemed to me that he was staring directly at Jill when the aviation fuel ignited.

The words formed in my head—*The Jabberwock with eyes of flame, came whiffling through the tulgey wood*—yet I couldn't manage to say them out loud.

Jill sat in Brand's canvas chair, a blanket wrapped around her shoulders. Someone had built up the fire, and she was staring into it. Her hair had dried some, yet it was still matted to her head. Her eyes were swollen from the crying she had done. I sat next to her and held her hand. I had been holding it for nearly two hours. I just didn't want to let her go.

The volunteer fire department had come and gone. There hadn't been much for them to do except wet the ground and extinguish all the embers they found. After the barrels had exploded, the fire burned off all the aviation fuel. A few trees had gone up with it, yet not as many as you'd think before the fire died out on its own.

The Mexicans were on their way to the Cities along with their weapons. The serial numbers of the guns proved that they belonged to a batch the ATF had lost in Operation Fast and Furious. There were only four of them, and Bullert seemed disappointed until his people searched the Mexicans' seaplane. Apparently they had enough ordnance on board to arm the entire population of Orr. The seaplane was licensed to an address near Thunder Bay, Ontario. Bullert conveyed that happy bit of news over the phone to his people in Washington, D.C. It was a pleasant conversation. When he finished he smiled broadly and announced he was going to Canada in the morning.

"Good for you," I said.

Meanwhile, his people searched the pontoon boat. They found the money all safe and sound, but not the bomb.

"Where is it?" Bullert asked. The woman I knew as Carolyn Rooney stood next to him. "We searched the pontoon from one end to the other."

"Where's what?" I asked.

"The bomb?"

"What bomb?"

"You're telling me there was no bomb?"

"Nice bluff," Rooney said. "Very nice."

"Half a bluff," I said. "There is a second bomb, it's just not on the boat."

"Where is it?" Bullert asked again.

"There's a shed near Lake Cody that's used by Deputies Eugene James and Allen Williams. Inside, you'll find an IED made with half a block of C-4 that you should be able to trace to our Mexican friends. When you apply for the search warrant you can tell the judge you're acting on personal observations by a credible confidential informant who has provided reliable information to the government in the past."

"Is that true?" Rooney asked.

"Does it matter? Oh, and if you look carefully, you'll find evidence of other crimes as well."

Bullert was smiling. "I have to tell you, McKenzie, this isn't the way I imagined things would go, but damn"—he patted my shoulder—"great job."

"We were lucky. Lucky that you understood what I meant when I told Daniel to strap on his sneakers."

"Sneakers?" Jill asked.

"We placed a GPS transmitter in the sneakers David Skarda was wearing when he escaped custody," Bullert said. "That's how we were able to track his movements, how we were able to track McKenzie once he put them on. It told us where he was going. I'm sorry it took so long to get into position."

"McKenzie," Jill said. "Is that your real name?"

"Yes," I said.

"You're an informant, a spy for the ATF?"

"Yes."

"Helping Dave, that was a lie, then."

"Yes."

"All the time acting like you were our friend, that was a lie, too. It's all been a lie."

"Not all."

She stared at the fire some more. I released her hand—I thought she would want me to—yet she continued to hold mine.

"We need to get you home," I said. "Everyone must be worried sick."

"I'll get you a car," Bullert said. He walked off. Rooney followed him.

"McKenzie?" Jill asked.

"Yes, sweetie?"

"When he . . . when the man said to give him the phone or he would . . . he would kill me—were you going to give him the phone, give it to him even though he said he was going to kill you? If the police didn't come, would you have given him the phone?"

"Yes."

"Oh."

A moment later, Bullert reappeared.

"I have a car," he said. "Carolyn will drive. She'll take you wherever you want to go."

"Thank you," I said.

When I rose from my chair, Jillian rose from hers. The blanket slipped from her shoulders, revealing her damp nightgown. She released my hand to pull it back around her. When she finished, she extended her hand to me. I took it gladly. She smiled. It was bright and warm, and I thought that after everything I'd done to her and her family for Jill to give me that smile—it was like the first time I went to confession at St. Mark's Catholic Church when I was a kid. I felt saved.

We turned to walk toward the car. I stopped when I saw a shadow emerge from the forest near the mouth of the road.

"Who's that?" I spoke loud enough that the agents were spooked; hands flew to the butts of handguns.

"It's me," the shadow replied.

I recognized him when he came closer to the fire.

"Fenelon?" I asked. I had completely forgotten about him. "What are you doing?"

"I've come to surrender."

"Surrender?" Bullert asked.

"Surrender for what?" I asked.

"For what I've done."

"What have you done, Brian? What have you done that falls under the jurisdiction of the Bureau of Alcohol, Tobacco, Firearms, and Explosives?"

"I betrayed you."

"From how your face looks, I can hardly blame you."

"I tried, I tried—they kept hitting me . . ."

"It's okay," I said.

"Whatever you've done, it had nothing to do with us," Bullert said. "That's between you and McKenzie."

"I have no complaints," I told him.

Fenelon's mouth fell open and his eyes widened like a poor student trying to comprehend the A on his term paper.

"C'mon, Brian," I said. "We'll take you home."

Jill squeezed my hand and leaned in until her head was resting against my shoulder.

"I was right, what I said before," she told me. "You are a big softy."

JUST SO YOU KNOW

Sunday morning I drove up to Ely. Nina had wanted to tag along, but I figured it was one of those trips I'd best take alone. I was surprised by how understanding she had become after I got past the explanation of why I called Shelby instead of her. I also explained that Shelby had been wrong when she suggested that I wanted to marry my best friend's wife and since I couldn't, I vowed not to marry anyone.

"That might have been so once, but it hasn't been true for four years, nine months, and seventeen days," I said.

"And what happened four years, nine months, and seventeen days ago?" Nina asked.

"I met you."

That seemed to make her happy; Bobby, not so much. He was furious that I had made Shelby my moll—those were his words, not mine—although his attitude mellowed somewhat when Nina said that Shelby could keep the dress.

Even though it was out of the way, I stopped at the Chocolate Moose to buy a couple of strawberry-rhubarb pies before swinging back down toward Krueger. I was driving my Audi

S5 partly because it was such a sweet ride and partly because the county sheriff's department still hadn't released my Jeep Cherokee. Apparently the sheriff wanted to arrest someone — anyone—for the armed robbery of the Mesabi Security Company's remote vault, the fact it was a front for an ATF sting be damned. Phone calls were being made, however, and I knew nothing would come of it.

I also knew I would find the Iron Range Bandits at the cabin on Lake Carl, although I wasn't sure I should call them that anymore. They were sitting on the redwood deck looking both pleased and forlorn, an odd combination, yet fitting, all things considered. They heard me climbing the stairs. Skarda made it clear that I wasn't welcome.

"You sure?" I asked. "I brought pie."

Jill hopped up from the picnic table and crossed the deck. Her arms circled my shoulders and she kissed my cheek. It was difficult to return the hug because I was carrying the pies in one hand and an envelope and newspaper in the other. From his expression, that was just fine with Roy.

"I never thanked you for saving my life," Jill said.

"You thanked me so many times I lost track," I said.

She hugged me some more as Roy crossed the deck.

"I'm grateful for what you did, Dyson," Roy said. "On the other hand, you're the one who put her in danger, so I don't know what to think about it."

"He didn't put me in danger, John Brand did," Jill told him. "And his name is McKenzie. Rushmore McKenzie."

I didn't know how pretty my name was until she spoke it.

Jill led me by the arm to the table. I set the boxes containing the pies on top of it. "I'll get plates and forks," she said, and disappeared into the cabin.

The old man was sitting in his customary spot at the head of the table. Josie, Skarda, Liz, Jimmy, and Claire were gathered around it. Roy remained by the door to the cabin as if he were guarding it. No one else seemed to have anything to say, so I asked, "Have you seen the newspaper?"

I dropped a copy of the Sunday *Duluth News Tribune* in front of them. They leaned in to take a look. There was a story beneath the fold. The headline read:

DEPUTIES ACCUSED OF ARMED ROBBERY, SUSPECTED OF BEING IRON RANGE BANDITS

Liz took up the paper and read aloud.

Two county deputies implicated in a scheme to smuggle illegal weapons across the Canadian border are now also suspects in a series of unsolved armed robberies that occurred throughout the Iron Range in the past year.

According to a government spokesman, a search of a storage unit owned by Deputy Eugene James and Deputy Allen Williams produced sacks of receipts and checks that were taken during a daring daylight robbery of a grocery store in Silver Bay, MN.

At the time, authorities claimed the robbery was the work of a group known as the Iron Range Bandits that had committed at least a half-dozen crimes throughout the region.

The storage unit also contained vehicles and merchandise valued at over $100,000.

The deputies admitted that the unit belonged to them, sources say. However, they could not explain the presence of the stolen sacks, nor could they produce evidence that proved ownership of the rest of the unit's contents.

"Apprehending the Iron Range Bandits and putting an end to their crime spree is a big win," said Assistant U.S. Attorney James R. Finnegan. "It shows what we can accomplish when federal, state, and local law enforcement agencies cooperate with each other."

It was during an initial search of the same storage unit that agents of the Bureau of Alcohol, Tobacco, Firearms, and Explosives discovered explosive devices that linked the deputies to a Mexican cartel that was attempting to sell stolen weapons to criminal organizations inside the U.S.

The arrest of James and Williams comes on the heels of a raid by a joint task force of ATF agents and Royal Canadian Mounted Policemen on a seaplane base in Thunder Bay, Ontario, that resulted in the apprehension of a dozen Mexican nationals and the confiscation of 392 firearms.

"What does this mean?" Jimmy asked.

"It means someone else is taking the fall for your crimes," I said. I glanced at Josie. "I told you I'd get the bastards."

She didn't reply; didn't even look me in the eye.

"You framed them?" the old man asked.

"You have to admit there's a certain poetic irony to it."

"How?"

"Remember the bags of checks and receipts we had after the Silver Bay job?" Josie said. She was speaking to her father and not to me. "Dyson put them in their shed."

"McKenzie," I said.

"You really are a spy for the ATF," Claire said.

"Was a spy."

"Not a criminal mastermind."

"Just a gifted amateur."

"What about Dave?" Liz Skarda asked.

"Dave's coming with me."

Skarda nodded his head even as he squeezed his wife's hand, a despondent expression in his face. "I told you, honey," he said. "I have to pay for my crimes."

"Oh, stop being so melodramatic," I said. "The charges against you for robbing the music festival in Grand Rapids have been dropped."

"What?"

"Turns out the evidence against you was obtained illegally and is inadmissible in court."

"Really?"

"It came as a surprise to the Itasca County prosecutor, too. You still have to face charges for your daring escape from justice, but Deputy Ken Olson is prepared to testify that I forced you to go with me at gunpoint, so . . . Just keep your mouth shut. You think that's possible? Don't say anything until you talk to your lawyer."

"I don't have a lawyer."

"Your lawyer is named G. K. Bonalay. She'll meet us in Grand Rapids."

"Wait a minute." This time Josie actually was speaking to me. "G. K. Bonalay is the one who just bought this lake cabin from the stockbroker's estate—I got a six percent commission. That's why we're here—to clean up the place before the new owner arrives."

"I wouldn't worry too much about that."

I handed the envelope to Claire. She opened it slowly as if she expected to find something nasty inside.

"This is . . ." she said.

"It's a purchase agreement," I said. "The deed will be in the mail in a few days. Consider it a wedding gift."

"You're giving us the cabin?" Jimmy said. It was both a question and an announcement.

"You guys were guilty of trespassing," I said. "Now you're not."

Everyone seemed happy to see me after that—well, except for Josie. Jill emerged from the cabin carrying a tray loaded with paper plates, silverware, a pitcher of lemonade, and several beers. I nearly choked—it was Summit Ale. We ate and drank and chatted. The Bandits all swore to God above that they were done with outlawing, even the old man, who quietly thanked me when no one was looking for keeping his secret. After a while, I made my good-byes and led Skarda to the Audi. He asked if I stole it. I told him no. He seemed disappointed. Josie appeared before we had a chance to climb into the car. She asked Skarda to take a walk. I told him to make it a short walk.

"So, all's well that ends well," Josie said.

"It would seem so."

"When I found out what happened, when Jill told us after you brought her home, I wrote you off as just another asshole who was stealing oxygen from the rest of us . . ."

"I can't blame you for that."

"You're not that guy, though—Dyson, I mean."

"No."

"Who are you?"

"I've been trying to figure that out for quite a while."

"McKenzie . . . they say your name is McKenzie?"

"Yes."

"Are you married?"

"No."

"Girlfriend?"

"Yes."

"Do you love her?"

"Very much."

"So, when you warned me that you would be heading out the door and down the street and that you wouldn't be coming back, what you meant was that you were going back to her."

"Yes," I said.

"And you prefer not to leave any misunderstandings behind."

"I'm sorry, Josie."

"It's not like you didn't warn me."

"I'm sorry."

She moved toward the cabin, got halfway around it, and stopped.

"Are you going to marry her, this girlfriend?"

"It's still undecided."

"If she won't have you, I will."

A moment later, Josie disappeared from view. I watched the spot where she had been standing for a long time. Bachelors, I told myself, and bachelorettes—we fall in love too easily for our own damn good.